DECEPTION:
Return of the Gods

by Stephen H. King

TOSK – The Other Stephen King

ISBN: 978-0-9989355-2-2

A SPECIAL THANKS

I owe a special debt to all those who've helped me make this series come alive. From a story inside my head to a book on a shelf is a long way to travel, and none of my efforts could've made it without the help of many of my fellow authors, nor the help of my wonderful group of readers.

Of course, no married author in his right mind would think he could've achieved half of what he did without the help and support of a loving spouse. Heidelinde, my wife, has been such a great help throughout this process.

Oh—and I should remind you that this writing, as with all the other creations in the Return of the Gods series, is a work of fiction. No dragons or apes were actually killed in its creation. Also, any resemblance to persons, living or dead, or places, or events, is most likely completely coincidental. And, um, so on.

Formalities aside—hope you enjoy!

Table of Contents

♋

Crystal faced her beloved husband, her eyes radiating anger and her arms spread wide to the side, raw elemental power coursing around her through the space that was their bedroom. Matt, in turn, loomed in challenge, his own face unreadable. Matt's body also pulsed immense and powerful flows of energy as husband and wife—god and goddess—warred one against another, both pressing the primal forces of natural magic back and forth between them. The floor shook with a rumble of masonry grinding against supports. Lightning flickered across the ceiling, both illuminating and marring the sky scene that had always seemed too real to Crystal. Bright bands of energy flashed once, then again, and then several times more from ceiling to floor, the god's and goddess's powers dancing nimbly around the room in a deadly magical storm. Encased in the cacophonic soup of energy, Crystal wasn't certain whether the strikes were the product of her anger or her husband's, or more likely both, but wordlessly the pair battled on, Crystal's expression furious while Matt's remained stoic. Tumultuous winds whipped about the bedroom, slamming the closet door shut and spinning the couple's beautiful four-poster bed around on the floor before sending it crashing into the wall. Temperatures alternately spiked and fell around the space in spots and in waves. Specks of light appeared everywhere, energy visibly flashing and twinkling as it built up, higher and higher, reaching a display of power on a scale that Crystal had never even imagined possible. Through it all Crystal, shielded by her powers, concentrated on the battle rather than its effects.

Twin screams cut through Crystal's concentration, the sound tossing a cold blanket of concern over the fire of her fury. Instantly losing her interest in the battle, Crystal dropped her attacks and shield, knowing instinctively that her husband would do the same.

All the energy in the tempest dissipated quickly as husband and wife released their flows and spun toward the door where their twin daughters, Heidi and Linda, stood side by side just inside the bedroom. The door was off its hinges and leaning against the wall, giving the girls full view of the domestic fury that had ensued. The teenagers, still dressed in their nighties, clung tightly to one another, faces wrenched into terrified expressions as their cries trilled on. With the elemental onslaught ended, their screams were the only sound as they pierced the uneasy quiet.

The sight and sound of her daughters' terror wrenched Crystal's heart out through her throat. Unable to face the reality of what had just happened, she gathered energy around herself once more and teleported out, fleeing magically to her sanctum. It was both husband's and wife's sanctum, really, the little cottage at the far end of the estate, but she was the one who needed it now.

Hastily Crystal raised one magical wall of force after another around the little stone structure. She knew her husband wielded enough power to easily swipe it all to the side if he dared, but she hoped he was smart enough not to intrude on her horrified self-recrimination. Everyone else, meanwhile, would be kept out, and the sound barriers would also prevent them from hearing the sobs that rushed past Crystal's lips even as she wove the cocoon of force around the getaway.

How did it get to this? She had her husband had never, ever fought. They'd never needed to, since any and all disagreements were always talked through rationally. Why now? She thought back over the past twenty-four hours, remembering the start of the debate from the night before....

A Little Lovers' Spat

It was definitely purple, Crystal had thought, staring down into the small cup of nectar, the liquor of the gods. She moved the glass in her hand, swirling the liquid gingerly around the sides and watching as the viscous purple liquor rose and fell in oscillatory patterns. She set the cup down on the table and watched from above, entertained for the moment by the effort of continuing the fluid's movement with her magic, using flows of air swirling around the inside of the cup.

"It's purple, mister," she said to the only other person in the bar she cared about.

"Brown, dear," Matt replied, though it was clear how little he really cared about the matter. They'd argued the point since the last trip to the bar in Olympus. Matt claimed that nectar, the drink of the gods, was the color of whiskey, while she swore it was more like a fine wine. It didn't make a lot of difference, of course, but it gave Crystal something to do.

Crystal couldn't recall the last time she'd needed to be given something to do. Growing up an only child to two parents who were very busy teachers, she'd had plenty of time on her own, but it had always been easy time to fill. She remembered being a curious kid, always getting into things just to see what they were about. Later, working her way through college had kept her plenty busy, and then marital life had kicked in with a whirl-wind of working and all the traveling they'd done as wealthy newlyweds. After the girls were born, a whole new level of time management came over her horizon, of course. From that point to the cataclysm, then, there'd always been something that needed doing.

Suddenly the cataclysm had—well, it had happened, was the best verb Crystal knew to describe it. Happened, with all its associated changes, terrors, and revelations. "Oh, yeah, beloved wife, I, your husband, am actually the ancient god of war," had been the hardest change to swallow, though she'd buried her angst from that under the reasoning that she'd lost far less in the bargain than the people who had lost dear family and friends. At the same time she'd been thrust into the role of first lady of a god's manor, but that first lady had had an entirely competent staff working for her while her husband and his staff did most of the administrative work. So then she'd buried herself in the insurmountable task of becoming an immortal goddess capable of standing beside her immortal god husband, and—she'd won. Crystal, the middle-class daughter of everyday schoolteachers, the ordinary California girl, had become—a goddess.

Unfortunately the win hadn't come with any further duties. There just wasn't a goddess manual of requirements. Matt had a thrakkoni servant who took care of his every need, and suddenly Crystal had one also.

Not only that, but what Matt had been hinting at was now perfectly clear. The human condition involved a constant quest to achieve, achieve, and achieve some more before you died. Taking the 'before you died' part out of the equation made it all tumble to the floor. All at once it had dawned on Crystal that she would live another hundred, thousand, million, and even several millions of years. In the very next instant, a calmness had settled over her that said she didn't have to worry about what she accomplished in the next hundred years, because she'd have the hundred years after that to finish it. That calmness had given rise to an entirely self-possessed pleasure that had turned to....

Well, it had turned to boredom.

Granted, there'd been a time when merely visiting the dive bar of the gods, wherever it was in the universe—Matt claimed it was in the center of the universe, but he also claimed Gaia's glade was in the same place—had made for such an incredible journey that her old friends back at the estate had had a hard time believing Crystal's story. Drinking nectar at the bar of the gods had seemed even more incredible.

Now, though, it was—well, it was becoming normal. Boring, even.

They're going to think you're drunk, Matt's telepathic message interrupted her musing.

"So what? Do you?" Crystal asked her husband out loud.

"No, I know better. And I guess I can't really answer your first question. I don't care a whole lot what the other deities think, either."

"We can hear what you're saying, you know," a gruff voice behind them said.

"So?" Matt challenged.

"Well, it's not enough that you two lovebirds give off the energy of telepathy the entire time you're here. One can only imagine ye're sayin' 'I love you!' and 'I love you too!' But to actually talk about not caring that we can hear is rude, my old friend."

"If you're that interested in participating in the conversation, Thor, you could always join us at our table," Matt said.

The huge god seated behind them laughed, his massive voice pealing through the room as his beard shook against the table. "I'd rather eat pure sugar, Tyr. At least sugar would make me gag less from its sweetness."

"I suppose if we're that intolerable we should leave. Crystal, are you going to drink your nectar or play with it?"

In response, Crystal lifted her glass, downed the liquor in one gulp, and returned the glass to the table, its bottom making a sharp report on contact with the wood. She leered at her husband. She'd never been a drinker before; at most, she would give in to a single glass of wine for special occasions. Now that she had met the tests to ascend to the pantheon to which Matt belonged, though, her liver was as immortal as she was. She couldn't actually get drunk no matter how much nectar she consumed due to the healing spell that had been set to permanently oscillate through her body, but she could—and did, frequently—enjoy the feeling and flavor of the smooth liquor served at the bar of the gods.

"Well, somebody's gotta get me drunk so I can have your way with you—er, my way with—or is it…. Whatever, Mister of War God, it's time for you to home me back carry and enjoy our ene— eve—evening together," she said, slurring the words in her best drunkenness act.

Matt smirked and downed his own nectar. As he reached across the table to teleport the couple, Crystal heard a deep guffaw from Thor and a disapproving snort from the side. She didn't need to look around as the pair of them popped back to Matt's estate.

Matt chortled as they reappeared in their bedroom. "Dear," he said, "as much as I enjoy bantering back and forth, you should think about how much you're vexing our peers."

"What? Thor liked it, unless he's taken to guffawing in vexation. And I haven't had a good night at Olympus unless I've gotten a snort from Hermes—who's usually acting rather drunk, himself, right? Oh, and a glare of daggers or three from your exwife, Aphrodite, which in turn seems to give your buddy Thor even greater pleasure. And that guy who never speaks, who sits regally in a conjured golden throne and sips nectar from a sake cup with his pet monkey. You know, the guy who stared at me all night. Am I supposed to worry about offending him too?"

"I've told you who that is, Crystal."

"I know, but you've never told me why the eastern pantheon has its own emperor, or why they make such a show of staying separate. Or why he has a pet monkey, for that matter."

"The Monkey King is far more of a drinking companion to the Jade Emperor than a pet, actually. They've had their battles out, in fact, and Monkey has won his fair share of them. And they need their own separate pantheon because—well, because they're different from us."

"Separate, but equal?" Crystal asked, referring sarcastically to a mindset used before the cataclysm to justify keeping different people at separate schools or on separate bus systems. It had been separate, but not really equal.

"Hmmph. No, nothing like that. They're every bit as powerful as we are, but they prefer to drink alone."

"Okay, so I don't care about offending them, then. And why should I worry about what the others think? I'm a goddess! I'm one of you!"

"Yes, you are, and the only reason I can really come up with for why you should worry is that a million years is a long time to spend on somebody's bad side."

Crystal glared at her husband for several long seconds. Finally, unable to field a suitable retort, she fell back on her standard response and stuck out her tongue.

"Excellent idea, my dear beloved wife," Matt said, his voice dripping with sarcasm. "The next civilization that pops up, we should introduce ourselves as the God of War and the Mighty Goddess of the Sarcastic Tongue. See? Problem solved."

Crystal grimaced. She had, in fact, been trying to figure out what she would be the goddess of the next time she was asked. The twelve elder gods, those who had been around since the Beginning, already had the big roles tied up. Her husband, for example, had always been and probably would always be the god of war, strife, and all things egotistical. Michael, or Apollo, as he had been known once, had the areas of magical arts and healing sewn tight because that was what he did best, and his twin sister likewise was the goddess of the hunt. Meanwhile, Ben'thra, who had been known as Hermes the Trickster to the only body of mythology Crystal had studied, played the role of thorn in everyone else's back side quite regularly and well.

Humans who had found the path to ascension later had filled in the gaps. Matt's first wife was the first to ascend and took the role of deity over love, or, more accurately and appropriately, sexuality. Thor, who had become like a big brother to Crystal in her stay at his estate, served as the barbarian thunder god to the civilizations who were interested in such things. Other aspects of nature, such as wind and sea and animal fertility, were also already taken, leaving Crystal with a big blank in her title. It was a blank she had been working to fill.

Goddess of the Tongue wasn't it, though.

"Thank you for your suggestion, dearest husband, but I shall continue seeking after something more in keeping with my natural talents and interests," Crystal said, mimicking the lofty tone she'd heard Gaia, the mother goddess, use with Matt.

Matt grunted in response. "Goddess of Boredom, perhaps?"

Crystal glared at Matt.

"What? You're bored, aren't you?"

"Bored? I'm a goddess. I can do anything I want anytime I want, and I often do. I have a beautiful and amazing horse to ride around the grounds, and a thrakkon who will take me anywhere I wish, and a loving husband who accompanies me to the most incredible bar in the universe. All that, plus a couple of pretty awesome kids. How could I be bored?" As she objected, though, she realized Matt was right.

"Mm hmm," he said. "A few months ago you were scared out of your mind, preparing to enter the arena against Aphrodite to face a battle that would determine whether you would ascend, or die. Now that's over, and your most significant challenge is what? Existing. Right? And that's not much of a challenge for a goddess, is it?"

Once again she found herself without a suitable retort. This time, though, it was because Matt was dead-on to the truth of the matter, and she knew it.

"Okay, so you're right. So what do gods and goddesses do to keep themselves entertained?"

"Oh, all sorts of things. Sometimes we go live among the people and wreak havoc from within. Sometimes we watch civilizations grow from on high, and sometimes we also play around with them a little. You know, start little conflicts and such. Sometimes we spend a lot of time at Olympus drinking and arguing about important stuff like whether nectar is purple or brown. Sometimes we busy ourselves administratively. Why do you think I set this estate up to run like a miniature duchy? Do you think it really matters to me how many cattle we have in the herd, or how our stock of flour is holding out?"

"You don't need any of it, do you?" Crystal said, realization dawning on her.

"Until you and the girls came along, no, all Sorscha and I needed was an occasional nearby herd of large mammals for her to feed on."

Crystal grimaced. Sorscha was Matt's personal servant and attendant, a member of the race known as thrakkoni—an old term for dragons. The thrakkoni had been made by the gods to be resistant to all flows of magic, but they could teleport and speak telepathically through their own native abilities. They also could shape-shift: normally Sorscha appeared in a spectacularly beautiful humanoid shape, but when either battle or hunger called she rapidly transformed into the fearsome form of a tremendous silver-scaled dragon.

Sorscha had, luckily, taken a liking to Crystal quickly and was thus her main source of information regarding the early days. Crystal had been shocked to learn that the beautiful silver-haired being who appeared to be in her mid-twenties was one of the oldest of her kind. Several hundreds of millions of years old, Sorscha had actually stood beside Matt back when the continents were forming, had actually fought beside him in every war he'd joined.

"So what do you suggest I do?" Crystal said as she shifted her attention back from her memories.

"Well, I'm glad you asked."

"I hate when you say it that way."

"With good reason. But this isn't something to hate. It's a long story, though, so I'll tell it in the morning."

"Why wait for morning?" Crystal asked. "It's not like either of us needs to sleep anymore."

"I didn't say anything about sleep, now did I?" Matt shot Crystal 'the look,' making her knees weak as only the god of war could.

Tumbling into bed, the couple entwined about one other. Crystal pulled her head out away from where Matt's neck had formed a perfect nook for it. A naughty expression in her eyes, she asked, "So, sex is a good cure for boredom?"

"Wasn't for Stacy," Matt said.

"What?" Crystal said, confused. She pulled back further, mood dissipating rapidly.

"Sex didn't seem to keep Stacy from looking for more interesting activities, is all I'm saying."

"What difference does that make? Why bring her up?" Stacy, also known to the Greeks as Aphrodite, was Matt's ex-wife who'd tried to kill her several times in the days just following the cataclysm, and had also put Crystal's daughters in danger. Later, when the time had come for trial by combat to enter the pantheon, Stacy had battled Crystal very nearly to the death, and had taken advantage of every opportunity to taunt Crystal while doing so.

"Well, you asked about boredom. You and Stacy are two peas in a pod, so to speak."

"You're kidding, right?"

"Kidding? No, not at all. I mean it; you and Stacy are exactly alike when you get bored."

"Excuse me?"

Matt shrugged, propped up on his elbow and watching Crystal move away. "Lookit, dear. Both of you ascended to being goddesses, and she got bored and cheated on me. Part of the reason—a large part of the reason, I must say—that I resisted your efforts to ascend is that I wonder how long it'll be before the god of war won't be enough for you, too."

"What the hell do you mean by that?" Crystal spat, rising from the bed. "I've never, ever, so much as thought of cheating on you, Matthew. How dare you?"

"Oh, come off it. You're the one who's going off the deep end. How dare you challenge me?" Matt rose to face her, both partners reaching for elemental flows. Crystal had seen battle lust in her husband's eyes before, but never directed at her that way. It terrified her, and the terror made her even angrier.

"I will not come off it," she said between her teeth. She lashed out angrily with a thrust of air, a move Matt diverted easily with a sneer on his face.

"You're—you're really going to fight me?" Matt said, his sneer deepening. He snickered.

You—snickered. At me! Crystal's mind screamed at her husband, who was clearly not listening to her in any way, not even telepathically.

Infuriated, Crystal responded with a barrage of forces and, mere minutes later, found herself weeping at her cottage, a mixture of fury and shame engulfing her being. She settled in to the corner, relishing the cold hardness of the stone wall while replaying the memory of the fight over and over while, at the same time, rehearsing what she would say when Matt came along, bashing aside her shields to bring her back, as she now realized she hoped that he would.

Making Up

She waited all night, alone.

As dawn flooded the windows with light, she unfolded herself from the corner. She hadn't really expected Matt to visit, but she'd hoped he would. It hurt, despite her knowledge that he probably needed as much time to brood on what had happened as she did. Her initial anger at being compared to the most evil woman in existence had burned down to a heated spot of rage, fueled through the night by concern over where her husband was and why he hadn't tried to see if she were okay.

Exercise would help clear her mind, Crystal figured. A romp around the estate on the back of her mare, Lady, would have been wonderful in any other mood, but Crystal knew better than to try to ride Lady when she was angry. She'd done it before, or at least she'd tried before, and Lady had told her in no uncertain snorts that Crystal needed to calm down before getting onto her back.

Instead Crystal took off through the trees on foot, running and leaping around the huge central meadow, exalting in the sensation of wind whipping through her hair as she manipulated tiny flows of air to spring her strides much farther than would have been possible before she learned to use magic.

Crystal lost track of the number of laps she ran, but after a while the goddess was finally winded. She knew she could refresh herself with a mere touch of the purple healing flows, but the run had given her the chance she needed to calm down and so there wasn't any point to continuing. She settled into a jog, headed back toward the estate.

Veering off at the last minute, she loped into a hedge maze she'd largely ignored in the past. It wasn't large, nor were the hedge rows much taller than a regular-height person. Still, she knew how much Matt adored hedge mazes; he'd often said that he considered them the ultimate display piece in a cultured estate's grounds. It hadn't surprised her at all, then, to arrive at his estate to find one out behind the main building.

Crystal slowed her pace to a walk, enjoying the sensation of being lost and slightly shut in as she strode down the narrow paths. Finally she found what she assumed was the middle, adorned as it was with a magically-powered fountain surrounded by benches. She sat, her still-tumultuous thoughts rushing and gurgling in time with the flowing water.

Being a goddess should mean being able to control her anger, she mused. It didn't, however, mean never showing it. There were plenty of instances throughout mythology where one deity or another had made that point. Looking back, she really felt like she'd been in control of her anger, displaying it rather than getting lost into it. But as her mind replayed the fight and the cold night against a stone wall, the renewed hurt boiled up into anger once again. She shifted her gaze up to the sky, where Matt's carefully-controlled climate wards created, as usual, a breezy warm day with blue skies and cotton-puff clouds. Grinning a wicked grin, Crystal tweaked the wards' energies slightly, and then a little more. She watched the sky turn grey, menacing clouds herding their benign cousins out of the overhead view.

Well. Matt had his powers, and she had hers.

The sound of a throat being cleared behind made her whip her head around.

RJ, dressed in his work coveralls, held up his hands defensively. "Just doing my job, Crystal," he said quickly. "No need to blast me or anything."

"Why would I blast you, RJ?" RJ had been her husband's boss, the president of the college, before the cataclysm that had thrown everyone's life into chaos. After a confrontation with Matt which hadn't gone well for the former president, he seemed to have settled fairly happily into his current role as chief groundskeeper. Crystal hadn't seen him very often, before the cataclysm, in anything less dressy than slacks and well-pressed polo shirts, but for some reason the overalls and t-shirts seemed to suit him better.

"I—um, I just don't know if you're still angry. At Matt, you know, but sometimes people—or gods—take that out on others."

"Angry at Matt? He told you about our fight?"

"No, no. I haven't spoken with him all morning. Haven't even seen him."

"Then how did you know about our little magical tussle?"

"Little?" RJ's look was incredulous. "You're kidding, right?"

As she slowly shook her head, confusion filling her expression, RJ continued, "Crystal, you two shook the entire mansion last night. It took a couple hundred of the thrakkoni zipping and teleporting about to notify us that you two were just enjoying a little tiff before people calmed down and went back to their quarters. Some were wondering if we hadn't just imagined the cataclysm and were now facing a nuclear attack. This morning we—my crew, that is—checked it out and found the side of the mansion newly decorated with long charred black stripes. You really didn't see it?"

Crystal used a column of air to raise herself so she could see over the hedge. Sure enough, the entire side of the building was blackened in long vertical streaks. It looked as though bolts of lightning had danced all along the wall. She hung her head, shamed. She'd spent her entire married life with Matt in a wonderfully peaceful, loving relationship, and now that they'd had their first fight it had made headlines in a great big sooty way.

RJ slipped easily onto the bench beside her and placed his arm around her shoulder. "It's okay, my friend. Nobody hurt, and my crew can repair the damage quickly enough. Besides, Krista and I have had plenty of good healthy arguments. Granted, we've never called down the vast powers of the universe during our rows, but they've been hum-dingers regardless. Hey, what's one blackened wall when you have so many more that are still white?"

She laughed in spite of herself, appreciating RJ's sense of humor.

"Yeah," she said, sobering, "I guess there are plenty more. But the girls walked in on this one. The look on their faces tore my heart in two."

"Scared 'em a little, huh?"

"Scared 'em a lot."

"Heh. Smart girls. Did I mention that you two shook the entire building?" When she nodded, he continued, "I thought I had. You two lovebirds just need to practice safe argument from now on. You know—whisper, don't shout."

She laughed again briefly, and then stopped as she broached the subject that bothered her the most. "He didn't come for me."

"What do you mean?"

"After the girls walked in on us, I teleported away to a spot on the estate that he gave me as my special refuge."

"That little stone cottage, right?"

"Yeah, how did you.... Never mind. I expected—hoped—I don't know, something—that he would come after me."

"Why would he do that, after you two nearly set the estate on fire?"

She turned her head to look at RJ, surprised at his reaction. "Well, because I wasn't there. I'd left angry. I would've been worried, if the places were reversed."

"Oh. Let me make sure I understand. You would've been worried if your husband had been off by himself at night? You do realize who you're married to, right?" Searching her blank expression for understanding, RJ continued, "You know, one of the primary gods. The freakin' god of war. The god who, in his anger, killed off all the dinosaurs, if I heard the story right. That god. That you'd be worried about him is quite commendably wifely, I guess, but I really don't see the point. Nor do I see why he'd be worried about you off by yourself, considering you're an immortal goddess yourself now. You've got some serious mojo, Crystal. Enough, in fact, to stand up to the freakin' god of war. And you're smart enough to know that the two of you needed cool-down time after. I don't get why you're upset over this."

"I...." RJ was right. Crystal had been away for months at a time learning the skills she needed to pass the tests of ascension. She'd even faced a goddess in a battle to the death, or so she had thought at the time, in order to earn the right to join the pantheon of deities. Matt hadn't been entirely pleased with her decisions then, but he'd stood behind her and never displayed an ounce of worry. Why, indeed, should she feel offended that he hadn't shown worry over her spending the night at the couple's private retreat on his own estate?

A grin spread over her face, her anger still wanting to seethe but firmly in her grip now. Kissing him on the cheek, she said, "Thank you, RJ."

He rose. "For that? Anytime, ma'am. But you still—I mean, I kind of sense that you're still a little bit peeved."

"Oh, I am. Trust me, I am. My husband stepped over a godda—a cuss—oh, dammit, why is it now that I can't even curse well without thinking of what it literally means to be the wife of a god? Whatever. Anyway, my husband crossed a line last night, and he and I still need to hammer that out. But you've done a fine job calming me down for the most part."

"Okay," RJ said, his tone suggesting that he didn't really believe Crystal. "Glad to help, then, at least for the most part."

"RJ, wait," she said as he turned to leave.

"Yes?"

"I don't get it. You, that is. You were always a proud, sometimes to the point of coming off as kinda arrogant, college president. Then we had the cataclysm. After that, you and Matt got into an argument and then he, you know, killed you. Granted, he brought you back to life, but now you run around looking like you're pleased as punch as you do grounds-keeping and wear overalls. What happened to the arrogant college president?"

RJ sat and looked at his palms for a while, moving his fingers, touching the calluses that seemed to be a new addition to the features on his hands. Finally he replied, "Well, nothing happened to the arrogant college president, really. I guess it might look like I changed, but I didn't. I mean, I made a damn good living for Krista and the kids before the cataclysm, and I did it in the best way I knew how. Everybody expects a college president to be arrogant in a certain way, and so that was the face I wore. And it worked, at least for the most part. As for your husband, well, let me tell you, honestly, that having your husband on my team was the best thing that happened to me. Yes, he and I got into it occasionally before the cataclysm, but I could always count on him to do what was right," Crystal turned her head slightly to hide the smirk she couldn't keep off her face. 'Occasionally' was a horrific understatement, though she had always assumed the friction she heard her husband's side of was due to both men's passion toward the college and its successes. She was successful in hiding the smirk, she noticed, as RJ continued without missing a beat. "That said, though—all that time, I really just wanted a simpler life. I always looked jealously at the people who could happily maintain a small flock of farm animals and call that good. I—well, I wanted that. Then the cataclysm happened, and all our lives were turned over. I was just as lost then as everybody else was. Lost my parents, and Krista's family, and the rest of —well, you know. It was hard. Since the cataclysm, I've slipped into the superintendent's shoes and absolutely loved this job. This is my ideal job, Crystal. I get to work out in the sun every day, and in a magically-protected environment to boot. I get to supervise a great crew. Have you seen what the thrakkoni can do physically? It's amazing. Plus your husband really isn't bad to work for. He's a good guy, you know. All said, this is a great life, and a great job. I can be proud of it—and I am proud of it—and I don't feel the need to come across as arrogant any more."

RJ held out his hand and helped Crystal rise from the bench.

"Thank you, RJ. You've helped me put things into perspective."

"Don't mention it."

Crystal walked a short distance away before she teleported directly into the center of her bedroom. Matt was there, sitting in the chairs facing the windows, staring over steepled fingers out into the world.

"Hi," she said, unsure and inexperienced in how to begin a conversation after an argument.

Matt rose mutely and walked over to her. With a single move, the god of war enfolded his wife in his arms, pressing her body to his. "Hi," he replied quietly.

"I missed you too, dear, but I need to breathe."

"Not really. You're a goddess, remember?"

As Matt released her from his grip, she reached out and behind with a flow of air and pinched his butt, baring down with the flows of air as hard as she dared.

"Ow!" he cried. "That hurt."

"Not really. You're a god, remember? Besides, I think you deserved that," Crystal said, smiling while hoping that Matt would agree. She looked into his face and her last ounce of resistance melted as he nodded.

"I'm sorry, my love. You're right, I shouldn't have compared you to my ex-wife. You're...."

"Oh, shut up about that," she cut him off. "You and I are meant to be together forever, bored or not, ex-wives or no. It's now behind us. Right? You're not going to do it again. Right? So we're done talking about it. Right?"

"Um, right?" Matt purposely put a querying tone into his words, a smile playing its way across his face.

"Right," Crystal said as both turned toward the sound of four paws racing across the floor. She grinned and leaned over, offering her arms as a landing pad, and Yuki accepted with a leap. She giggled as her Chihuahua licked her face and neck.

"Therapuppy, hard at work," Matt observed with a grin.

Crystal smiled, keeping her mouth tightly closed against the onslaught of her dog's tongue. In the initial days following the cataclysm, the estate had seemed a dark place as the survivors grieved for lost family and friends. Everybody had lost someone. Crystal had taken it upon herself as the lady of the manor to visit those who were having the worst of it, and she brought Yuki along initially just for the companionship. It had turned out, though, that the white Chihuahua's antics could bring smiles to faces much faster than anything Crystal could say or do, so Therapuppy had become her quasi-official title.

"Where were you last night?" Crystal asked, knowing she wouldn't get an answer. The last she remembered, the four-pound, long-haired dog had been curled up at their feet as they settled into the bed.

"Therapuppy is, of course, excellent at sensing moods," Matt replied for Yuki. "And pretty darn smart, too, but don't expect me to admit that often. At the first sign of agitation, she high-tailed it into the closet. Then when the battle got really heated—um, literally—I closed the closet door.

"Well, Therapuppy says thank you, daddy," Crystal said, her smile growing. "So how are the girls?"

"Right now, quite unwilling to talk to me. You want to try?"

"The god of war can't get two teenage girls to talk to him?"

"As a matter of fact, no, I cannot. They get that from you, I think, and dealing with it wasn't in my god of war training manual. Other than torture, of course, but I find that strangely inappropriate in this situation. Let's both go try, I guess, and see what the god of war and the goddess of the tongue can accomplish together."

Hand in hand, Crystal and Matt walked into the entry. Crystal's breath caught when she noticed the burn marks gouging their way down all four walls. "Matt," she whispered, "let's agree right now that any more fights between us must be held down in the battle room, okay?"

Crystal was referring to a special room only she and her husband had access to, a room shielded from the remainder of the estate both by ancient magical wards and by feet-thick granite walls.

"How about we just agree not to have any more fights, dear?"

Crystal swiveled her eyes to look at her husband. "Can't promise that anymore, Mister of God War." She stuck her tongue out to punctuate her error. "Besides, I hear that make-up sex is incredible."

"Mom! Eww." Heidi said, her door opening.

Matt and Crystal both chuckled. "Come on out, dear, and get your sister. We need to talk," Crystal said in her most persuasive voice.

The family gathered in the anteroom. At first the girls' eyes darted around to all of the scorch marks on the walls, their expressions painting a portrait that Matt finally noticed. He gestured and the walls immediately reverted to their colors from prior to the fight. Sorscha joined them, standing silently behind and between Matt and Crystal.

"You know, girls, married couples, no matter how much they love each other, occasionally disagree," Crystal started, her voice quiet and tentative.

"Most of them don't burn the house down or blow it up with their anger while they're disagreeing," Heidi objected.

"Now, we didn't really burn the house down," Matt said, earning him a glare from all three women. "Okay," he capitulated. "We almost blew it up. Better?"

"I think what our daughters are looking for, my darling husband, is some sort of assurance of safety for themselves, their parents, and all their neighbors, in the years ahead."

"Our daughters need to go read more Greek mythology about Mars and his temper, I think," Matt said.

"You're. Not. Helping," Crystal barked from under arched eyebrows.

Matt's gaze traveled from his wife's commanding expression to his daughters' scared faces. He sighed. Holding his hands in the air, he said, "Okay, okay, I was joking. Well, mostly. Look, girls, I love your mother with all my heart. Yes, I have a feisty side to me, one that I've been developing for hundreds of millions of years, and so it's not going to change anytime soon. So when your mother and I found something—something really stupid, I admit—to disagree on, I found the challenge—well, fun. Exhilarating. After all, your mother is not only a beautiful woman and a wonderful partner and an intellectual equal to me, but she's also an extremely powerful mage. I—well, I am sorry for letting the contest get out of hand, though, and I am perfectly willing to promise never to let it do so again. Aren't we, my love?"

"Exhilarating? Now that's a unique way of describing a domestic disturbance that nearly destroyed the domicile," Crystal said, arms crossing in irritation.

Matt spread his hands in supplication. "I am who I am, my love. Can you forgive me that much, at least?" On his face he held a parody of remorsefulness.

Crystal gave in to a smile and a chortle at Matt's expression, and then said, "We all are who we are, and there's nothing to forgive unless you've been keeping other secrets from me. Any more goddess ex-wives, mister?"

"Nope, no more hidden secrets," Matt said. He surreptitiously lifted his right arm and looked under it. "Nope, nothing there either. So how about it, girls? Ready to put this behind us and move on as a family? Say, to a horseback ride?"

"We're always up for a horseback ride, Dad," Linda said. "But next time you two disagree, how about a game of tic-tac-toe rather than global thermonuclear warfare?"

"Agreed," Matt said, laughing as he rose from the chair.

"And by the way, Dad, the Greeks didn't know who Mars was. You were Ares to them," Linda said.

"Oh, yes, so I was," Matt said, beaming a smile at his more studious daughter. "Glad someone was listening."

"Thhffffpfpfpft," Crystal said, and then they teleported themselves and the girls directly to the stables.

"So, are you feeling like taking another trip to Olympus?" Matt asked Crystal after dinner. Crystal smiled back; the ride around the estate had been—well, exhilarating—and then the family had spent some wonderful time together in Matt's expansive library. It had ended up being a grand day, truth be told, a stretch of time when the family had come together and enjoyed each others' companies. She could think of only one way to end such a phenomenal day, and drinking at the dive bar of the gods wasn't it.

"Actually, I've only ever heard, second- and third-hand, about how good make-up sex is. How about we skip the journey to the bar at the center of the universe and instead find out the truth, first-hand, so to speak?"

"Oh, an experiment! Sounds brilliant to me, especially the part about the hands," Matt said, making a grand gesture out of kissing the top, and then the palm, of her hand, and then leading her into the bedroom.

A Mission

Crystal rose after Matt, as usual, the next morning. While her body didn't actually need sleep due to the energy oscillations she had learned to set in place during her magical studies under Apollo, she still enjoyed the peacefulness and the restfulness of it. When, that is, her husband allowed her the opportunity, as he hadn't for much of the night.

Matt had risen with the sun to hold court upstairs in his throne room, as he always seemed to on a particular day of the week. Crystal never quite knew which day of the week it was; she hadn't cared enough to either track it or ask about it, and in a world without labor laws—or real labor, for that matter—or paychecks, or anything else related to normal timekeeping requirements, the general use of calendars had faded away. Of the thousand (ish) human inhabitants of the estate, a couple hundred were identified as battle mages of various strengths, and these were all required to practice magic every day no matter whether they called it a weekday, a weekend, a Thursday, a Thor's Day, or by any other term. The rest all had their duties to perform in the kitchens or on the facility and grounds crews, and with the work spread across so many hands no one seemed to mind the few hours of effort every day. At least, if someone did mind the lack of regular days off, no one dared complain about it to the god of war.

Crystal had wondered why the god of war held his receptions in a simply-decorated room; a plain mahogany throne was its only decoration besides the pretty gold circle on the floor that served as a teleport target and the golden bell he used to notify other gods of his impending presence. It seemed to her, after all, that the god of war should well be able to afford the finest of golden thrones beset with bright red rubies, his favorite stone. After their discussion, though, she thought she understood. The court—Matt's court—wasn't about ostentatious finery or a display of powerful identity as she'd assumed initially. Instead, it gave his immortal mind, and also his long-lived thrakkoni servants, something to do through the eons.

Crystal left the bedroom by teleporting the other direction, away from the stairs that led up to the throne room. Instead she let a small sigh of relief escape as the door closed behind her in the war room downstairs. Initially she'd had to sneak down the hallway used by the novice magicians to get to their training area, find the special brick to open the secret door, and dart in and down the hall to the war room without being seen by questioning human eyes. Her clandestine trips had become much simpler, though, since she had learned to teleport directly to the hallway leading to it. Granted, there had been the matter of modifying Matt's wards that were set up to detect teleportation on the estate grounds, as well as further wards designed to prevent teleportation to that room in particular, but her pride had demanded that she figure out how to shift the wards to ignore her energies rather than ask Matt to make the necessary change. He'd mentioned once that he noticed her revisions, but it had been clear from his voice that he was rather proud of her achievement.

The room had become as much her room as it was Matt's, anyway. He rarely worked out down there, busy as he was teaching the novice mages and attending to other matters of the estate. Crystal, meanwhile, exercised her battle skills in the granite room every day. Not only was it—what was the word he'd used, exhilarating?—to test her skills against opponents in all sorts of situations, but she also still had yet to come down from the highs she'd experienced while being trained by Thor to defeat Aphrodite in the Olympian arena.

She worked out in the war room for a long time, using Matt's figurines both as they were and also with her own variations. Matt had molded the figurines on his desk using ka, the pure white essence of magic that was only used by deities, and only for works of great creation or great destruction, to replicate the various warrior and mage archetypes he had observed over the eons. When activated, the figurines would spring into the room in life-sized realistic form with all of the weapon skills and toughness they would've had in real life. While that was useful to some of her practices, she occasionally modified them to replicate the barbarian warriors she'd faced while training under Thor's hand at Valhalla or the casters with whom she'd sparred at Apollo's estate while training in the use of magic.

"Excellent! Very nicely done!" Matt's cheer startled her. She spun to face him, still holding the enchanted hammer that Hephaestus, the smith of the gods, had made for her after she passed his tests and apparently won a spot in his heart.

It had been nicely done, she admitted to herself as she relaxed from the battle stance she'd assumed in her surprise. She'd just finished taking down two dual-wielding barbarian warriors without either of her opponents getting a hit in and also without resorting to the use of magic. According to Thor's lessons it was supposed to be impossible to do so without a shield in her offhand, but—well, she was a goddess now, after all. A Thor-trained goddess, at that. A goddess who, thanks to Thor's always-painful teaching methods, could take on just about anything with her divine hammer in one hand and a short sword in the other.

"Just keeping my skills fresh, my love," she said with a leer.

"Mm hmm, and that's quite important, with all the wars going on these days."

"Mm hmm," she countered. "Except there aren't any. Sounds like the god of war is slacking, mister."

"Actually," Matt said, his tone growing serious as he conjured a chair into the room and sat down, "that's what I came to talk about."

"You're going to start a war? Or you want me to start a war?"

"I'm going to try to prevent one, actually. Or I want you to, anyway. No, I'm not kidding. I don't normally worry over whether there's a war going on, but this situation is—delicate. It needs your delicate touch."

"Go on." Crystal wasn't used to Matt delaying his approach to a point of discussion.

"Love, remember our first trip to Atlantis? When you met Prince Dhri?"

Crystal nodded, wondering where Matt was going. She had enjoyed the trip to Atlantis. She'd enjoyed seeing the diverse architecture of the city, for one thing. For another, the naga race that populated the city was so foreign to Crystal that the visit had been fascinating. They were cold-blooded reptilian creatures with intellects that rivaled and even frequently surpassed that of the human race, for one thing. For another, the naga figurines in Matt's war room were among the toughest to defeat due to their towering seven and eight foot tall frames and tremendous strength, and Crystal could only imagine how difficult fighting the real thing might be. Additionally, the fact that they actually hibernated for the two thousand years of each technology cycle was completely alien to Crystal. During their visit, the hum of activity in the huge bazaar had captivated her, and the silk merchant she had met offered some wondrous garments not available anywhere else in the world.

Unfortunately, that trip had been cut short by a dangerous visit to the estate by Aphrodite, when Matt's ex-wife had put the twins in grave danger for reasons Crystal still didn't understand. Matt and Crystal had traveled back immediately, the mother terrified for her girls' sake, and much of the rest was fortified into Crystal's memory as an ever-present source of anger.

"His brother has gone missing," Matt said.

"Oh. His brother, the king? So—why do you care that much for the safety of the naga king, as often as I've heard that you smashed his palace to rubble. And if you really care, surely you could just fly over there and find him yourself, right?"

Matt shrugged. "Probably not. He has always hated me, and goes out of his way to disguise himself from me or to cause me trouble. His servants and the nobles close to him, other than Dhri, won't talk to me either. So no, I don't stand much chance of finding him."

"Okay, but if he has always hated you, again I have to ask: why do you care? Some sort of allegiance you owe to the prince?"

"Allegiance? From the god of war? Of course not. I admit, I've developed a bit of a fondness for Dhri over the years, and so I don't like to see him torn up as he is. But there's also a certain amount of self-interest involved. King Takshaka is a brilliant and head-strong military leader who remembers all slights, and is thus a perfect ruler to have against me."

"The god of war would be nothing without war, is what you're saying?"

Matt shrugged again. "There will always be war, Crystal. It's just that Takshaka provides so much opportunity for it, while his younger brother Dhri is too level-headed."

"You do realize how twisted that sounds, don't you?"

"Well, yeah, but Dhri is also entirely against the idea of being king, himself. And it is his brother, a bond that transcends even the disagreements those two have often had. He really is grief-stricken. He reached out to me personally, sending a missive in the hopes of securing my intervention, though he knew it would be useless for me to do so in person."

"But—if it's useless for you to do so, why did he even try?"

"Because he knows that I will do what I can, and he trusts that I am smart enough to figure something out. I am a god, after all. You remember that, yes?"

"How could I forget?" Crystal smirked at Matt and then continued, "So that's where I come in, obviously. But why will I have any more chance of success than you?"

"Well, you're not me, for one thing. Naga don't really hate humans; in fact, the human race has served them well for a great many cycles. They don't trust us western gods much and most of them really don't like me. Granted, that might have something to do with me flattening a city or two of theirs in the past, but you know how faulty my own memory is in such cases. In any case, you can go in as a visitor, a human mage doing the dirty work, and you'll be for better or worse accepted into the palace with Dhri's help. You can pass yourself off as a powerful mage visiting from—oh, probably best to use Apollo's name for this. He's largely ignored the Eastern gods and civilizations, and as a result they have a bit less enmity for his mages."

Crystal recalled what he'd told her several months earlier during their first trip about the reason for the disappearance and reappearance of Atlantis. At the beginning of each technology age, it sank deep into the sea, and at the beginning of the next magic age, the island ascended again to rest above the water level. Its inhabitants, being cold-blooded, were able to survive for the two thousand years of being beneath the ocean by entering a deep sort of hibernation that left the inhabitants groggy for a while after resurfacing.

"They've gotten over their sleepiness now, right?"

"Most definitely."

"So will they act more irritable or less?"

"They're going to be naga, Crystal. Saying a naga acts irritable is like saying a mountain acts tall, no matter whether it's groggy or not."

"A mountain can be groggy?"

"You know what I mean."

"Yeah," Crystal said. "So, are there any clues that they've found?"

"Dhri could give me none. According to his transmitted report, one I place very little faith in, by the way, the king went to bed a couple of nights ago and didn't emerge from his chambers the next morning. No one saw him leave, and his guards were questioned thoroughly."

"Did he have concubines?"

Matt gaped at Crystal. "He's naga."

"I figured that out all by myself. What does that have to do with concubines?"

"They're—sort of snakes. Snakes don't have sex."

"How do they reproduce, then?"

"Eggs."

"And eggs get fertilized how?" Crystal crossed her arms.

Matt looked confused for a moment. "Hell, I don't know. I'd just assumed that the male goes and sprays stuff over them. That was—someone else's area of interest, anyway."

Someone else as in Matt's ex-wife, the goddess of love. Someone else, indeed, she thought.

"Okay, fine. So do you want a report on the naga mating habits while I'm over there doing your dirty work?"

"No, it's not like that, Crystal. Dhri actually requested that I ask you to come over and look into it. It's not that I don't want to investigate; it's that I can't. They honestly won't let me into the castle without me having to blow a hole in the side, which would kind of defeat the purpose."

"Of course I'll do it, Matt. But—won't they recognize and suspect Sorscha, too?"

Matt thought for a moment then shrugged. "She is a shape-shifter."

"But her hair won't change," Crystal said. The trademark metallic hair was the most recognizable trait the thrakkoni had, and she was pretty sure that the gods had graced them with it in order to make the race of servants more recognizable in the first place. Dragons bore scales of any of the bright hues of the rainbow; Sorscha's were glittering silver but other dragons shone in other colors. Thrakkoni hair, in humanoid form, was the same metallic shade that their scales were in dragon form. That was why Sorscha's hair always glimmered like tinsel. Crystal found it soothing and attractive. Surely, though, the naga would be sophisticated enough to recognize the metallic hue of a dragon's hair.

"You and I would see that," Matt said, "but I doubt the naga would be smart enough to notice."

"Still, I'll take Breenda, instead. Her hair is no less recognizably thrakkon, but at least it's not recognizably your thrakkon. She's offered herself as my own personal thrakkon, anyway, and I'd like to see how that works out. Besides, without Sorscha keeping your calendar, I'm not sure the kids would get fed."

"Not fair."

"Not fair is you sending me away again so soon after our first and best session of makeup sex. So tell me everything you know about the situation I'm going to be walking into."

Prince Dhri

Less than an hour later, Crystal found herself standing in Prince Dhritarashtra's study with Matt, Breenda, Sorscha, and the prince. Matt's briefing had consisted of very little else she found useful; the man could lecture her for hours about the fighting tactics of the naga warriors and sorcerers, but that he knew as little of their inner politics and machinations as he did of their reproductive methods was exasperating. A short and irritating discussion later, then, he had teleported the pair to the prince's home in order to prevent them being seen flying in. Sorscha had, in turn, helped Breenda zero in on the teleport target.

"I am very happy that you agreed to assist, Goddess Crystal," Dhri said formally.

"As much as I love my new title, can we just go with first names?"

"Absolutely. Please, call me Dhri."

"Well," Matt interjected, "Now that the two of you have gotten on so splendidly, it's probably time for Sorscha and me to get back to the estate."

"What, are they going to lose count of the cattle in your absence?" Crystal asked.

Matt chortled. "Probably not. Would you prefer I stay for a while?"

"Well, I do like spending time with my dear husband."

"And he likes spending time with his dear wife. But keep in mind that I'm gonna ask you again in a million years."

"Okay, fine. Leave if you wish."

"And miss Prince Dhri's fine telling of the tale of his brother's disappearance? I wouldn't dream of it, now. Besides, I'd miss you too much."

"Oh, bite me."

Matt started to comply, but Crystal pushed his face away, causing both Dhri and Sorscha to chuckle. She found the combination of the naga's airy hiss with the thrakkon's throaty huff oddly amusing, so she began laughing also.

As the laughter died down, Matt said, "Okay, so seriously, now, Dhri, why don't you relate what you know of the details surrounding your brother's disappearance to Crystal?"

"There's really not much to tell, other than it happened at night, and you obviously did it."

"Me?" Matt asked, a confused expression on his face.

"Someone who could only have been a god made his way into the castle without causing our teleportation alarms to go off. He'd been there before, too, because he teleported directly into the king's antechamber. The doors were closed magically so no more guards could come in while he slew the two who were in the chamber by cutting them in half, a feat that is difficult to imagine without one of those large swords you're known to carry around. The doors from the antechamber to the bedroom were then blasted down, in a style that, again, you are well known for. And then whoever it was teleported out, apparently taking the king with him."

"Huh," Matt said. "It does sound like my handiwork, doesn't it?"

"But you didn't do it, did you?" Crystal asked.

Matt turned to regard his wife with a surprised look. "Do you seriously need to ask that question?"

"Well, no, I don't. I was just—well, trying to get that much out in the open, at least."

"Huh. Well, for The Open's benefit, no, I didn't do it."

"Somebody's gone to a lot of trouble to make us think you did, my husband."

"Not necessarily," Matt shrugged. "I'm hardly the only god who knows how to teleport, or how to blast a wall down, nor are such feats out of the range of humans by this point, especially if they've got some help from a god's trinkets. And big swords aren't that unusual, either. Granted, mine are the biggest, but size doesn't always matter."

"But why would somebody with that much magical power to command use a sword to kill the guards?" Dhri asked, seemingly oblivious to Crystal's tongue sticking out at her husband.

"Oh, that would be a stylistic thing," Matt said. "It's—well, I guess you're right. It is the sort of thing I would do."

"But you didn't," Crystal repeated.

"No."

"And somebody wants us to think you did," Crystal said.

"Possibly. I'm still not sold on the idea, but it has merit."

"Why aren't you sold on the idea?" Crystal asked.

"Well, who would benefit from going through such an elaborate ruse to kidnap someone who is difficult to kidnap, while making it seem as though I'd done it, when it'll just make the naga hate me more without giving them a way to take it out on me?"

"I was going to ask you that question, actually," Crystal said.

"There you have it. Why invent a conspiracy when one isn't called for?" Matt asked.

"Hold on, there, my husband. Just because we don't see a motive initially doesn't mean one doesn't exist," Crystal said.

Matt sighed. "Good point, love."

"So when, exactly, did the kidnapping happen?" Crystal asked the prince, shifting gears to questions that could be answered.

"Yesterday morning, an hour or so before dawn. It's the quietest time in the castle."

"Anything unusual happen the day before yesterday?"

"I have heard of nothing."

"Have you searched for your brother since then?"

"Of course. We turned the castle upside down."

"What about the surrounding homes? The bazaar?"

"No. The private property is illegal to enter physically without a search decree signed by the king, and that decree is difficult to acquire without the king."

Crystal looked at Matt and asked, "Any reason I shouldn't try scanning for him the same way you scanned for survivors after the cataclysm?"

"No, not really. The scanning can be warded against, but there's no danger in it. I'm not sure how successful you'd be, though. Scanning looks for energy—an aura, if you will. When I was scanning for survivors I was looking to find human life forms in groups, rather than a specific life form. Looking for the existence of an aura is very different from looking for a particular aura, and besides, you've only met the king once."

"Right, but it wasn't all that long ago, and he was putting out a pretty massive aura at the time," Crystal said. Soon after her ascension to the ranks of deity, Matt and Crystal had returned to Atlantis to buy a silk dress she'd fallen in love with on the first trip. On the way, they'd run into the king and his personal guard, a dozen naga warriors and mages who looked ready to attack Matt at the slightest provocation. When Matt explained the touristy economic reason for their visit, the king had grudgingly let them pass into the bazaar with a mere warning.

"Held against his will, though, his aura will change over time," Matt objected. "If you go in looking for the same blazing force you saw at the entrance to the bazaar, odds are that you won't find it no matter whether you're looking directly at him or not. If you go looking for something more, um, muted, then you'll find every naga in the neighborhood."

"Well, I'll still try," Crystal said. "I'm not sure what else to do."

"Make sure you ask questions of everyone," Matt said. "Your unfamiliarity with naga facial expressions means you'll notice pretty much everything, which is a good thing to a point. Granted, you'll go into overload if you try to remember every detail, so consider it more of a comparison thing. Keep track of what's different. Oh, and read any energy resonances left behind."

"Left behind?" Crystal asked, confused.

"Yeah, the eddies. Apollo didn't teach you about the eddies left behind, did he? I shouldn't be surprised, since he knew that he was teaching you for battle rather than magical forensics, and of course the twit wouldn't teach you one ounce more than I was asking him to. But yes, when spells are cast, energies are displaced, and there is a small but noticeable energy eddy left behind. If it's a simple spell using small or moderate levels of energy, like a fireball or the lifting of a rock, it creates a minor eddy that dissipates within minutes. Teleportation eddies, meanwhile, last a few days. The energy to blast fortified doors down will probably leave eddies for a week or more. The problem is that up to now you've only been concerned with gathering energy, not detecting what already exists. To read the eddies, you need a little bit lighter touch. What's so funny?"

Crystal stopped snickering and said, "The god of war is telling me to have a lighter touch. That's...."

"Ironic, I know, but it's what is needed now. Think of it like the surface of a pool. Casting major spells is like dipping your arms in and wiggling them around, splashing water where you want it to go. Reading the spells that have been cast is more like hovering just over the water, watching the path and rhythm of the ripples that already exist without touching the surface. It's a challenge, but I'm sure you can figure it out. Once you can see the ripples, of course, you can tell the mixture of energy that was used for the spell to be cast, and since most of us have been casting our spells in our own particular way for millions of years, that knowledge, in addition to knowing the magical habits of the gods and goddesses out there, might give you a clue who was behind the attack."

"But I don't really know the magical habits of the gods and goddesses out there," Crystal objected.

"No, but I do," Matt said. "If you can get a good read, let me know what it looks like and I can help interpret it."

"They won't let you into the castle, though."

"You haven't forgotten how to do telepathy, have you?"

"You will have help in the castle itself, by the way," Dhri said.

"What? Who?" Matt asked, his head whipping around.

"The god you call 'twit' already has a senior mage on site," Dhri said. "She seems fairly competent."

"Well, if Apollo is already on the case, why do we need to be here?" Matt said, crossing his arms.

"Because I trust you more than the human or the western god whom I hardly know, so I am asking you for your help. Additionally, I assumed that you'd prefer having someone with a vested interest in your own innocence on the case to a human who has no such interest."

"That's true," Matt said. "Still, I'd like to meet those who are investigating my case in my stead. Can a meeting be arranged between me and Apollo's senior mage?"

Dhri hesitated, and Crystal decided to take charge and intervene. "He does prefer having a goddess with a vested interest on the case," Crystal said, looking at Matt. "I'll be happy to mediate all discussions as necessary with the mage from Apollo's camp, having been trained there. Now, may I have the honor of your escort into the castle, Prince Dhri?”

“Absolutely, Goddess Crystal,” Dhri said.

Crystal walked over to her husband, who was still glowering at her and the prince. Taking his head between her hands, she pulled his lips to hers for a kiss.

“Relax, dear. I’m going to prove your innocence,” she said, “and then you’ll owe me when I come home.”

“Mmm, a debt I will gladly pay,” Matt said, replacing his glower with a leer as he and Sorscha disappeared through dual teleports.

Just—be careful. I love you, Matt’s telepathic message came to Crystal as the teleport closed.

Unwelcome In The Castle

Breenda donned the deep-hooded cloak that Prince Dhri gave her to hide her shiny blue hair for the walk, and then Crystal and Breenda followed him through the streets of Atlantis up to the castle. As they walked, Crystal was once again struck by the diversity in the architecture that wound its way through the city. The construction was consistently of a grey granite stone; she assumed it was the only material that would withstand a two-thousand-year plunge to the bottom of the ocean. The material was the only consistency, though, as the design ranged from classic Greek columnar to Asian pagoda and nearly everything in between. Clearly, the Atlanteans traveled the world in their years above the surface, and they brought much of the architectural variety back with them.

The crowded city street narrowed as it climbed up the long hill that led to the highest point on the island, upon which rested the massive stone castle. Crystal noticed that there seemed to be no room in the city's space planning for what she would have considered recreation. Each building was constructed right next to its neighbor, and the closeness continued right up to the grey stone wall that surrounded the castle. From what she could tell, there was a little space, but only a very little, between the castle itself and its defensive wall. Not that the naga seemed to need parks or other recreation; every one they ran into was industriously headed somewhere, all giving the most efficient of nods to the prince on their way to whatever business awaited. They were clearly a very industrious race.

The guards at the gate crossed arms, clearly averse to letting the pair pass even in Dhri's company, but they relented after a few minutes of discussion with the prince in their strange hissing speech. Crystal had managed a translation spell on her own before starting out across town, an accomplishment she was proud of, but the nuances in the magic with which she wasn't familiar caused some difficulty in catching the words quickly. She caught some dire threats in the prince's voice, though, just prior to being allowed to pass on by the guards.

It was only a dozen steps from the gate through the thick granite wall to the entry doors of the castle. Crystal glanced to the sides as they stepped across the short path. As she'd guessed, it was a narrow space with just a roadway punctuated every so often by what could only be guard posts.

The castle itself loomed immediately over them. From the front it looked to be of a simple box design, its austerity strange in its juxtaposition with the wild diversity of architecture of the rest of the island. That wasn't really surprising to Crystal based on Matt's frequent descriptions of the naga as a pragmatic military society. It was impressive to approach from the front, though, as she imagined she could see the tiny tips of arrows poking out through the tall slits in the castle above. Crystal also saw the small openings in the wall and ceiling of the sally port leading up to the main entry door into the castle proper. It would make an excellent killing field for anyone rushing the doors.

She really was beginning to think like Matt.

The chamberlain in the entry was more accommodating than the gate soldiers, but not by much. "Ssstill digging for exsscusssesss to use for avoiding blame for the wessstern god of war?" he asked Dhri. "And ssso you wisssh me to let thessse followersss of the war god ssstay here and help the exsspertsss sssearch?"

Dhri drew himself up to his full height and replied, "My brother's disappearance must have you very rattled, chamberlain, to forget your place when speaking with one of the royal house."

The chamberlain sniffed and bowed. "My prince will forgive my lapse, I pray. The human and her pet can, with His Highness's oversight, stay in the east wing in whichever of the rooms she most desires, as they are all vacant at present. Except, that is, the room where the other human is staying, but she can feel free to stay in that room if she wishes. We have no suitable food for humans at present, so His Highness will hopefully be able to find a way to provide board for their stay. They are free to move about the castle as they will, since they have the prince's blessing to do so. Does my prince have anything more for this lowly chamberlain to attend to?"

Dhri held his presence for several seconds in silence. Crystal mentally catalogued the expression he wore as what must pass for regal. Finally the chamberlain turned and slunk back toward the inner area of the castle.

Speaking in English, Crystal asked Dhri, "How many of the castle residents speak my language?"

"Very few, as contact hasn't really been made yet for our own sorcerers to work out the translating devices. Don't assume that no one does, though. It wouldn't surprise me that the chamberlain or the head sorcerer might have arranged it somehow. And if you're overheard speaking in English, you can expect the distrust of you and your motives to increase even further. You should speak in our language as much as possible." The last sentence was in Atlantean, spoken as they walked through the antechamber into an inner courtyard.

Along the way, Crystal asked in Atlantean, "Prince Dhri, why did the chamberlain's speech pattern change so abruptly?"

"What do you mean?"

"At first, he had a lot of sss sounds in his speech, and then after you upbraided him he did not."

The prince looked sideways at Crystal and said, "That was very observant of you. The emphasis on the s sounds is the distinction between highborn and lowborn speech among us. His speaking to me as a lowborn would was intended to be explicitly insulting to me. Everyone in the castle should speak as though highborn, and so if you hear the same from someone else, you know they are insulting your station."

The courtyard was furnished with sculptures of naga, benches, and a few pedestals on which rested glowing light orbs. Despite the presence of the orbs, the area was mostly lit with skylights above. The floor was a brightly-polished version of the same stone that all the walls in this and every other building were constructed from, as was the high ceiling. Glancing around, Crystal noticed that the statues were the only addition that might pass as artwork in the bare-walled castle. She used that to try to make small talk with the prince.

"Do all the statues represent famous naga of the past?" she asked in Atlantean.

"Yes."

"Do you have any statues of your gods?"

"No, of course not. Statues of the gods only impress humans."

Crystal felt her face flush as a few nearby naga laughed at her expense. Dhri's biting sarcasm wasn't intended for her ears, she knew. He had a reputation among his own kind to keep, and she was just a human as far as any except him knew. She followed Dhri silently the rest of the way into and down the corridor of rooms that constituted the east wing of the building. He stopped at the end of the unornamented hall and opened one of the doors.

"In here, I believe you will find the largest unoccupied room. Is it to your liking?"

Crystal walked in. It really was quite a large room, nearly as big as the entire suite she shared with Matt at the estate, and it looked to be furnished for royalty. In addition to a round, oversized bed, the room featured several stone seating benches, a dresser, and a beautifully-carved wardrobe. All the furniture other than the benches appeared to be made of a fine dark lacquered wood, though as she looked closer it appeared to be more of a wood veneer over something, probably more stone. A line of square columns built up into brackets at the ceiling were used to separate the bedchamber from a side room that was less well-apportioned and apparently meant for a servant. Each wall was decorated in stone and tile murals depicting naga in various situations.

"Are these murals history, art, or both?" Crystal asked.

"Yes," Dhri said.

Crystal looked back from the art to see if the prince was smirking, but he still held the strange regal-ish expression from before. Recalling that she was playing the part of a regular human mage, she inclined her head and said, "This one is very beautiful, Your Highness. May I ask which this mural is: art, history, or both?"

"That one is both, as are all the ones in this room. Our history is far too involved to discuss now with my brother's disappearance so fresh, but the short answer is that the mural depicts in an artistic manner some of our forces taking part in what came to be called the Battle of the Ten Kings. It was an epic melee. But now I must ask again: does this room meet with your approval?"

"Oh, yes. It is very nice. Thank you, Prince Dhri," Crystal said formally.

Dhri closed the door and said, "The other human appears to be staying across the hall, according to the mark on the door frame, so this suite should suit you well in your combined efforts towards concluding the investigation. I will have your luggage brought here, since the wards prevent teleporting it in. Since the chamberlain cannot find the grace within himself to feed you, I will have food brought also."

"Food won't really be necessary, Prince Dhri, as...."

Dhri cut her off with a hiss. Looking meaningfully up at the corners of the room where Crystal realized listening devices or spells would likely be placed, he said, "I would not want you to go hungry regardless of the length of your stay. And now, may I escort you to my brother's chamber where the abduction occurred?"

Crystal mentally kicked herself. Dhri and Matt had both warned that the rooms would likely be spied on, and yet she'd forgotten it in the time it took to walk across the city. Some sleuth I'm making myself out to be, she thought. She nodded her assent for the prince's escort.

"Stay here, Breenda, and draw me a bath for my return, please," she said as she walked out. There was no point bringing a thrakkon into a magical investigation because the thrakkoni immunity to the flows of magic meant that they could neither sense nor direct the flows for gathering the evidence she needed. In addition, Crystal had needed reminding once too many times about sticking with the script they had decided upon before coming. Breenda would never be disguisable due to her metallic hair and extremely angular features. The naga tended to look down upon the thrakkoni in their role as a subservient race, so it would be easiest to pass Breenda off as a human Crystal's thrakkoni servant—which, was, in fact, close to the truth, except that Crystal was no longer a human. The naga, though, wouldn't know that thrakkoni never bent their knees to humans.

Crystal followed Dhri back through the hall, up a grand flight of stairs that circled the courtyard, and then along the hallway that led away to the north. Down the hall were evenly-spaced doors that were open into what appeared to be simply-furnished guard rooms, and at the end was a doorway that stood open. It was guarded by two large naga who let them pass without protest.

"My brother's chambers," Dhri said levelly as Crystal drew up beside him. The bodies had been removed, but two large spots of blood still stained the rich rug, and black marks from flame singed the entire wall opposite the entrance. The door, she saw, hadn't just been blasted off its hinges as she'd previously thought, but rather the entire frame and surrounding stone work had been caved through. Stones still lay on the floor in the bedroom, where a round bed similar to but much larger than the one she had been offered downstairs lay unmade.

"And now I shall leave you to your investigation, Crystal. I will check back in with you from time to time, and if you have need of me you have but to ask the friendly chamberlain. Oh, and don't hold his churlishness against him too heartily. He is not only a distant cousin but also a good friend of my brother's, and is likely taking the king's disappearance much harder than he indicates on the surface." Dhri nodded once more to Crystal and departed.

"Well, then," Crystal said to herself in English. "I just have to figure out where to begin."

"The beginning is usually the best place to do that," a voice carried from the king's bedroom.

Crystal followed her ears and, rounding the corner, saw a young and very thin girl who turned a captivating smile toward Crystal and bowed, her black curls framing her face.

"Hi," the girl said. "I'm Melissa."

Melissa

"Melissa," Crystal said, allowing the syllables to spill over her tongue. She'd always loved the name. "So Apollo sent you, I understand?"

"Yes," Melissa said, her face brightening. "You know the great lord?"

"Quite well," Crystal said.

"Oh? Are you a—a goddess?" Melissa stammered.

"Who, me? Noooo," Crystal said, running her eyes meaningfully around the room, lacing just enough sarcasm into her tone to make her meaning clear. As much as she needed to keep the naga in the dark, she wanted Melissa to understand her position. The young girl gave Crystal a subtle nod; good, she got it.

"You're only a novice?" Crystal asked, looking at Melissa's white dress. She recalled her own training with Apollo, in which she had been required to wear a scratchy white dress until she'd mastered Apollo's test and graduated to the level of adept. Adepts always wore robes that were colored the same as the energy they were studying: red for fire, yellow for air, blue for water, green for emotions, purple for healing, deep indigo for earth, and orange for prophecy. Crystal couldn't help but grimace thinking about orange; she'd hated the prophecy work they'd done. Apollo had said, and Matt had confirmed with a laugh, that the prophecy the mage received was always completely correct, but rarely useful in any real way.

As luck would have it, the first prophecy Crystal received had shown her the battle she'd fought against Matt's ex-wife in the arena in Olympus. After, she had only seen commonplace things like herself riding Lady or sitting in the anteroom of their chambers at Matt's estate, but the first vision had stuck. It had honed Crystal's resolve to learn all she could as fast as she could in order to ascend.

"Me? Of course not," Melissa said.

"Of course not what?" Crystal said, coming back from her memories to realize she'd completely forgotten the question Melissa was answering.

Melissa's smirk infuriated Crystal, but it disappeared as quickly as it had come, replaced with the same pleasant smile Melissa had worn since their meeting. The girl said, "Of course I am not a novice. Lord Apollo just sends us all out in white gowns for neutrality purposes. But surely you knew that, Miss—um, what did you say your name was?"

"I'm sorry. I'm Crystal," she said, letting her irritation drop. She had no reason to be irritated at the little girl, she told herself.

"Miss Crystal, then," Melissa said smiling.

"Just Crystal, please. Miss Crystal reminds me too much of my teaching years, and I—really don't want to be reminded of those." Merely mentioning them brought a lump to Crystal's throat as she remembered a time surrounded by young kids clamoring to learn. Granted, it hadn't always been that way, but who remembered the less-than-great times?

"I see. Crystal it is, then. What kind of a teacher were you?"

"I taught elementary school for a while. Then I had my girls, and I mostly just stayed at home taking care of them. I still volunteered in their classrooms fairly often. You know, you can take the teacher out of the classroom, but you can't take the classroom out of the teacher. So what did you do before the cataclysm, Melissa?"

"Oh, a little of this, a little of that. Did some acting, and some other stuff. My passion, prior to my discovery of this incredible power of magic, was being a massage therapist."

"Oh, a masseuse. That sounds exciting."

"Not so much exciting as fulfilling. And we therapists, just so you know, are rather offended to be referred to as masseuses."

"Oh, I didn't know," Crystal said. "I'm sorry if I offended you. Why is the term insulting?"

"We're therapists."

Crystal waited for a few long moments to see if there would be more to the explanation, but Melissa stood quietly, the same pleasant smile on her face. Finally she gave up on understanding and said, "Well, therapists it is, then. I suppose the trail isn't getting any warmer. We should get to the investigation."

"We should, indeed," Melissa said. "I just arrived a few minutes ago, myself. Perhaps we can work together to scan different parts of the room for magical residue?"

"Sure. Are you—did Apollo teach you how to scan for residue?" Crystal asked.

"Am I competent, was what you were going to ask? I am the best student in the universe's all-time best magical instruction academy. The great lord has told me so several times. I believe it's safe to say that I can handle this investigation quite well on my own, but I'll be glad for your help anyway. You know what they say about two sets of eyes."

As indignant as Crystal wanted to feel at that, she let it pass. She still felt too new at being a goddess to smite a human for impertinence, and she really had been about to ask Melissa if she were competent. Besides, the girl's smile had an uncanny quality about it that made it hard to become or stay angry with her. Crystal decided to try diplomacy.

"Can you teach me what Apollo taught you, then? He is the master of the arcane, from what I've heard, and undoubtedly his teaching was strong."

"Certainly," Melissa said, "though I'm not certain what Lord Apollo could have taught me that your own master would not have taught you. It is a straightforward process."

"My husband, actually. Not my master."

"Considering who your husband is, aren't they much the same thing?" Melissa asked.

Crystal, unable to field a good riposte, settled for a shrug.

Dining, Atlantean Style

By the time Melissa finished delivering a lengthy lesson on reading magical residues, Crystal wondered why the girl hadn't been a teacher. The girl showed real talent with her explanation, giving it to Crystal in a practical and visual manner that Matt hadn't and taking time to point out specific flows in her analysis.

"You should've been a teacher," Crystal said as Melissa wound down.

"I was, sort of," Melissa said. "Therapists are teachers to our clients. And I made a lot more money doing that than I would've made in a classroom."

"Good point," Crystal said and walked over to the spot where the wall had stood. "So, I'm reading a lot of fire energy here."

"A lot of a lot," Melissa agreed.

"Isn't that strange? I would've thought to use air energy to batter down a wall."

"And you batter down walls often?" Melissa asked.

"Well, no, but if I were to try, I'd push air against it," Crystal said.

"When battering down a wall, the heat works to soften the joints between the materials so that the push of the air will be more effective."

"Ah. So you batter down walls often?"

"No, I don't, but were I to give it a try, I'd use a combination of fire and air," Melissa countered, her pleasant smile turning up into a playful grin.

"Touché, I suppose," Crystal said. "But this energy signature is entirely fire, and a whole lot of it."

"So it is."

"So what do you make of it?" Crystal asked, hoping that Melissa would have an idea. She sure didn't; her own detective skills were proving woefully inadequate, and standing in the king's chamber bantering about the proper way to take down a wall using magical energy seemed a waste of time.

"I make of it that whoever did this used fire energy. It's not like there's going to be a signature down on the corner."

"More research required, then?" Crystal asked.

"And what did you expect? You know the king's magicians already tried this and came up empty, do you not? It's the only reason we're allowed to come in and play—they've already given up."

"Well, I'm not giving up."

"Of course you're not. I'd make fun of the way you said it, but I'm not giving up either. Now, what we need to do is comb the room in search of smaller eddies before they all dissipate. Look, let's do a criss-cross pattern. I'll follow that wall and go north and south, you follow the wall behind us and go east and west. After each pass, step a foot or so to the side and repeat. Let's take our time and look."

Crystal wanted to rebel at the human mage's stepping into the command role she deserved, but Melissa seemed to know what she was talking about. She went to the wall the young mage had indicated and started stepping slowly across the room, un-focusing her eyes and reading the elemental flow patterns.

"So, didya find anything?" Melissa asked, smiling at Crystal as they collided coming back to the original walls. Both had been walking and not paying attention to physical surroundings.

"Look! I found a mage," Crystal said.

"Ha ha. I take it you found as much in the way of magical eddies as I did."

"Unless you really meant to say as little, then no."

"Hmm. As little, then. It's more accurate, I suppose."

"Yep. That's pretty much it. Next pass, then."

The two women criss-crossed the room entirely. Crystal was discouraged that they found very little. She shook her head as they met back in the middle of the room.

"It was too much to hope for to find something here right away," Melissa said. "We're really just getting started."

"Oh," Crystal said and then heard Melissa's stomach growl. She reckoned it had to be nearly dinner time, after the long slow process of sweeping the room. "Hey, I'm hungry too. Time to go find some food?"

"Sure," Melissa said. "It'll give us a chance to strategize."

"The prince is supposed to be sending some food to my room, since the chamberlain said they don't have food for humans in the castle."

"Better to go try the dining room, food for humans or no. There's no telling what we may learn in a public place like that, but I'm sure our chances of learning anything at all are greater there than they would be in a private guest chamber. The naga digestive systems are enough like ours that they wouldn't eat anything poisonous to us, I would think, so he's probably just thinking that he has nothing he would serve to human royalty. We should be fine."

As the pair walked down the hall toward the dining room, Crystal mused, "I wonder what naga eat."

"Fish and seaweed, probably, at least till they build up some trade," Melissa said. "I didn't see many herds of cattle or amber waves of grain on the island."

"Oh, have you toured the island?"

"I'm going to have to work on my sarcasm face around you, aren't I?" Melissa asked. "How about, next time I mean something in a sarcastic way, I smile like this?" Rotating her visage toward Crystal, the girl twisted it into the most bizarre mockery of a grin that Crystal had ever seen.

"It will benefit our ongoing friendship more if next time you mean something in a sarcastic way, you just not say it," Crystal lectured. "And—look out for the pole."

Without changing her expression, Melissa deftly stepped around the narrow column that stretched upward to the high domed roof of the chamber they'd just entered. "How," Melissa asked, continuing as though the column hadn't even existed, "did we manage to cultivate an ongoing friendship when I was neither consulted on nor informed of the matter?"

"It sounded nicer than 'ongoing sarcastic antipathy,' I suppose," Crystal said drily, eyebrows raising as the corners of her lips turned downward.

"There! See? Now that was a good sarcasm face," Melissa said, clapping her hands gleefully, her own expression slipping back into the disarming smile Crystal had come to know. "Maybe I can just start mimicking the expression you used."

Crystal sighed as she opened the door to the dining hall. "Maybe," she said.

"Besides, antipathy is such a nice-sounding word. It rolls off the tongue cleanly with some ups and downs—antipathy. Antipathy. Antipathy," Melissa said, repeating the word several times with varying inflections and vowel sounds. "Never mind that antipathy is as difficult to build in such a short time as friendship is, of course. It's still one of the prettiest words. You do pick the best words."

"Was that your sarcasm face?" Crystal asked.

"Bingo! Good job!" Melissa said and then both turned their attention to the servant, a finely-dressed naga who brought plates of food and set them down in front of the women while clearly refusing to acknowledge their presence.

"Not very welcoming to humans, are they?" Crystal asked.

"No, that they're certainly not," Melissa said quietly and picked around at the food on her plate. "But that said, you'll be pleased to note that I'm pretty sure our charming serving staff member pulled these plates at random off of the tray over there, and so I doubt that the food is poisoned."

"Well, that's comforting," Crystal said. "What is it, though?"

"Food."

"I'm trying to see your sarcastic expression again."

"No, not sarcasm," Melissa said. "It really is food."

"Okay, not sarcasm, but not an answer, either. What kind of food?"

"Now why would I know that? You could go ask Grumpy-face, but I doubt she'd answer. Not in any intelligible way, anyway. By the way, would you like my fish?"

"Fish? Is that what this is?" Crystal looked at the oily slab of cream-colored flesh on her plate. "It doesn't look like they cooked it enough."

"Doesn't look like they cooked it at all. It's not unusual for sea-based societies to eat their fish raw, Crystal. I believe before the cataclysm it was called sushi and cost more per pound than the cooked fish did. You've never had sushi?"

"I—never developed a fondness for it, no, especially when it was served—um, slab-style like this. And there's no wasabi or soy sauce."

"You should go ask our charming serving staff for the full sushi set-up and see what happens," Melissa said with a coy smile. "Regardless, one of us needs to at least cut a few pieces off it and push it around the plate, and I'm a vegetarian. Which, I believe, leaves exactly one of us to fulfill the 'don't insult your hosts by wasting food' rule. Therefore, Crystal, I'm awfully glad you're stepping right up to take one for the team. And besides, what's the worst that might happen?"

"The worst? I might find it so foul-tasting that I spit it out onto you, and then we'd have to fight right here in the cafeteria. That wouldn't be good at all, would it?" Crystal said, her own smile turning coy.

"No, probably not. But at least you could taste it and let me know what I'm missing. The greens are quite yummy, by the way."

Crystal lifted a few of the stringy green strips off of her plate and looked at them closely. She lowered her voice and said, "It looks like somebody picked that green crap up off the beach and chiffonaded it."

"Ooh, a culinary term! Used incorrectly, though. Chiffonade is a noun."

"No, I'm pretty sure it's a verb. I watched that show about good eats and stuff before the cataclysm pretty regularly. Regardless, you and I are the only two people on the island who speak the language, so we'll just have to wait till the investigation is concluded to find out."

"Okay, that is a valid point. Not many copies of English dictionaries to be found here on Atlantis, I suspect. In any event, seaweed is quite nutritious, you know," Melissa said, munching on another bite of the green slimy vegetable. "And this is well-seasoned. And besides, what did you expect, potato salad and slaw?"

"Mmm," Crystal said, putting as much facetiousness into a single sound as she could. She popped a fork full of the seaweed salad into her mouth and chewed carefully. Melissa was right; it was tasty. The seaweed itself was like a sweeter version of a chewy kale, with a rich saltiness to it. "Tastes like it was sautéed in sesame seed oil."

"Definitely, I'd agree on the sesame seed oil, but can't you also taste a hint of flavorful fish oil?"

"Hmm," Crystal said, closely examining the signals coming from her taste buds. "Yes, I guess I can. Hey, aren't you a vegetarian?"

"I am," Melissa said, and then took another bite of the salad.

"Can you eat fish oil as a vegetarian?"

"I can eat anything I want. I choose not to eat the flesh of the animal inhabitants of the planet, but that doesn't give me the right to march into the kitchen demanding to know, and then change, the methods the cooks are using to make their customers happy, now does it?"

"I see," Crystal said, choosing not to answer what was probably a rhetorical question.

"So watch closely. This is me taking one for the team," Melissa said, gleefully downing another bite of seaweed salad. "Speaking of, aren't you going to try the delicious fish?"

Crystal popped a chunk of the white flesh in her mouth. "There," she said around it, "I'm trying the fish. Go team, go." She chewed, preparing her brain to receive all of the wrong signals from her taste buds. Those signals didn't come, though. The fish flavor was there indeed, and it was strong, but it was offset just enough by a tart citrus aroma she hadn't expected. It was actually pretty good.

"Mmm," Crystal said, finishing her bite and picking up another. "It's quite yummy. It tastes like—like vegetables, in a firmly-packed form, with fish oil added. You should certainly try it, dear."

"Nope! I am quite certain that I should not," Melissa said. "I'll be happy to give you my slab, though."

"Don't you dare," Crystal growled under her breath and finished chewing, glaring at Melissa's satisfied smirk across the table. She managed a few more bites before deciding she'd taken enough—for the team, whoever that was—and was done eating from the slab of fish ceviche.

Trying To Find A Kidnapper

"So? Strategizing time?" Crystal asked once both women had slid their still-burdened plates away from them toward the middle of the table.

"Nap time sounds better," Melissa said, stretching her entire body out straight, arms angling over her head as her back came away from the chair.

"I'm sure it does, but we're here to solve a mystery and prevent a war and become the heroines of our age," Crystal said. "So far all that we know is that the people who were attending the king are dead, and that the magicians tried and failed, and that whoever did it used a lot of fire-based magic."

"You're right, on all counts," Melissa said. "So now what?"

"Well, whom do we know who uses a lot of fire-based magic?"

"We?" Melissa asked. "Unless you know a lot of deities that I do not, I believe that we've passed out of our realm of expertise here."

"Good point. I'll ask Matt, and you can ask Apollo when you next speak to him. But I am hoping for any obvious clues that can be drawn from that, and I don't see any."

"Neither do I. Keep in mind that we only looked at one room. We still need to investigate the entire area," Melissa said. "Plus, at some point, we need to ask the mages what, if anything, they found. Did that husband of yours teach you anything about naga body language? Anything useful, that is, that doesn't involve showing fear and supplication toward a war deity."

"No, nothing," Crystal said. "He didn't even bother with the fear and supplication part."

"Hmm, I'm a little surprised. But that means our inquiries might be difficult to process. We should both probably be involved to make sure we don't miss anything. Let's work on interviewing mages next, then, and if that doesn't turn up anything we can go back to the king's chambers."

A couple of hours later the women walked back toward the king's chambers shaking their heads. The interviews with the mages had gone poorly; the naga, it turned out, were so certain of their own race's superiority that they expressed disbelief that the humans were even attempting to investigate. Prince Dhri had to be called in to sit with them to force the magi to speak.

After the fourth naga had ignored the women and spoken only with the prince, Crystal had sighed in frustration and asked, "I don't suppose we could try talking to a female mage, could we?"

Prince Dhri looked at her with what could only be shock on his face and said, "Well, no."

"Why not, Your Highness?" Crystal asked.

"We have no female mages. That would be—unthinkable. Your ways are different from ours, I fear."

Crystal sputtered and turned to Melissa, who was calmly applying a warm and sympathetic smile to the situation. "Did you know that?" Crystal asked.

Melissa nodded once and said, "It is not important now. Prince Dhri, is there anyone else we can interview?"

There hadn't been.

Walking back, Crystal said, "Sorry I almost lost my cool there. Misogynistic attitudes make me furious."

"Well, let it go. Misogyny refers to hating women, so it isn't really appropriate. The naga don't really hate women, they just have certain roles rigidly defined, and women rigidly don't belong in the role of magician. I guess when you live that long, it's...."

"Don't you go defending them," Crystal complained.

"Oh, I'm not. I'm on your side, remember? I'm just pointing out that when you have something as ingrained into a culture as this, there's no way California girls are going to change it."

"Oh, Are you from California, too? Most of Apollo's mages in training were from Britain, as I recall."

"No, I'm more of a big northeastern city girl, myself, but there was a song—oh, never mind. Point is, we're not going to change the naga's attitudes in anything close to the timeframe that we have available to us," Melissa said.

"Well, I understand that, but it seems now like we've wasted an entire day," Crystal said.

"No, not wasted."

"Tell me one thing we've learned."

"Okay, it was fire energy that was used to blast the wall down."

"Right. But what does that tell us?"

"Well, I don't know yet. But we have, in fact, learned something, even if we don't know the ramifications at this point," Melissa said, her smile turning up into a smirk.

"Fine. So this morning wasn't a total waste. What about this afternoon—what else have we learned since?"

"We learned that the teleportation alarms didn't go off."

"No, we already knew that, or at least I did. Besides, I suspect the alarms are possible to defeat somehow. Anybody who can blast through a wall with fire energy is probably powerful enough to fool the alarms, isn't he?" Crystal said.

"I'm not so sure," Melissa said. "Do you know how teleportation alarms work?"

The question brought Crystal up short. "No, I don't, actually. I've never thought to ask about it. Do you?"

"Well, yes, at least in theory. Teleportation works by translating from matter to energy in one spot and back again in another. That requires a tremendous amount of power, which is why only the strongest mages—and deities like your husband, of course—can manage it. The teleportation alarms look for the eddies caused by an energy-to-matter conversion, which frankly aren't that hard to find due to the hugeness of the spell. I don't know of any way the sensors could be fooled into thinking that the conversion wasn't happening."

"You don't know of any way."

"That's pretty much what I said."

"But it's possible they could be fooled in a way that we're not privy to," Crystal said.

"It is, but it's just as possible that the kidnapper just walked in instead. Occam's razor and all, you know."

"Seek the simplest solution, I know. But they barely let me walk in, and I was with the king's brother," Crystal said.

"You weren't toting along an illusion, were you? It's entirely possible that a good illusionist would be able to fool the guards into thinking he was a naga."

"So now we're suggesting that somebody adopted the illusion of a naga, learned their customs and mannerisms, and sneaked his way into the stronghold by himself while staying away from the magi who could certainly have read an illusion. Now, what were you saying about seeking the simplest solution?"

"Okay, granted," Melissa said, "The illusion idea isn't simple, per se. But it's still simpler than somebody teleporting in while disabling the teleportation sensors."

"Well, if there was a teleportation, shouldn't we be able to sense the eddies?"

"Possibly. Let's try," Melissa said. Their discussion had taken them all the way through the castle to the king's chambers once again, and so both women immediately put their senses to the test looking for residual proof of teleportation.

Suggestion From the God of War

"See?" Melissa said gleefully once the pair had criss-crossed the area outside of the king's chamber twice searching unsuccessfully for the energy-based stain left by teleportation. "I told you. No teleportations were harmed in the making of this mystery."

"Okay," Crystal admitted. "So I'll buy that somehow the kidnapper came in bearing some sort of disguise or illusion. But that doesn't explain how he got out with the king without teleporting. Surely the guards would've stopped them from walking out?"

"Not surely. Well, surely that they couldn't have just walked out, but don't also assume they didn't teleport out. By that point the kidnapper had blasted a wall down and managed to set off every alarm in the building besides the teleportation sensors. Everybody was on their way to this chamber—well, all but the stationary guards in charge of things like the treasury. That's what the mages said at the beginning of their stories, remember? So by that point the whole castle was up in arms and getting a headache from the massive chimes. The outward-bound teleportation alarm added in at that point wouldn't have meant anything," Melissa said.

"Okay, but shouldn't we have read some residuals of the kidnapper's teleport out, alarm or no?"

"There is that," Melissa said, her gleeful expression darkening with the admission.

"I wonder…." Crystal said, looking through the hole where the blasted-out wall had once stood.

"What?" Melissa asked, following Crystal into the other room.

"Right here!" Crystal said, reaching the middle of the room. "Here's our teleport spot."

"It's—yeah, I guess so. I'd looked here earlier, by the way, but this isn't exactly a teleportation spell. At least, it's not a teleportation spell as I'm—well, as I've seen them done."

"What's the difference?" Crystal asked.

"Don't you know? You're the—the student of the god of war," Melissa said, punctuating her pause with a glance around the room that mimicked Crystal's stance when they had met.

"Heh," Crystal said, "funny. Very funny. But no, I'm not really an expert at this kind of spell."

"Oh. Well, neither am I, really," Melissa said. "I really was just hoping you'd know. It's just that this spot feels different from the spells I've seen used to teleport."

It felt different to Crystal too; most of the time when Matt teleported he used ka, and she'd learned the spell from him. This spell, though, had used a tremendous mélange of energies with a foundation of fire energy. Still, it was clearly a teleport; she could sense the mass to energy conversion that had happened. "Okay, then, let's recap. So far today we've learned that the naga don't think women should be magicians, and that the wall was battered down with an unusual amount of fire energy, and that the teleportation spell used to leave wasn't—well, normal. Oh, and that the naga serve fish raw and seaweed sautéed. Is that about right?" Crystal asked.

"Pretty much," Melissa said.

"Well, I'm sure the god of war will be pleased with our progress," Crystal said.

"You think?"

"No, not really."

"Well, pleased or not, I need to get some sleep," Melissa said. "You probably should too, and we'll reconvene here in the morning."

"Sleep? I...."

"I know, I know, you can hardly feel tired as important as this investigation is, but you have to accept the fact that you're only human, Crystal. Sleep is a requirement if you're going to stay sharp through tomorrow."

Crystal gritted her teeth. As much as she hated it, Melissa was right. Crystal no longer needed sleep, but if she stayed up and worked tirelessly through the night it would destroy her cover.

"Don't we have a deadline?" Crystal asked Melissa.

"Not that I know of," Melissa said. "So far it's just a matter of a case that needs to be broken. That can always change, of course, but if it does I'm sure we'll know. Till then, we need to keep pace for the long haul."

"Okay, fine," Crystal conceded and faked a yawn. "I'll see you back in here first thing in the morning, right?"

Melissa nodded through a yawn and left. Crystal glanced around the king's chambers one final time, hoping to glimpse some sort of magical 'I did it' calling card and thus solve the riddle. When nothing caught her eye she growled under her breath and left, heading back toward her own room.

"Ma'am, the prince had dinner delivered for your enjoyment," Breenda said when she walked in, pointing to a tray that boasted a covered dish.

"Oh. Damn, I forgot about that in all the researching effort," Crystal said. She really had no desire to see another slab of raw oily fish, to be honest. Better to make up something—anything!—than to face that again.

Breenda continued, "The prince's servant explained that he realized that naga fare might not be appreciated by our race."

Oh, right—Breenda was supposed to be a servant to a human. Crystal mentally kicked herself for forgetting that detail in favor of the investigation at hand. She lifted the cover from the plate. Dhri had done well. Fruits, primarily, greeted her, but there was also a selection of sliced cheese on the side.

"Are you hungry?" Crystal asked, knowing the answer already.

"No, ma'am. The prince sent a separate tray for me. That one is all yours, too, as I am not particularly hungry."

Crystal popped the flesh of an unidentifiable fruit—papaya?—into her mouth and relaxed as she allowed herself a moment of wondering why she was doing so poorly remembering her own cover story.

"So what did you find out today, ma'am?" Breenda asked. "Are we close to an answer yet?"

"Not much closer than we were this morning, no. And please drop the ma'am," Crystal said. "I appreciate the honor, but the use of the honorific doesn't do much for me."

"Very well, Crystal," Breenda said, the smile on her face reminding Crystal of a similar conversation she'd had with Sorscha, Matt's thrakkoni servant, when she'd first arrived at his estate. Sorscha had had a good reason for the shield of formality, though, as she'd apparently developed an aversion to Stacy, Matt's first wife, and the thrakkon's initial assumption had been that she would dislike Crystal just as much. Crystal had, luckily, proven the assumption wrong, but it took time and effort on her part, as well as Sorscha's. Now the two were as close to dear friends as a human and a thrakkon could be, so Crystal still held out hope for the fledgling relationship she and Breenda shared. Crystal had never had a servant, didn't know what to do with a servant, and was fairly well convinced that she had no need of a servant. Still, it seemed to make Breenda happy to be useful to a goddess.

Thinking of Breenda.... Crystal came back to the present to realize that the thrakkon loomed still as a statue, eyes unblinking. It was an unnerving ability of her race, something about their cold-blooded shape-shifting bodies being able to become rigid for hours at a time. Sorscha had worked beside Matt for so many millions of years that she never dropped into "stonestance" as Crystal called it, but other thrakkoni did it regularly. Breenda was doing it now, and while it was perfectly natural for her race as a matter of conserving energy, it ruined the illusion of her humanity.

"I have no further need for you this evening," Crystal said. "I can turn down my bed myself; you should get some sleep so that you're available early tomorrow as I rise to continue the work."

Breenda nodded, bowed, spun, and walked wordlessly to her room.

Crystal thought back over the day's lessons as she snacked on fruit, both exotic and less so, from Prince Dhri's tray. The apple was pretty obvious. What was shaped as melon chunks had a yellow skin and a pinkish flesh that Crystal had never seen before. It was good, though, despite being less sweet than the melons she was used to. The cheese was all white, fairly firm, and very tangy, and it contrasted with the fruit very well. Before Crystal realized it, she had eaten the entire tray.

Who cares? I can't get fat now, she thought to herself and smiled as she danced to her bed. It was finally time to call Matt.

Yes, love? Matt's voice came across the telepathic connection once she'd made contact. Crystal allowed herself a moment to feel proud of herself for establishing a mental link across several thousand miles of separation. His mental voice was full of apprehension, though.

I—thought you'd be happy to hear from me, Crystal transmitted.

Oh, I am, my love.   I am always happy to hear from you. But the connection was made with a forcefulness that suggested that the island was sinking.

Oh. I'm sorry. I had no desire to do that. The island is fine. I was just really looking forward to talking to you after an entire day here, so I pumped a little too much energy into the spell. That was only a partial truth. It was her first time establishing the link herself; every time prior it had been through the use of a blue glass bauble that Matt had enchanted for her. But she was tired of admitting her own inexperience with spell weaving, tired of not being good enough.

It's okay. The tone of telepathic communications can take a while to get just right. So Matt hadn't bought it. Was she really expecting her own mate to not see through the mistake for what it was, she wondered?

So tell me, what has happened in the long day you've been there?

Crystal told her husband about the meeting with Melissa and the pair's findings, leading him chronologically through the day. Matt chuckled over the raw oily fish—*it really is their normal fare, love, and I'm impressed you tried it,* he said. *It's quite tasty, though, don't you think?*

The fact that the magi wouldn't speak to women neither surprised nor shocked Matt as much as Crystal thought it should. *Crystal,* he replied, *the naga have been how they've been for hundreds of thousands of years. Some of the ones you've met today, in fact, probably have been around nearly that long themselves. If not, then they at least smell like it. There's really no point getting upset over their attitudes. Perhaps now, though, you can understand my joy in the occasional dalliance with blasting their island to rubble?*

Perhaps, Crystal replied, a smirk glimmering on her face. *But I still think it's because you just like blasting things to rubble.*

Well, yes, guilty as charged. Speaking of, let's get back to this part about the energy signature—are you absolutely certain it was nothing but fire energy?

Absolutely, Crystal replied.

And this Melissa agreed?

Yes.

Well, that's troublesome.

Why? Crystal prompted after waiting several long moments. She could sense Matt's disquiet, but it wasn't like him to not be forthright.

I'm probably the only deity who would blast down a wall with fire energy.

Why would you do that?

To watch it melt, of course, Matt said, and then he continued, *no, it's certainly not the best way to bring a wall down if that was what you were wondering. I'm sure that twit Apollo could tell you the specific mix of energies required to most efficiently bring a wall down, or to build one up, or whatever the clever little twit-exercise of the twit-day was. But you know me. I don't get into the efficiency of magic thing. Never have. I like to see it work. I like to feel the force of it. I'm the god who would stop a flood with fire rather than earth, just to watch the steam rise.*

That forcefully direct part of your personality has always been one of your most endearing, even when we didn't have magic available. It just never occurred to me that it might manifest itself in wall-melting. But—you didn't kidnap the king, though, did you?

No, of course not. Why do you keep asking that?

Because that's what will be asked of me, somehow by somebody, I'm sure. So if not you, then who? How do I approach an investigation where the only evidence leads to my own husband, a guy I know to the core of my very soul is innocent, when I haven't yet found anything to the contrary?

Hell if I know. If this were easy we could've just sent in the kids from Hogwarts.

Very funny, Matt. Fine, I'll keep on tilting at windmills here. Sooner or later one of them has to turn over, right?

Well, no, but…. Thank you, Crystal.

You're welcome. So back to topic, are you the only god who could bring down a wall with flame, or are there any others?

We all could, Crystal. I bet you could right now, in fact. You shouldn't try it, though.

Why not?

It pisses the wall owners off, and right now you're not in a great position to have a thousand angry naga coming at you. I'm sure you could handle it, of course, but I wouldn't want you bearing the guilt of that much naga-death. That's just me looking out for my darling bride's psychological well-being.

Thanks, babe.

Free god advice from your loving husband, and I get sarcasm back?

You reap what you sow, mister.

Well, you got me there. Anyway, melting a wall down isn't as big a deal as you have it wrapped up to be. Half of my battle mages could probably manage the feat as well.

So you're telling me that I might be looking for a human instead of a god?

Technically you're looking for a naga. I'm less concerned with who done it than with where the king is. Solve that mystery and the other one will play out. But back to your question, yes. The kidnapper doesn't have to be a god, despite what Dhri said when you started yesterday morning.

Oh. Right. Damn.

So what about the sword?

Sword? What sword? Crystal was at a loss.

The sword that the kidnapper used to kill two guards. Remember?

I remember now, but why is it a big deal?

Well, if there's any one thing your husband knows well, it's swords. The sword in question was big enough to cleave two naga warriors. That doesn't necessarily mean it was particularly large as swords go, but it still couldn't have fit in an overnight bag or down someone's sock. Since you're convinced that the perp didn't teleport in, that means the sword was either carried in or conjured on the spot.

And nobody saw anybody wandering around with a sword.

You don't know that, Crystal. Anybody you've talked to so far, you haven't remembered to ask about the sword. And if anybody is going to walk into and around the palace, and ultimately up to the king's bedroom doors, with a naga-cleaving sword strapped on his back, at least without meeting heavy resistance and raising some major alarms, then there's no way he's going to succeed unless he uses a fair amount of compulsion magic. You remember how that works, right?

Crystal did remember; the green flows of emotion magic had been one of the most intense learning experiences that Apollo had pressed upon her. The ability to control someone else's base emotions had seemed downright cruel when wielded by an expert. Apollo had watched Crystal gleefully bouncing up and down in a completely baseless expression of pure joy, and then writhing on the floor to the rhythm of heart-felt sobs, and in several emotional states in-between, all while looking on with his ever-present smirk.

I remember, Matt.

Good. Then you'll recall that you can't actually erase someone's memory, you can only make them desire not to recall it. It's kind of the same thing, effect-wise, except that nobody is perfect, not even us gods. While a guard under compulsion would refuse to remember an intruder, he probably wouldn't have any problem remembering a great big sword, and I, myself, would probably forget to spell-weave the guard into forgetting that.

Oh. Okay, so I need to do another round of talking to people who won't talk to me.

Not necessarily. What might work better is if you set yourself up to be captured.

What? That sounds crazy.

Oh, come on, Crystal. You're immortal. Surely you're not scared of a few naga. What you ought to do is wrap yourself in a cloak and wander around the castle at about the same time the abduction happened day before yesterday. It's a safe bet that you'll eventually bump into somebody who will question why you're skulking around the castle, and whoever that is will be the one to look for compulsion with.

Okay, so assuming I do succeed at this thing, how do I detect the eddies of a compulsion spell? There's no way it would require the expenditure of enough energy for those eddies to still be around two days later.

You're right. You can't detect the eddies of a compulsion spell two days after, but you won't have to. You won't be looking for eddies, but rather for the actual spell.

Oh, right, the perpetrator will have locked the green magic into a resonance field. I can find that.

If it's there, Matt cautioned. *It's a delicate search you'll be doing, and the kidnapper taking the sword in with him is only one of the possible scenarios.*

The other being that he conjured the sword in the room, Crystal replied, trying to establish herself in the conversation.

Right.

But Matt, I won't be able to detect a conjuring eddy at this point either, will I?

You won't be able to detect most conjuring, no, but the conjuring of a naga-cleaving sword, yes.

Why the difference?

Well, most conjuring spells are simple and small, but it takes a fair amount of raw power to make steel of the right composition for a sword. Specifically, it takes a lot of earth and air energy and then a tremendous whammy of fire. That, or you can use ka, but it's the same difference in terms of size of eddies.

Okay, now I'm feeling better about the future of the investigation, or at least about the investigation having a future to speak of. Now I just have to figure out which possibility to look into first, Crystal said.

Not hard to do. The wandering around to see who you bump into can only be done at a particular time. The searching for sword-conjuring eddies can be done at any time. Which you do first, then, depends on what time you get out of bed, my love.

I'm just never going to be as smart as you, am I?

Probably not. I do have a few—um, million—years on you, Crystal.

I know, Matt. I just feel so stupid sometimes.

Well, don't. You've never done this sort of private eye work, for one thing, and you're pretty new to magic, for another. Besides, there's no way anybody who had even the slightest bit of stupid in her would have become a goddess in just a few months. This investigation is actually a good way for you to learn more, you know, though I'd still prefer you not having to do it this way, with so much riding on your shoulders.

Well, thank you. How long did it take Stacy to become a goddess?

What's that got to do with anything?

Call it a jealous wife's morbid curiosity, I guess. I've refrained in comparing myself to the goddess of love in so many other ways, I figure the Time To Goddess rating might be a fair and relatively undamaging comparison to look at.

There's no comparison between the two of you, though. One of you is dearly beloved by the god of war, and the other is his ex-wife.

Aww, that's so sweet. So how long did it take her, Matt?

Through the link she could hear him snort before he answered, *Honestly, I have no idea. We separated when she was still a human, and it took me a few thousand years before I was willing to talk to her again. Sometime in the midst of all that, she became a goddess.*

Oh.

You could try asking the twit, though. Michael would probably know.

No, he kind of scares me.

And I don't?

Of course not. You're the love of my life. So how are the girls? Crystal asked, changing the subject to one she was more comfortable with.

The girls were definitely, Matt explained, full-on teenagers, having spent nearly every moment of the day with Steve and Corey, the twin boys who were very nearly the same age. Crystal worried; it was probably impossible, after all, for any mother to remember the things she'd done as a teenager and not worry that her daughters would be just like her. Still, she did trust her daughters to do the right thing in important matters of growing up, and she had some awfully strong and fast thrakkoni spies watching in case they didn't. Trust, but verify, her teaching program advisor had once said.

Crystal realized that most of the conversation had been held with her standing motionless. Grinning as she wondered what anyone spying on her would be thinking, she padded over and slipped into bed, still talking with Matt about the girls, his day, and anything else she could think of. It was like when they had been dating, she thought with a smile, only now she didn't have to hold a phone to her ear. She could talk all night without neck cramps, she realized, and the thought made her very happy.

Interrogated

Crystal woke with a start. Someone else was in the unfamiliar room, touching her shoulder. Jerking up, she called a light into being.

"Oh. It's you," Crystal snapped.

"Good morning," Breenda said with a worried smile. "Sorry for startling you like that; I didn't realize how soundly you were asleep. It is now the time that you asked me to awaken you."

Crystal reached back through her memories. Yes, she vaguely remembered asking Breenda, sometime between disconnecting from the conversation with Matt and slipping off into a deep slumber, to roust her early enough that she could wander the halls. She groaned. "I don't suppose I asked you to do it with a cup of coffee, did I?"

"No, but it's my job to be prepared for all situations," Breenda said, walking over to a stand where a steaming pot rested. She poured a few teaspoons of milk into the small cup and then filled it the rest of the way with a steamy black beverage and presented the result to Crystal.

"Mmm—cinnamon?" Crystal asked about the aroma. Not waiting for the answer, she took a sip. "Oh my, that's strong stuff."

"Most Atlanteans prefer tea, of course, but those who do drink coffee apparently enjoy it strong and spiced."

"Not complaining; it's good. It's making it much easier to rise and shine, that's for sure. I just wasn't quite expecting it."

Crystal sipped her coffee until it cooled, and then she rose and dressed quickly. Slipping her cloak's hood over her head and shrouding her face, she stepped quietly out into the hall. Wrapping herself mentally and physically up into the stealth required for the morning's walk was somehow invigorating by itself.

"Nice cloak," Melissa said from behind her, surprising Crystal enough that she jumped and gasped. She spun around angrily, preparing a retort for the scare she'd received, but then started chuckling when she saw that Melissa also stood in the hall, her own hand on the door handle to her room, her own features shrouded in a full cloak. "I see we go to the same clothing store," Crystal said.

"And read the same detective novels," Melissa agreed.

Crystal quietly filled her in on the plan that she and Matt had crafted the evening before. Her suspicion was borne out when the girl detailed a nearly identical plan for the day's research. Melissa must have reported to Apollo while Crystal was talking it over with Matt. The two men—gods, actually, and elder gods at that—were far more alike than either of them cared to admit.

"So, let's divide and conquer," Melissa said. "I'll...."

"No, let's not," Crystal argued. "There's not that much ground to cover, and having two of us there means you can keep him occupied while I look for compulsion spells."

"Or you can keep him occupied while I look," Melissa said.

"Yes, yes, whatever. Whoever he's talking to can talk to him while the other searches. Happy?"

"Absolutely not," Melissa said.

"Why not?"

"You haven't wished me a good morning yet."

"Neither have you," Crystal said.

"I wished myself a good morning quite some time ago. I just made sure it was totally silent because I wouldn't want anyone seeing me talk to myself."

"You know what I mean. You haven't wished me a good morning."

"I said nice cloak. It's much the same thing," Melissa said.

"No, it's not. 'Good morning' would've made me feel—happy. 'Nice cloak' nearly gave me a heart attack."

"Well, fine. Good morning, Crystal," Melissa said with the grandest faked smile Crystal had yet seen from her. It was—almost creepy.

"Good morning to you too, Melissa, and I must commend your most excellent work on your smile of sarcasm," Crystal returned with what she hoped was a similar expression. Despite her efforts, though, it morphed into a sincere grin. Stressful situation aside, she was beginning to be taken in by Apollo's protégé's charm. "Now, can we get started?"

The pair didn't have to walk far before they found what they were looking for, or at least it found them. As they started down the hallway leading toward the king's chambers, four pairs of naga hands shot out from behind and roughly grabbed each woman's arm, the pair on the outside yanking toward the hallway wall followed by a pair from the middle grabbing the other as the women fought for balance. Crystal instinctively reached for the energies to cast a fireball, but she stopped short just in time. Their mission was to investigate, not fight. Besides, as roughly as they were being handled, she was a little surprised it wasn't even rougher here in the castle from which the king had been kidnapped just a couple of days before.

"What are you doing here?" a naga who stepped into the middle of the hallway growled in English. At least, Crystal assumed he was a naga; he could just as easily have been a very large humanoid turtle with all the armor he wore. Shoulders that were easily seven feet above the floor took up nearly four feet of the width of the hall. That mountain of naga warrior might intimidate even Matt, she thought. Still, she fought through her intimidation to look for green magical energies and continue the investigation.

"WHAT ARE YOU DOING HERE?" the tank-sized naga bellowed again.

"Sir, these are..." the naga beside Crystal, who had pulled off her hood as another naga had removed Melissa's, said in Atlantean.

"I know who they are," the leader growled, this time in Atlantean. "Bring them," he said as he spun, lumbering off down a different hall that Crystal hadn't seen before.

The four naga threw Melissa and Crystal into a holding room and shut the door, closing them into a small eight foot by eight foot cell. The door they'd been tossed through had no knob on the inside, so unless one of them used magic they were stuck until someone else rescued them. The cell held a few small chairs, two of which the women sat into.

"Well," Crystal said and looked at Melissa, who just shrugged in response.

A short wait later, the door opened and the chamberlain huffed his way in. He looked at each woman sternly and asked, "Are you two quite done upsetting the palace guards?"

"We were merely walking to the king's chambers to begin our investigation for the day," Melissa said, her voice holding an edge.

"Dressed like thieves? Even if I believed your story, you were caught on listening devices laying out a plan to 'bump into' the guard forces. Well, you accomplished that. Congratulations. Now I have to decide whether to kick you out or let you go back to the silly façade of investigation you were clinging to," the chamberlain said.

"The decision will be simpler if you wait for...." Melissa started.

"For the prince. I know. You somehow have His Highness's faith that you will actually find something that the true professionals haven't. Rest assured that his faith is not generally shared, but he is the ranking sovereign in the king's absence. Fine. Go. I'll arrange for escort to the king's chambers for you, and if you deviate from there to your rooms again I'll kick you out immediately and quite physically and worry about explaining to the prince later. Do you understand me?"

"I do," both women said at the same time. They allowed the naga guards to lead them to the king's chambers quietly.

"No evidence of compulsion," Melissa said when they were back in the investigation area.

"No, none that I saw either," Crystal said. "I guess that means we look for...."

"It's right here," Melissa cut her off. Crystal opened her mind to the ambient streams of magic in the room and saw what Melissa was pointing to—clear eddies left by a powerful conjuring spell. Now that she knew what to look for, in fact, Crystal could see it very easily.

"I'm surprised we didn't notice it yesterday," she said.

"Yesterday we were looking for a teleportation spell that requires certain elements. I wasn't really even looking at air or earth energies."

"Okay, so now we have someone who didn't teleport in but was instead able to walk into the king's antechamber unmolested, create a sword out of ambient energies, slice two guards in half, and then blast a hole into the king's bedchamber and teleport away with the king rather than slicing him in half with the same sword. Right?" Crystal asked.

"That's about it," Melissa agreed.

"Why doesn't that make any sense to me?" Crystal asked.

"Which part? The bit about the perp being competent enough to conjure a killer sword yet patient enough to merely walk into the castle, or the part about him blasting a hole in the wall between the rooms using fire energy instead of just opening the door? Or maybe you're pondering why someone would be willing to set off alarms by casting tremendous spells after carefully not setting off teleportation alarms? Or perhaps you're confused by the kidnapper's willingness to kill guards and yet not to kill the king?" Melissa asked, one eyebrow arched.

"Yep, pretty much," Crystal said. Everything Melissa had pointed out was truly on Crystal's list of things that didn't make sense.

"Me too," Melissa said. "Let's at least closely investigate the spell eddies so that we can clearly understand the order in which everything really happened. Once we have that down, then we should probably report back to our respective libraries for further research."

A Truth Comes Out

Crystal and Melissa both looked up from their work as a loud rumble sounded from out in the castle. It grew louder and seemed to come closer, resolving itself eventually into loud argument and shouting. The two looked at each other, eyebrows raised curiously, and then turned back to the closed doors leading in. Crystal pulled together a flow of fire and watched Melissa do the same as they waited for an attack.

Before long the source of the rumble revealed itself as Matt stormed in followed by Birch and Phoenix, both dressed up in what could only be described as wizard-y robes. Crystal turned and smiled; both of her friends actually looked the part of powerful human magic-users. Birch's robe, tied with a golden cord, was white velvet with embroidered trees lighting up each hem. Phoenix's black robe, also cinched about her waist with a glimmering cord, glistened with suns, moons, and stars stitched into its borders. Each carried a carved staff that Crystal didn't sense much power in; she assumed they were mostly for appearance.

A visibly enraged chamberlain, the tank-sized captain of the guard the girls had briefly met that morning, and several dozen naga, all holding weapons at the ready, held their positions outside the room glaring in. Matt turned and pointed threateningly at the huge naga captain, a gesture the mighty warrior actually shrank away from.

Prince Dhri serenely followed Matt's party into the king's chamber, turned to face the guard, and imperiously ordered the door closed.

"Well, that was fun," Matt said in a voice that was joyous rather than sarcastic. He turned and greeted his wife, and then his eyes focused on Melissa. "Well, fancy that," he said, lips turning upward into a grin. "Hiya, Stacy."

"Stacy? No, this is..." Crystal said, her voice dying away as she watched the charming little girl transform into her nemesis. "How did...."

"Hiya, lover-boy," the newly-revealed goddess of love purred, her demure thin frame and straight black hair replaced by voluptuous curves and explosive red locks. "Come to rescue us poor women-folk with your grand pow-pow and your powerful human battle magi?"

Phoenix's reaction didn't surprise Crystal; her friend was the most hot-headed priestess she knew. Before the cataclysm the pair had spent a great deal of time together; while Matt worked the long hours required of a dean, Phoenix had done her best to raise Crystal up through the ranks of the Wiccan coven she ran. It hadn't worked; Crystal was too interested in the practical world to spend hours learning spells and magical incantations that she never saw bearing any fruit. Nevertheless, the hours the pair had spent together, both teaching and learning, had morphed into a strong friendship before the cataclysm and a stronger one since.

It was Phoenix, then, who immediately recognized Stacy for who she was and reacted. Crystal watched in horror as her friend quickly pulled together a ball of fire to throw at the goddess, knowing from experience how little good it would do against her.

Before Crystal could stop her friend, Phoenix loosed the fireball only to watch it dissipate harmlessly. Melissa—or Stacy, or Venus or Aphrodite, all names that now tasted like vinegar to Crystal's tongue—flicked her hand.

Phoenix died.

"NOOOO!" Crystal heard herself wail as she forced her legs to move. She rushed to her friend's side faster than Phoenix's body crumpled to the floor, catching her in a blanket of air. Crystal seized angrily at the violet energy of healing magic.

She could heal Phoenix. She just had to figure out what Stacy had done, and quickly.

The memory of Matt's killing of RJ helped. Way back then (had it been that long ago?) Matt had used the shocked silence of his trainees as a lecturing opportunity to explain that the heart had a switch that could be stopped and started again at will. At the time Crystal hadn't been able to identify the energy flows her husband had used, but now she could. She could sense the trail where Stacy had reached in and shut off Phoenix's heart. Tentatively, she reached into the same spot with a tendril of purple energy and flicked the chemical switch back on.

Her friend gasped and jerked. Crystal had accomplished what she'd thought impossible; she'd raised the dead. She would have celebrated if she hadn't felt as worried as she did about Phoenix's recovery. What was it like, part of her wondered, coming back from being dead? She knelt and watched the color return to Phoenix's face, silently willing her to come through it, to be okay.

Once Phoenix's heart rate and breathing were back to normal, Crystal relaxed a little, let out the breath of air she'd been holding, and pointed a relieved expression toward Matt. Then she turned her head a little further to release a withering glare at Stacy.

Both god and goddess peered down at her with the same expression of dismay. Why?

"Dear," Matt said in the lecture voice she'd heard him take on with students, "Please keep in mind that you're a goddess now."

"So?"

"So you're not supposed to care that much. About them," Matt said.

"About—them. Them? Humans, you mean. Our friends. You're joking, right?" Crystal asked, daggers creeping into her voice.

"No, he's not," Stacy said. "I'm sure they're cool and make you happy and all with their ridiculously short-lived concept of friendship, sweetie, but they're just humans."

"And this is just a wave," Crystal said, angrily flipping both god and goddess off.

Matt sighed and said, "Look, my love. You've only just recently been raised to goddess status. Your attraction is to be expected. Some day, you'll understand."

"I can't believe I'm hearing this. If that wasn't the most condescending bulls..." Phoenix said, starting to rise from the floor.

Matt waved his hand as though to bat away a mosquito. "Oh, shut up," he said, and she died again.

"Stop it!" Crystal screamed and started Phoenix's heart again. "Look, you two, if anybody's going to kill my friend, let it be me, okay?"

"That's kind of a strange deal to work, but I'm good with it. Stacy, what say you?" Matt asked.

"Oh goddess," Phoenix said, sitting up slowly from where she had lain sprawled across the floor, hands rubbing her temples.

"Yes?" Stacy asked, the superiority in her voice not matching the smirk on her face.

Phoenix ignored her. "Matt, I find it a bit ironic that at different points in history you decided you cared enough to marry each of the goddesses in this room, and both when they were just human too, and yet now you're all high and mighty about she's just a human. And you know, none of you left me dead long enough to find out about the whole white light of heaven thing, and yet the headache I have now is pure hell." She rubbed her temples harder, her eyes closed. Finally she rose slowly and continued, "Lookit. I know I'm only human and crap, but please do me a favor. Either leave me alive, or leave me dead. This back and forth thing hurts like hell."

Matt shrugged. "Fine with me."

Phoenix glared at the god of war and muttered "asshole" under her breath.

Stacy sighed aloud as Matt's laughter filled the room. "Why," she said, "dear god of war, do you put up with them like this?"

"She's cute," Matt said, shrugging while still chuckling.

"Cute?" Phoenix's voice dripped with indignation.

"If that's cute," Stacy asked, "then what is that?" She pointed at Crystal.

"She is my lovely and talented, and now exalted, bride. Who, I must point out, owns quite a powerful backswing with a war hammer, as I suspect you'll recall rather vividly, my exalted but exasperating ex-wife."

Crystal couldn't help, despite the insults being hurled, snickering at Stacy's momentary flush. She recalled every moment of the battle in the Olympus arena when she'd proven herself the combat equal, and then the superior, to Stacy, and she was sure that Matt's ex-wife recalled it as well. Part of the proof she'd offered had been a particularly painful reverse combination Thor had taught her. It was devastating when landed on armored combatants, and it had very nearly crushed the unarmored goddess of love's ribcage when Crystal had executed it perfectly.

"If she were half as quick with that wit as she is with that blasted, Vulcan-blessed hammer, we might have been done already," Stacy said with daggers in her voice.

"Hmm, seems to me that there's been two goddesses working here, neither of them solving the question. You know, if either of them had been half as quick with their wit, and so forth. Which reminds me," Matt said. "Why are you here, Stacy?"

"Besides attempting to prevent a war among the gods? Oh, no reason," Stacy said, surreptitiously cleaning under a fingernail.

"Where's...."

"Michael? I have no idea, but thanks for asking, asshole," Stacy snapped.

Matt cocked an eyebrow but otherwise did not respond. Crystal thought back to the tale Sorscha had once told her of how Michael, the primal god who had been known to the Greeks as Apollo, had in the earliest days been Matt's best friend, but that a woman—the goddess of love, apparently, and the very woman who stood in the room with them now—had come between the two.

Crystal snickered at the memory; both Matt and Stacy turned quizzical expressions toward her.

"You two are funny," Crystal said, shrugging.

"If I may," Birch interrupted, his voice small and tentative, "um, thou, um, exalted ones, this humble human must ask, are we not here to find out what happened to King Ta—um, Tassa— um, Tallahassee?"

"King Takshaka," Matt corrected gently.

"How'd you get a gnome?" Stacy asked, directing a curious smile toward Birch.

"Birch is perfectly human," Matt objected. "He's a mythology expert."

"Since when do you need a mythology expert? You wrote most of that crap, or at least you influenced the people who did. If I recall correctly—and I usually do—you arrange for that type of influence every cycle, just to prove that you can."

"We figured that out already, exalted goddess," Birch said. Phoenix muttered something under her breath and glared at Birch, whose plaintive shrug seemed to serve as his response.

"You figured it out because I told you," Matt snapped. "So how else would entire civilizations come to fear me as the war god?"

"Well, you are awfully damned powerful, and a nearly perfect asshole to boot," Phoenix chimed in. "Maybe they'd just fear you for your sweet ole' self once they come to know you?"

"Hey, on second thought, I kind of like you," Stacy said, her face twisting into a leering grin. "Sorry about that killing stuff, but—well, you know. A goddess has to do what a goddess has to do."

Matt leveled an intense glare at Phoenix, but could only hold the expression for a few seconds before he burst into laughter again.

"Yep," Birch agreed with Phoenix, his full beard rattling as his head bobbed up and down. He shrank behind Crystal as Matt stopped laughing and turned a glare his direction.

"A timid gnome," Stacy observed. "You obviously haven't taught him much of your battle mage pow-pow, have you, Matthew?"

"He's learned quite a lot of pow-pow, actually, Stacy. He's pretty damned good at it, in fact. You should lead an attack against my estate some day, so you'd see."

"Oh, right, because as we all know, the goddess of love is famous for leading frontal attacks," Stacy said.

"Right, I forgot that the goddess of love prefers insertions from..." Matt said.

"Don't say it, lover boy," Stacy interrupted, daggers in her voice.

"So what have you found?" Birch pressed, stepping through the glares to look Crystal in the eyes. "We're here to help figure out where the king was abducted to."

Stacy said, "I see why you like the little gnome, Matthew. He's tenacious. In answer to your question—Birch, is it?—we've found that someone worked their way into the primary guard area through trickery, and then used a massive blast followed by some pretty wicked swings of a large summoned sword to deter the guards over there. Then he teleported out from over here."

"The magic residue feels like Ben'thra," Crystal said, feeling somehow left out. "Hermes," she explained when she noticed that Birch's face was blank.

"Oh, I know who he is. Matt told us...."

"It does?" Stacy interrupted, and then nodded and said, "Oh, yes. Yes, it does."

Matt looked at Stacy quizzically and asked, "Really? It feels like Benny?"

Stacy's nod quickly changed to swing the other direction as she shook her head. "No. At least, it doesn't to me. But perhaps your young bride is onto something. It actually feels a lot like you did it, but if you did do it you wouldn't be here so seriously wondering who did do it when you didn't do it. In a strange, twisted way, it does feel like Benny—um, he did do it. Benny, that is. Ah, hell, I'm twisting myself around my own words now. That, if nothing else, is proof that Benny must be involved somehow."

"Matt, haven't you had some problems with Hermes in the past?" Birch asked.

"Yeah, you could say that. Benny wasn't at his best playing Hermes to the Greeks, though; he also played Loki against my Tyr to the Norsemen."

"One could argue that the most significant part of his role in the pantheon of deities wasn't that of trickster," Stacy mused.

"Oh, really?" Matt asked, his face darkening as it swiveled toward Stacy. "I thought the trickster aspect was the primary source of disagreement between the two of you."

Stacy shrugged, a half-smile barely showing on her face. "He was, after all, considered the god of trade, the god of messengers, and other things that required quick feet, hands, and tongue." She drew out the last word so that it carried a heavily-laden meaning.

"Uh huh," Matt and Crystal both said at the same time.

"Well, so why haven't you gone there to ask him some questions? It seems pretty obvious," Birch asked, seemingly oblivious to or else ignoring the hidden meanings.

"No, no, no, Birch," Matt said. "That's exactly the problem. We're talking about the primal trickster of the gods. If he had done it, he wouldn't have left clues that clearly indicated so. The fact that it's obvious means that it's not obvious."

"But the clues indicate that you did it."

"Precisely. The clues indicate that I did it, but I didn't do it. That means he left clues indicating that I did it which clearly indicates that he did it."

Birch continued, excitement in his voice, "But, but, but— what if he left clues indicating he had done it through you not doing it, knowing that you wouldn't suspect him of doing it because he'd left clues that indicated he'd done it through you not doing it? What if the clues were too obvious to be obvious?"

"Well now—wow," Matt said. "Just wow. Wow! That's some pretty impressively circular logic there, Birch. I don't even think I quite followed it through to the end. Regardless, it still just doesn't feel to me like he did it."

"Your gnome has a point, though," Stacy said. "We should at least visit Benny to ask him."

"Just ask him if he's involved? And if he says no, he's involved, and if he says yes, he's not involved? Is that the game we're going to play?" Matt said.

"How about instead of accusing him, maybe we—as in you—just talk to him?" Stacy asked.

"Why me?" Matt asked.

"Matt, did I just hear the ancient and all-powerful god of war whine?" Stacy asked with her hands on her hips.

"Of course not," Matt said, his voice deepening slightly as he deflected the accusation. "I was asking why you considered me the best choice of the assembled deities. Surely someone with different arts than mine would get a more useful and readily-interpreted response."

"From Benny? He's never been affected that much by different arts," Stacy said, looking at her own and Crystal's chests meaningfully.

"You would know, I suppose," Matt said.

"Matter of fact, I would," Stacy said, arching her eyebrows over the glare she directed Matt's direction.

Crystal, despite everything she'd gone through over the past several months, started feeling a kinship to Stacy. A small and strained kinship, but a kinship nonetheless. Granted, the goddess of love had entered Crystal's life wanting to kill her over a man, but then again that man was Crystal's husband, the god of war, and Crystal had to agree that the man was worth fighting over. They'd stood side by side and investigated to save the man, though admittedly under false pretenses, for hours. And now that the goddess of love was carrying on a repartee that Crystal could easily hear herself in, she seemed far less of a threatening force to be feared and hated and more of a woman to be—understood, of all things.

"Matt," Crystal interjected, "joking aside, you're the senior god, aren't you? You're also the one with the most to lose, and besides, you've got the most experience of us all in dealing with Ben'thra. If anybody would sense whether or not he's lying, it would be you."

"Too bad you can't ask the question in Breidablik," Birch mused.

"And what do you know of Breidablik, my precious little gnome?" Stacy looked at Birch, who cowered away slightly despite the good-humored tilt of her lips.

"See?" Matt crowed. "Told you. Mythology expert, right there."

Birch, realizing he had an audience, cleared his throat and said, "Breidablik was—is, I suppose—the home of Baldr and the hall of truth and light in Asgard where no untruth can be uttered."

"Asgard? Asgard can't be—is Asgard real?" Phoenix asked, an incredulous look on her face.

"Why wouldn't it be?" Birch asked his compatriot, his voice sounding stung.

"Oh, well, it's just that—well, no offense, Birch, but the stories of Yggdrasil don't exactly mesh with the Greek or Roman mythology that we've seen come to life. I kinda thought it needed to be one or the other. Sorry. So—so it's real, Matt?"

"Of course it is. Well, sort of, anyway. It sounded like a good idea, and so we created it long ago as back-story for a population that was very similar to the Norse. And yes, Birch, there have been hundreds of races similar to the Norse across the millions of years. Odin, the Father and Creator, obliges these sorts of things sometimes and just kind of thinks the fantasy areas into existence."

"Unlike the rest of us, who have to really work at it," Stacy said.

"Right. And once it's created, it doesn't really go anywhere, so—well, yeah, Asgard, and Yggdrasil, and the rest of it, it's all still there."

"And when I went to Valhalla, that's where I went?" Crystal asked.

"No, that Valhalla is on this realm, near here in the Himalayas—look, we're getting awfully far from the topic at hand. Birch, your idea has some merit. I'll go talk to Benny, and if I feel like he's not being honest—no, change that. If I feel like he's not being forthright, we'll move the conversation to Breidablik. Crystal, would you come with me? I'd love the companionship and the second set of eyes and ears."

"Sure," Crystal said. "But—wait. This Breidablik is interesting. Are you actually saying that there's a place where even gods can't lie?"

"Nope," Matt said.

"So why this talk about moving the conversation to Breidablik?"

Matt glared at Stacy as the goddess of love emitted an impatient sigh. "Give her a break, Stacy. She just ascended." To Crystal, he continued, "The core of the matter is in the difference between can't and won't. There is a geas set into the walls of Breidablik, to be certain, one that makes inhabitants and guests alike strongly desire to tell only the truest of statements. But you've studied green energy, right? Michael said you were incredibly adept at it, in fact. If you know green energy is being used against you, you can counter it. Breidablik's magic can be overcome with a simple twist of energy. A very simple one, in fact, yet we do not. It's a matter of convention rather than imposition. Does that make sense?"

"It does," Crystal said, nodding sharply as she glared at Stacy also. "But wouldn't you know if the person you were talking to was countering the geas?"

"If you were sensitive enough, sure, but keep in mind that a counter to a large flow of green magic is another smaller flow of the same stuff, and it's easy to lose one inside the other. Plus, if you really wanted to deceive, you would constantly toss about random flows of green energy so that nobody would be able to see a real counterspell."

"How devilish."

"Some would say strategic, actually. Well, then. Phoenix and Birch, unless you wish to stay here and keep Stacy company as she researches the crime scene more, let's teleport you back to my estate while Crystal and I go question Benny. I presume that you do not wish to come along, Stacy?"

"You presume correctly. I certainly have no desire to talk to him."

"Then in that case, we'll be right back."

Matt gathered energy twice; first the humans disappeared, and then Crystal and Matt followed. In the haste of her departure Crystal almost missed Stacy's sing-song dismissal, "Toodles!"

Hermes

Crystal blinked as her eyes adjusted to the bright light of her new surroundings. Several large dazzling golden chandeliers cast dancing lights around the room. That illumination was multiplied many times over by reflections from sparkling gold inlays set into the white marble wall panels, around the matching marble columns that were spaced evenly about the circular room, and on the side of each of the five steps that led up to the vacant gold throne. Other than the repeating rectangular pattern that had been tooled into the wall panels, there was no art to be seen. The gold was meant to be the art, it seemed.

The glare was nearly blinding.

"Matthew, how nice it is to have you visit me here in my humble home," a familiar, silky voice purred from behind. Crystal jumped in surprise and then turned.

She had met Ben'thra in the bar at Olympus. She knew, both from watching him in the bar and from listening to tales spun by Matt and by Sorscha, that the primal god of trickery was a never-ending source of trouble for his fellow deities. He was the god whose ferocious battle with Matt, sparked over a quarrel that Matt either couldn't or wouldn't recall, had changed the entire surface of the planet. It had also heralded the need for a ban on direct conflict among deities, or at least on conflict using ka, the essence of magic.

Stacy, if Crystal had gauged the love goddess's reactions correctly, hated Ben'thra, though Crystal hadn't had the opportunity to ask why. At the same time, she seemed to have had some sort of relationship with him in the past. Sometimes the actions and attitudes of the gods mystified Crystal, but she imagined that a million years was long enough for even the most powerful enmities to fade, or to be kindled. Or—both.

Regardless, Benny was trouble. The very incarnation of trouble, apparently. He was literally the original incarnation of it.

And he was naked.

Not completely naked, she was kind of glad to see. The Trickster wore a hat and his famed golden winged sandals, Crystal noticed as she shifted her eyes away from other areas, happy to have somewhere else for her eyes to rest. He also hefted a golden staff about which two golden serpents were entwined, but otherwise his body was entirely unencumbered.

Crystal couldn't help gaping; when she'd seen him in the bar at Olympus he'd always been draped in rich finery. Here in the apparent comfort of his own dwelling, though, he was flaunting a physique that she would once have innocently described as "like a Greek god." Now, she was married to a Greek god, but Matt's physique wasn't as—godlike.

Benny leered at her and said, "Ah, Crystal. It's grand to see you again, considering that you met the challenges of ascension so resourcefully and joined our ranks with such grace and aplomb as you did. And an incredibly lovely addition to our ranks you do make, I must add. Lovelier, perhaps, than even the goddess of love, and that is definitely a significant accomplishment. I see you're admiring my staff; do you like it?"

"My wife has seen just about enough of your staff, Benny," Matt growled.

"Pity. It was a grand gift, you know. Our brother Mi…."

"Yes, we know," Matt interrupted even more pointedly than before. "Could we impose upon you to put some clothing on? Please." The last word sounded to Crystal as though Matt had swallowed bleach.

"Oh, I suppose," Ben'thra said, and a white, gold-accented robe suddenly appeared around his form. It hung barely low enough to cover his private parts, and it accented his muscular shoulders and legs to an advantage that his brute nakedness hadn't managed.

"Now that I have bent, so to speak, to your expectations, may I ask the purpose of your interruption of my solitude in my own, formerly-happy home?"

"That is a nice staff," Crystal blurted out, still curious about a thought she'd had regarding the short, golden, serpent-entwined rod with the golden bulb at the top. "But I don't recall anything in mythology indicating that you were the god of medicine or healing."

Ben'thra's laughter pealed through the room, careening back and forth between the gold-clad walls, for several moments. It had to be the gold on the wall, she thought, that made the sound ring as vibrantly as it did. Finally he answered, "I was not the god of medicine, you are correct. Asclepius bore that questionable honor, at least to the Greeks. I see your confusion, though, as his staff has one serpent; mine, being better, has two."

"So why is your staff—the caduceus, right?—often used as the symbol of medicine?"

"Oh, Crystal, you are such a peach for your recall of the myths of your cycle. My staff wasn't used universally as the symbol for the practice of medicine. In fact, most used the single-serpent staff correctly as the symbol of the healer for a long, long time. My staff, the caduceus, was used by a small group of people because—well, because they got it wrong," Ben'thra said, his eyes lighting up and his voice merry, its pitch dropping nearly an octave as he sang the final word.

"They had help, though, didn't they?" Matt snarled.

"Oh, of course. What's the fun of being a god if you can't help the humans along a bit? It's not like you never talked to

Snorri, after all. Hey, speaking of Snorri, how did his brother, Sleepy, do in his own myth-writing?"

"Snorri Sturluson was a wise poet who just needed some help interpreting—. Oh, hell," Matt said. "Look, asshole, we're here to talk about the king of Atlantis."

"Temper, temper," Ben'thra purred, rebuke dripping from his voice. Matt let the silence draw out for several moments, and finally Ben'thra said, "Oh, fine, I guess that playing along is the fastest way I'll be able to get rid of you. King of Atlantis it is. Nice chap, as Atlanteans go. I've met him once or twice. Kind of scaly, rather large and grumpy, and he doesn't think very highly of western deities of war and such who smash his city to rubble, if I recall. King Takalaka, or something like that. Didn't he recently disappear?"

"It's King Takshaka, and yes, he recently disappeared. Some of the evidence at the scene points to your involvement," Matt said evenly.

"My involvement," Ben'thra said with a chuckle. "Well, now that's a fascinating way of delivering some very interesting news. Kind of a nice way of accusing, 'someone kidnapped him and we believe that someone was you,' isn't it?"

"Oh, wow! You know, you won't hear me say this often, but you're right," Matt said. "I can't believe how short-sighted we were coming here and being all nice like we are. Pretty silly of us simpletons, ain't it? Maybe it would be better if we just asked 'hey, asshole, did you kidnap the king?' Better?"

"Ah, now there's the war god we all know and despise. Succinct to a fault, arrogant, and hateful in every way."

"Mm hmm. Arrogant, eh? You have no room to speak of anyone else's arrogance, my fine bloviating fellow. Succinctness, on the other hand—now there's a quality I could see you being quite jealous of, if you weren't downright hostile toward it."

"Well, if succinctness is what you desire, then in that quality's name I shall bid you good day. And, I must say, it gives me pleasure to add—good day, asshole."

"Oh, come on, say it like you mean it, not like my thirteen-year-old daughter would."

"Oh, hah. Hah, hah. Good one. You got me. Crystal, I must say that my esteem for you grows greatly every time I consider what such a lovely lady as you puts up with in a husband."

Crystal started to reply, but Matt clasped her hand and the pair teleported back to Matt's throne room.

Regaining her balance from the sense of vertigo that was standard post-teleportation fare, she rounded on Matt. "Could you have made it any harder to accomplish our goal, dear?" she asked.

"What do you mean?"

"I've never seen, nor have I ever imagined seeing, two adults, much less two deities, go at each other like third-graders as I just witnessed. And while you two were trading jibes, did you not notice that he avoided answering the question about the king?"

"No, he didn't. He answered the question."

Matt's response brought Crystal's rant up short. "When—what—how—did he answer the question?"

"My dear, my darling, and now apparently my Ben'thra-esteemed wife, it wasn't just a tricky person we were dealing with. Benny is the original trickster. If I'd asked directly and he'd answered no, he wasn't involved, it would have told us that either he was involved and was lying about it, or he wasn't involved and was trying to make us think he was by telling us he wasn't. But by continuing with the insults rather than prancing about the disappearance of the king, he answered indirectly. Look, did you see his palace? He leaves rarely, and then only to get a drink at Olympus. The only reason he would have bothered with Takshaka's abduction in the first place would be to hurt me. Then, with me right there in his face in the safety of his own chamber, there's no way, once I mentioned it, that he would've been able to avoid gloating. He didn't gloat, so therefore I must conclude that he didn't do it."

"Oh. Well, that last bit makes sense, I guess," Crystal said, feeling a little confused and a little foolish at the same time. "By the way, our daughters aren't...."

"Thirteen. I know that, but he doesn't."

"Okay. So you fooled him. What difference does it make?"

"Everybody knows how thirteen-year-olds are," Matt said.

"Ours weren't like that," she contradicted.

"No, and it's likely that most really aren't. But the insult works best with thirteen, so that's what I used."

Crystal sighed. Her husband had shown far more finesse than she'd given him credit for. "I'm sorry, I...," she started.

"There was a time, not so long ago," Matt interrupted, "when you seemed to accept it as a given that I knew what I was doing or talking about. Now I'm getting the sense that either that acceptance was faked, or now you're thinking that Matt the god is somehow not as smart as Matt the human husband was."

Crystal started to object. "No, it's—," she got out before she stopped herself. He was right. She told him so, and explained, "It's not that you've changed, dear. It's me. Once upon a time you took the young daughter of a pair of public school teachers away from her simple lifestyle, after which she found herself married to a multi-millionaire professor who took her traveling around the world. She was living a life that revolved entirely around her husband. You really did seem invincible, all-knowing, and even all-powerful then, Matt, and compared to everyone else who'd ever been in my life up to the cataclysm, you actually fit those descriptions. Since the cataclysm, you're still the wealthiest, most intelligent, strongest man I know, but I've also seen a world I only ever dreamed of before. It's an amazing world, but the sudden transition and revelation have made me question everything I ever thought I knew to be true. You've never given me reason to, but the questioning everything includes you sometimes. Like I said, it's not you. I should've trusted you to know what you were doing back there, but—well, I just...."

"Questioned it," Matt interrupted. "And to be honest, that's a good thing, irritating though it may be when turned my direction."

"Peace, then?" When Matt nodded, Crystal changed the subject. "You know, some day you'll have to take me to see this Asgard place with its shining palaces and stuff."

"Shining palaces and stuff?" Matt said with a twinkle in his eyes. "It was created to meet the needs of the deities to barbarians, who are much more impressed by massive stone and wood structures than by shining palaces. Or shining stuff, for that matter. I'll take you some day, but you won't be that impressed, trust me. Anyway, speaking of travel, we ought to get back to Atlantis."

"Don't we have time for a little diversion here first?"

"I was hoping you'd suggest that," Matt said and led Crystal down the stairs to their bedroom.

"Don't lie to me. It didn't occur to you till I mentioned it," she said, her voice playful as he magically turned down the lights and slipped under the covers.

A Clue From Old Stories

Later the satiated pair emerged from their bedroom into the antechamber to see Sorscha entertaining the girls in her usual way, combing and braiding their hair while telling them stories of times gone by. Matt smiled pleasantly, but his smile was short-lived. Suddenly he turned to Crystal and said, Just received a call to a congress in Olympus, my love. It's just the elder gods, and it didn't sound like it was anything major, so I should be back quickly. Winking, he disappeared.

Crystal stopped just inside the antechamber to wait for her husband's return and to watch her young ladies interact with the dragoness and enjoy the sensation of nostalgia. The girls were growing up so quickly!

The twins, Heidi and Linda, had been thirteen when they'd left their home to come to the estate. They'd been—girls. Girls who were pretty from the day they were born, of course, but at thirteen they'd still been a little gangly, a little tentative. A little silly, too, and oh, so cute when they got serious. They'd started puberty but it hadn't really hit; they still had freckles atop dimples and thirteen-year-old chests that didn't quite fill out A-cup bras, a fact that Matt, being Matt, teased them about.

Then she'd missed a birthday; the girls, of course, had understood because mom was away being heroic and trying to become a deity just like dad. It had been hard on her despite the comforting presence of the blue glass, ka-imbued bauble that Matt had given her that allowed communication across the miles whenever her training schedule permitted. But since she'd returned and immersed herself in riding and trips to Olympus, the girls had grown even more. Now fifteen, they were well on their way to being women.

Oh, Crystal could look closely and still see her cherubic (a cup of angel with a dash of trouble, they joked) daughters in the young ladies that now withstood Sorscha's petting, but Heidi and Linda were girls no more. Their bodies had leaned up, and neither had to worry about teensy-cup jokes from their father any more. Their laughs had deepened. The looks that at one time had spelled trouble for mom and dad now hinted at tremendous promise—or a great deal more, deeper trouble—for the two twin boys they held in their esteem, the sons of a physicist and librarian whom Crystal and Matt had rescued early on.

Steve and Corey were the boys—young men, actually. Crystal had accepted them, pleased that her daughters had selected boys with good character after watching the respect and solemnity with which they'd laid their younger sister, a casualty of the cataclysm, to rest.

They came from solid stock, too. The boys' mother, Natalia, had some relatively minor magical talent but was an impressive librarian, so much so that Matt's three-story-tall research and historical library was her primary work place despite the god's prohibition against his mages doing any work besides mage-training. Matt had a thrakkoni librarian who had been and undeniably still was in absolute charge of the collection and its preservation—some of the works were millions of years old—but Natalia served as the face and the personality of the library, and everyone, including Matt, went to her for research questions. Even when she wasn't working, she made a wonderful friend to chat with.

The boys' father, meanwhile, was an accomplished physicist. Matt had made a special trip to Stanford to rescue him after meeting the boys and Natalia. The two men—well, more than men, the god and the physicist—had hit it off pretty well. Matt had relished his own physics fetish for as long as Crystal had known him, a fact that seemed strange because his chosen career as a dean didn't allow him to actually do any physics. Now she knew, though, that he'd spent much of nearly every cycle over the past several hundred millions of years studying the physical action of the world around him—or, more accurately, watching the humans study it. The study of the physical universe seemed to fascinate her husband nearly as much as the clamor of battle did.

Today the boys weren't around. For once, Crystal thought with a small internal cheer that surprised her a little. She liked Steve and Corey, and of course she adored their mother, but she missed mom and daughter time. She missed it a lot, in fact. The recent changes to her daughters' bodies and countenances only served to intensify the notion that they wouldn't be her little girls for much longer.

True to form, the girls squealed and rushed over to their mother. Heidi rushed, anyway; Linda was in the middle of a Sorscha braiding session so she just squealed gently and craned her eyes over that direction, twisting her smile halfway across her face. Crystal was certain that interrupting a Sorscha braiding session was similar to interrupting a Michelangelo painting session—Sorscha really was that good.

Arms enfolded her and Heidi from behind as Matt popped back in. She turned her head to smile at his quick return, and as she did she saw a somber expression evaporate from his face, replaced almost too quickly to see by a fatherly grin. She told herself to remember to ask him about the trip when they were clear of the girls, but let the question rest for the time being.

At her daughters' request, Crystal sat with Matt and began laying out the story of her investigations in Atlantis. They nodded and smiled through most, and then....

"Stacy? Mom, Dad, tell us that you beat her up or something," Heidi said.

"Or something," Matt said, the fatherly smile sticking stubbornly to his face.

"Dad! How could you not just—hate her?" Heidi said, face screwing around into a powerful frown.

"Dear, she is your father's ex-wife, and she was serving on our team, helping to investigate the king's disappearance," Crystal said, hoping to defuse the tension.

"So? She almost got us killed," Heidi said.

"Well, now, killed is a bit of a stretch," Crystal said, realizing that she was losing the fight and wondering why she was instinctively coming to Stacy's defense.

"Look, girls," Matt said, commanding their attention as only their father could do. "Stacy, or Venus, or Aphrodite, or whatever you call her, has her faults, but she's an immortal goddess too, a peer to your mother and father. Most important, she's helping with the investigation. What was done, is, at least for now, done. If we find the king and return him, all will be fine, and we'll have plenty of time to hate on my peers, but if we do not we'll have a calamity on our hands. Trust me, it'll be horrible. We need all the help we can get."

"What kind of calamity, Dad? King or not, he's just a mortal, right? I thought gods and goddesses didn't care much about mortals."

"Has Phoenix been talking to you?" Matt asked.

"Phoenix? No. Why do you ask?"

"Oh, no reason. At least, none that matters right now. But girls, of course we gods and goddesses care about humans, especially when they're our beautiful daughters," Matt said, touseling her hair as he had frequently when she was young. It was harder to do with a Sorscha-braid running through it, but he managed and then continued, "Regardless, there's another issue with this case, one I just had to go to Olympus to discuss. The naga live very nearly as long as thrakkoni, and they're a regal and warlike race, and so they're the favorites of the eastern deities, gods and goddesses who are now quite upset that their favorite king has gone missing. Their intention is to blame me, since much of the evidence on site apparently points my direction. That, and it was known that the king and I held a bit of a mutual animosity, so to speak, as do some of the eastern gods and I. If they do blame me, then the western gods will most likely circle wagons, to use a really bad cliché, around me. We'll end up with a war of the gods, one that nobody will win and the planet will lose."

"Has there ever been a war of the gods?"

"No, Heidi. At least, not like that. Skirmishes, yes, but the only time any of us have ever gone head-to-head is when Ben'thra and I pretty much ripped the world asunder long, long ago. That was just the two of us, and we moved continents and killed entire species in our wrath. That's the reason we don't battle directly now. We sort of decided to take it easy since then."

"But all the stories about the Norse gods, and the Greek story of the battle of the titans versus gods. Were those not real?"

"Well, yeah, sort of," Matt said.

"Yeah, they were sort of real, or yeah, they were sort of not real?" Heidi asked.

"How many double negatives do you need?"

"I didn't use a double negative, Dad. And you're avoiding the question," Heidi said, putting her hands on her hips and glaring.

"Well, yeah, sort of," Matt said, a grin creeping into his expression.

"Why?"

"Well, because. And I'm sorry, hon. What were we talking about?" Matt asked, his expression becoming a parody of innocence.

Heidi groaned in disgust. Crystal said, "Matthew, answer your daughter's question."

Matt sighed and said, "Well, okay, it's complicated. No, actually, it is. I'm not just saying that. The world has been around a long, long time, as have many of us deities. And it's not like we're all the nicest, most stable, most honest beings. Some gods are pretty cantankerous and contrarian, in fact, and they have quite the propensity toward making stuff up, especially when the stuff they make up makes them sound more awesome or makes their adversaries sound less so."

"Like you, Dad?"

"Oh! Oh, I'm injured," Matt said, pointing his deepest pout toward Heidi.

"Uh huh. So what you're saying is that mythology is a lie," Heidi said.

"No, I'm not saying that. Some of it's fictional, but much of mythology is true. Especially the characters involved. The stories themselves may not be completely true, but the actors in them are right, which is why the stories get distorted when it's the actors in the stories that are later telling them. I guess you have to look at it like a set of folk tales—always some truth in there, but you can't take it all at face value. Or, in the case of Atlantis, it's more like a set of fish tales."

Crystal and the girls all groaned at the bad pun.

"Okay, I guess," Heidi said, her expression still tenuous. "Your, um, tales, don't explain the whole gods versus the titans thing, but I guess there's something more important to worry about now. So, how do we find out who really took the king?"

"Nice segue."

"Thank you, Dad."

"I was joking, Heidi," Matt said, and then when his daughter stuck her tongue out at him, he turned to Crystal. "That's one she gets from you, dear."

Crystal stuck her tongue out at him.

The family laughed for several long minutes. Heidi came back to the present first. "Seriously, Dad," she said, "How are you going to figure out who took the king? Isn't it important?"

"Well, yes. It is," he said, his own laughter drying up. "At first I hoped your mom would find a clue, either a physical leftover in the debris or a magical trail through space. She's found neither, though, and she's had some pretty competent help at that."

"What do you mean by a magical trail through space?"

"When a god—anybody, really, but especially a magic-user with godlike power—does something that violently powerful, there are magical residues left behind in the elemental magic flows. It's kind of like the eddies that trucks leave behind them."

"Why would eddies left behind direct you to the king?"

"Well, they wouldn't, necessarily, but they give you a clue as to who cast the magic, and possibly what that person was preparing to face. Each god manipulates the same energies, but in slightly different ways, and we all shield from threats in different ways too. Since we've known each other for millions of years, for the most part, we know the signatures."

"But you weren't there," Heidi objected. "Why would Mom have known the signatures without you there?"

"That's why it was good that Stacy was there. She's been around nearly as long as I have," Matt said.

"And Mom and Stacy together couldn't determine who cast what," Heidi said, face looking pensive.

"That's right."

"So who hasn't Stacy seen the signatures for?"

"Well, you ask good questions, little one. The answer is, nobody. She wasn't originally a goddess, but she was around for the first cycle, and ascended right after. She's been around all the gods and goddesses, even the eastern ones. There's nobody she wouldn't recognize."

"So she would have known which if any of the gods had done that," Heidi pressed.

"Probably, but...."

"Yes, probably," Crystal interrupted. "What are you getting at?"

"Well, I remember somebody a long time ago teaching us about Occam's Razor."

"Yeah, that's right. I liked William of Ockham," Matt said, smiling. "He wasn't afraid to...."

"Dad, this is important," Heidi interjected, fixing her father with a stern look. "No time for side stories. Now, Occam's Razor says that the simplest answer is probably the most correct, right?"

"Numquam ponenda est pluralitas sine necessitate," Matt said sotto voce. "Plurality should not be suggested without necessity."

"Dad, quit it," Heidi said impatiently. "This is serious."

Matt sat back, arms crossed with one eyebrow cocked in irritation—or curiosity. "Well. Fine. Go on."

"So Mom and Stacy didn't find anything indicating that it was one of the gods who kidnapped the king."

"Correct," Matt said.

"So it wasn't a god," Heidi declared, her hands spread before her in a call to truth.

"Impossible. The power involved...."

"Wait, Matt. You told me earlier that the blasting down of the wall could've been done by any of your battle mages," Crystal said.

"That could be, yes. Blasting down a wall isn't hard. Conjuring a sword is a bit harder, and teleporting while carrying a large naga is really tough. Doing them all in rapid sequence while holding doors shut against a powerful defense force—well, some of the human sorcerers I've met in the past could probably accomplish all that, but it's way too early this cycle for anyone to have learned enough to have built up that much power. There isn't a human alive at this point who could've done that, I'd say. So, Occam's Razor and all, you know. It must have been a god."

"Didn't you say most of the characters in mythology are real?" Heidi asked.

"Yes," Matt said. "Go on."

"Well, I remember a whole set of characters outside of the category of gods from my classes. There are the ice giants from Norse mythology, and the titans from Greek mythology. What about them?"

"What about them?" Matt asked.

"What if it was an ice giant who took the king?"

"It couldn't be," Matt said.

"Why not?"

"They don't exist. They were made up in Norse mythology to give the gods a tremendous foe."

"What about a titan, then?" Heidi asked.

"Couldn't be."

"Why not? Do they not exist, also?"

"Actually, they do," Matt said.

"So why couldn't it be one of them?"

"The titans are all imprisoned in the Underworld, that's why. Not," Matt said.

"They could've escaped, like Sisyphus."

"That's a story, not real history."

"Gah!" Heidi shouted in frustration. "How are we supposed to figure anything out when we don't know whether what we already know is true?"

Matt shrugged. "I'd suggest just asking someone who was there, dear."

"Oh. Okay, so has anyone ever escaped the Underworld?" Heidi asked.

"No one who's been imprisoned there," Matt said.

"Imprisoned, like for giving fire to humans?" Heidi asked.

"Metaphorically, yes," Matt said. "At least, one of them. See, the titans aren't like you and me. They're pure energy beings who stood against us flesh-based gods at first as we set about shifting the planet into its transitional phases. You know, the two-thousand-year cataclysms when the earth changes from technology to magic and back again. They—Prometheus, in addition to the rest—wanted humans to keep growing and learning right up to what would only have been the humans' own self-destruction."

"I don't get that, Dad. I mean, I remember you telling us the whole Tower of Babel story our first night here, but I didn't get where that caused shifts in the planet."

Heidi's question brought Crystal back to that first evening after the end of the world that she'd grown up knowing. There'd been a jumble of emotions flying around through the room, all nearly tangible in their intensity. She had been relieved that everyone who held a spot close to her heart—even Yuki, her Chihuahua—had been preserved through the disastrous cataclysm that had wiped most of civilization away. At the same time, she'd been outraged that everything she'd known about her husband and partner was turning into a lie. Her fury turned to shame when she realized how much more the other people who'd made the journey had lost than she.

So strong had her feelings been, in fact, that she'd only really heard part of Matt's speech that evening as he'd done his best to answer everyone's questions. Later he'd confided in her how difficult it had been to reconcile their beliefs in their various religions with the fact that a Greek god had just come to life and saved them. It always was the same, he'd said. He'd used the Tower of Babel story, one that he was certain that they all knew, as a way to get them to understand the basic purpose behind the cycles of the planet and the periodic cataclysmic disasters.

"Well, girls," Matt started explaining it again. "Lemme 'splain. No, there is too much. Lemme sum up," he said, his grin and fake accent making it clear he was mimicking a movie the family had watched, several times, way back when. Back when life was understandable, before it had been completely flipped over on its head, Crystal was reminded.

"Ooh, Daddy, we get to hear you summarize. I didn't think you even knew how to do that," Heidi nailed her father in her sweetest voice.

Matt glared playfully at his daughter and then continued, "Alright, you asked for it now. So way back in the early days of the earth, after we'd done the whole experiment with the dinosaurs and all, and after it'd been decided to create a learning, thinking race with free will, we realized the problem that we'd created. You know what it was?" As both girls shook their heads, he said, "The humans could think. At least, most could. Physicists and mathematicians could think, and engineers could replicate the task within appropriate tolerances. That's a joke, by the way," Matt said as he grinned at the girls' uncomprehending looks. When they failed to laugh, he mumbled, "Rough crowd tonight, ain't it? So anyway, as I was saying, the humans could think. I mean, that was the point, of course. And it's not terribly bad at first, because we stopped short of creating a hive-style learning process. You know, where the entire human race would've been granted the telepathic connection that thrakkoni share, thus allowing the entire collective to learn as its members do. But humans quickly figured out that they didn't need collectivistic learning patterns if each individual would just record what he learned in a way that the others could also learn from."

"Books!" Linda said, obviously excited to be able to take part in the conversation.

"Well, yes, books. Books are the key, in fact. We deities watched the human race growing more and more powerful, each generation building on the recorded knowledge of the previous one, and realized that there would come a time when the race would know just enough to destroy Gaia."

"You mean Gaia, the goddess that Mom met?" Heidi asked.

"Sort of. She met the personification of Gaia, not the actual goddess. And so did you, the night of the cataclysm. Remember how she joined in with the teleport magic? There were physical challenges with moving so many, including such sticky issues as how to lift several hundred people into the air while protecting from wind and water, but there were also some severe forces ripping around us that she shielded us from. What would've been challenging for me was pretty easy for her, because the forces actually were her. Gaia is a goddess, but she isn't just a goddess. Gaia is called the earth mother, but in reality Gaia is the earth, and beyond that, she is the entire plane of existence. Destroying Gaia means destroying everything that you know exists—planet, moon, stars, everything. Does that make sense?"

The girls nodded, so Matt continued, "And so back to the case of the human race, the problem is that we'd already agreed that one of your key charms is your free will. To a great extent, you're masters of your own destiny. For us to let you get to the brink of destroying the mother and then allow you keep your free will was unthinkable. To let you get to the brink of destroying the mother and then take away what makes your race uniquely fun to work with was also unthinkable. Do you see the problem now?"

"Sure, Dad," Heidi said. "You wouldn't take away our ability to destroy the world, and yet if we had the ability then you couldn't accept the chance that we might do it."

"Exactly. Precisely! Yes!" Matt clapped; Crystal smiled. She loved seeing the old Matt the Professor bubbling out of him. He continued, "but do you see the core of the problem? What caused it, in other words?"

"Our free will?" Heidi asked tentatively.

"No, no, not really," Matt said. "You have free will now, but that doesn't scare me or any other god in the slightest. But...."

"The knowledge of how to use it in a disastrous manner," Linda said. "Or, more specifically, the ability to eventually learn such knowledge."

"Exactly. And that ability to learn how is based on what?"

"Books?" Heidi's gaze traveled off into the distance as she thought it through.

"Well, sort of. More general, though."

"I get it," Linda said. "Our ability as humans to record our knowledge proved to be a threat to the gods. If you took that ability away, then the threat was gone too."

"Right. But not just a threat to us; it was a threat to the Mother."

"Okay. So why not just take away our books?"

"Because you'd just reinvent them. There are hundreds of different ways to record information, sometimes scrawled on paper and sometimes written into magnetic spots on an electronic medium of some type. Or it can be geometric patterns burnt into fields."

"So you're saying that the crop circles were...."

"Nah, the crop circles were just us screwing with the humans, actually. This time. But to get at your ability to record information, we had to in turn get at the very language you used. Now do you see where the Tower of Babel story came from?"

"Because they all spoke different languages, none of them could communicate information. None could learn from the others. And none could then build any more towers to the gods," Linda said.

"Yes. But the human race has another annoying ability."

"Annoying? Dad, remember that we're humans, too."

"Of course, dear. You're not annoying. Except—well, that stunt in Brazil was more cute and expensive than annoying, I guess. But I was talking about the race as a whole and your ability to learn and decipher languages. We actually tried translation spells, warped a little bit backwards, to confuse their speaking at first, but humans figured it out within days. So we made it more complicated, and this time it took months. We figured, though, that at some point we were headed toward losing the game."

"So you changed the underlying technology for two thousand years. That's brilliant," Crystal said.

"Of course it is. It was an idea of the gods."

"So, every two thousand years, you guys basically dumb us down?" Heidi asked.

"Well—yeah, I guess. Look, in the very first cycle, after all of the setbacks we tossed in front of them, they started to record all information on nuclear resonance film devices. For comparison, the entirety of the space age's information from your cycle would've fit on one storage cell for them. We had to strike at the underlying ability to record information, because no matter what else we did they would've figured out a way around it. So we held what was probably our most riotous meeting at Olympus to discuss the matter, and when we finally walked away we'd decided to switch electrons out for elemental flows every two thousand years. It's an easy switch, really; Gaia does it almost in her sleep. As much as humans were confused over the nature of the electron as a particle and a wave, the sorcerers hundreds of years from now will be confused over the same duality in magical flows, because they're fundamentally different flavors of the same thing. We decided on two thousand years because that's more than enough time for any devices made during one cycle to have decayed to the point of uselessness before the next similar cycle."

"So Gaia just flips a switch every two thousand years?" Crystal asked, intrigued.

"There's more to it, of course," Matt said. "Flipping a switch wouldn't lead to a cataclysm, but rather just things that no longer worked. We also have to cause major disruptions to human activity. Electrons go away abruptly, but the magic flows come back in stages. That's how the outer atmosphere loses its coherence for a couple of days and allows the heat of the surface to drop perilously. It's also how the inner-crust flows that are generated by the magnetic fields slow down, which in turn causes major eruptions, earthquakes, and tsunamis."

"I thought you said the gods and goddesses cared about humans, Dad," Linda accused.

"We do. That's why the meeting where we lined this plan up was so contentious."

"So where do the titans come in? Was Prometheus in this meeting?" Linda asked.

"No. We'd already sentenced them to the Underworld. Their being purely elemental beings made it impossible to resolve any other way. They didn't have a reason to care whether the Mother was destroyed. After all, without the guiding intellect of the gods, the elements would be primary and unruly forces. We had to stop them."

"You stopped them by imprisoning them for eternity?" Heidi asked, a shocked look on her face.

"Well, yeah."

"Isn't that a bit harsh?"

"No. Why would it be? They're elemental beings, dear. It's not like they want out to go to the pool on a Saturday afternoon."

"How do you know, Dad?"

"Because.... Um.... Well, I just know. Hey, isn't it time for dinner? I'm starved."

"I thought you didn't need to eat," Linda countered.

"I don't, but sometimes the metaphysical corrugations in the plenary occuli in my stomach contract around the benevolence and make me feel hungry. Now let's go," Matt said and immediately spun for the door, leaving Crystal, his daughters, and Sorscha no choice but to follow.

"Mom," Linda whispered as they walked, "he made that stuff about his stomach up, didn't he?"

"Yes, he did. I'm not sure what a metaphysical corrugation would be, but I'm pretty sure there's no benevolence there," Crystal answered, winking at her daughters as they followed.

"Crystal, have you made contact with Breenda?" Sorscha asked.

"No! I got—well, that was pretty rude of me, wasn't it? I've been away nearly all day. Did she contact you? Is she worried?"

"No, ma'am. We thrakkoni assume that we'd know if our masters were in trouble. Anything that serious, after all, would be pretty noisy. But she is still in the castle in Atlantis without any companionship."

Crystal opened her mind, pressing the elemental energies to spool outward in order to find and connect with Breenda's mind. It was amazing, she thought, how her newfound powers allowed her to send her thoughts all the way across the planet.

Crystal! Breenda replied as their thoughts brushed against one another. *Is everything okay? You've been out all night.*

The thrakkon was right. Atlantis and Matt's estate were on opposite sides of the world, so the afternoon that had lazily passed for her had been overnight there. Some things about teleportation took a while to get used to.

Everything's fine, Crystal said as soothingly as possible, sensing the tension in Breenda's thoughts. *Is all well there?*

No significant changes. There was some booming yesterday, and I thought I heard your husband's mages' voices. But the castle has slept quietly.

Did you know that Melissa is actually my husband's ex-wife? Crystal asked, curious.

No. She is? You mean the goddess Venus, right? Why would she pretend to be a human?

For the same reason I am, Crystal said, satisfied. She hadn't thought that Breenda could have known, as unaware as thrakkoni were of magic and its subterfuges. Still, Crystal was still getting surprised fairly frequently by things she didn't know, so it was worth the probe.

My husband and his mages did visit yesterday, and we decided to go ask Ben'thra about his involvement. Matt is satisfied that Benny wasn't involved, though I admit that I'm still harboring some suspicion. But after the infuriating questioning period we came back here to the estate to check in on the girls. I'll be back there right after dinner and tell you all about it then. Do me a favor and check my room in about an hour from now to make sure there's nobody in there to see me pop back in.

Will do, and enjoy your dinner with your family.

Crystal withdrew the energy. Talking telepathically with thrakkoni felt strange. Matt and Crystal both used the same energy strings, and so it was possible to control the communication to a much greater extent. When so controlled, complex ideas, pictures, and emotions could be passed in addition to the simple words that served as the building blocks of communication. The emotions in particular presented a many-fold addition to the advantage of telepathic communication over verbal talking. When communicating with Matt or the girls, but Matt especially, Crystal found it useful to inject green elemental energy into the flow so that she could more directly get at what she really meant. She could also transmit, she had found, the secondary emotions like anger and love through the pipeline, despite the lack of direct energy flows supporting them. That, in conjunction with being able to transmit actual pictures, sounds, smells, and other sensations, made her and Matt's mental communications so much richer than even their whispered pillow talk. It was an amazing feeling.

At the same time, direct access to thoughts and feelings meant she'd also had to learn to shield the message flow—with Matt's help, of course. His mind was like a teddy bear stuffed with a steel sphere in the middle: soft and fluffy with an impenetrable core. He'd explained that he was guarded that way after millions of years working with other telepathic beings, but he'd also made a strong case for the benefits of not knowing everything even a lifelong partner was feeling at any given time. That too much sharing could be bad she had tentatively agreed with, especially when "for all eternity" was added literally.

The thrakkoni, though, were foreign. The gods had created them with no ability to touch or be touched by the magical flows of elements, as a way of protecting each god's servants from the machinations of every other god. But they'd also built into the race an entirely different mechanism for teleportation and telepathy—for the gods' convenience, not the thrakkon's—that Crystal still didn't quite understand. She could pass pictures and some minor sensations through her link with Breenda, but emotions weren't possible.

Sorscha had once explained to Crystal why that was a good thing. Thrakkoni weren't touchable by green emotional energy and thus didn't have emotions, she explained, and so for the gods to transmit them would be too foreign. Crystal had seen Sorscha angry one too many times to believe the explanation, though. That they had different emotions she could buy, but not the total absence of emotions.

She's fine, Crystal passed along to Sorscha, hoping to see a hint of emotion that might help her learn more about the thrakkoni mind.

Of course she is, Sorscha's thoughts sounded dry as she responded. *We're not kittens to be worried about when left alone. No offense intended, of course.*

And none to you, Crystal said, trying to project her happiest smile along the connection. When she received nothing back, she gave up.

Ultimatum

Dinner done, Crystal tucked her daughters back into bed, said lingering farewells to Matt, and blinked back to her room in the castle.

"Good morning, Crystal," Breenda's voice behind her made her jump.

"You snuck up on me," Crystal laughed, shaking off the surprise.

"Actually, you teleported in. I was just standing here watching. To sneak is an action verb, so technically, you snuck up on me."

"True. You win, I guess. But why were you standing here watching for me?"

"To make sure nobody else was in your room, as you had asked. I can't sense magic like you can, so I had to stand and watch. It's my race's...."

"I know, I know," Crystal interjected. "Sorry, I'm really not used to this, and sometimes I forget what you can and cannot do."

"You need not apologize to...." Breenda started, then cut off as both received a mental transmission from Stacy.

GET IN HERE NOW.

Crystal would've objected to the direct command from Stacy except for its tone of heated urgency. She took the distance from her room to the king's bedroom at a sprint, Breenda behind. The problem with teleporting was that you never knew who or what you might be teleporting into, and Stacy's urgent message suggested that their destination might be more dangerously populated than usual. It turned out she needn't have worried; when they entered the room they found Stacy facing off against just one other person, a tall Asian man in green robes.

God, not man, Crystal corrected herself. She'd seen him at Olympus once or thrice, most recently the night of her and Matt's last fight (was that two nights ago, now, or three? she asked herself) his haughty features always severe as he sipped a clear variety of ambrosia out of a crystalline sake glass.

The god stood silently, surveying the two goddesses along the pointed ridge of his nose.

"Well, hi," Crystal said, shattering the cold silence. "I don't believe we've been properly introduced."

"Please forgive me," Stacy interrupted, her voice sounding far more metered and formal than usual. "I should do the honors here. Emperor, this is Crystal, a junior goddess of Olympus, a champion of the Olympian arena, and thrice-blessed wife of Matthew, the Ever Triumphant God of War. Crystal, please be honored to meet the Jade Emperor, Supremely High Emperor of the Heavens, Holder of Talismans, Container of Perfection, and Embodiment of Dao."

The god's scowl deepened as he swiveled his head to glare directly at Stacy. "You are in no position to insult me, young goddess," he said.

Oh, my, oh myohmy, Breenda's telepathic voice floated to Crystal's mind, shaded in feelings of worry. Absently Crystal picked up on the emotional strain interwoven through the telepahy and wondered how it happened, but she was too busy watching the god Stacy called the Jade Emperor swirling powers around himself.

What? Crystal beamed a narrowly-focused telepathic signal Breenda's way.

She insulted His Imperial Majesty the Jade Emperor greatly by introducing him to you first, Breenda answered. *This won't go well.*

Hey, I'm a goddess, too.

You're a goddess, he's a god, and that's an important distinction in his realm. He's the top of their pantheon, too. He and your husband are direct and equal peers. Your husband would make no issue of it because he cares little for status levels among the brethren, but the Jade Emperor seems to have gotten all of the concern over status that the pair of them might otherwise share.

How do you know these things?

I'm talking to Sorscha now.

Oh, right. Forgot you could do that.

Should I call for Matt? Crystal asked Breenda, and then pushed the same question to Stacy's mind.

No, I'm letting Sorscha know. The Emperor won't be able to sense communication between thrakkoni, Breenda said.

No, we got this. It's two on one. Even better, it's two goddesses plus your dragon on one, Stacy replied.

Crystal liked Breenda's answer better. She knew first-hand how powerful Stacy wasn't against a deity in a fight, and there wasn't enough space for Breenda to transform to dragon form. The Jade Emperor represented a big question mark, but if he commanded as much power as Matt she wasn't sure two goddesses and a dragon could pull off a fair fight against him.

"So," Crystal said, keeping her voice light in an attempt to defuse the tension, "are you here to help with the investigation?"

The Jade Emperor snorted. "Here to help you cover up your husband's crime, you mean?"

"My husband didn't do this."

"And you came stealthily back to the scene of the crime disguised as mere humans just because you wanted to prove that he didn't, right? How—believable."

"Well, believe it or not, yeah. We did," Crystal said, not sure how else to respond.

"Let's cut the pretense," the god said. "Tell your husband that he can end his little prank now by returning the Atlantean king, and all that we'll ask in return is that he go into exile for a cycle or two."

"Well, since I believe him when he says he doesn't know where the Atlantean king is, I have to ask what you're going to do when he isn't able to comply with your demand," Stacy said.

"It will lead to his death."

The words chilled Crystal. There'd been a time when she wouldn't have believed that an immortal god could die, but after the battle with Stacy she'd had the truth explained to her by Gaia. If enough deities pounded on one of their own with enough power, using ka, they could in fact destroy him. Even Matt, with all his strength, probably couldn't stand up to the combined might of the Eastern pantheon.

A light pop beside Crystal startled her, but her surprise turned to relief as she heard Thor's booming voice cut into the conversation, "That will lead to war, you know." The mountain of a god, covered from head to toe in his fighting furs, twirled his famous hammer Mjolnir to punctuate his declaration.

The Jade Emperor snorted and twirled his own staff twice in reply. "Should it lead to war, then so be it," he said. He looked directly at Crystal and stated, "A warning, then. Three days your husband has to end this folly. If the sun sets on the third day without the king's successful and healthy return to his throne, war it shall be."

He clapped his hands and a narrow column of smoke erupted in front of him. When the smoke cleared, he was gone.

Crystal turned to Thor and buried herself in her old trainer's bear hug. "Thank you," she said quietly.

"Of course, lass. But we do have a problem, and a big one at that. What the Jade Emperor declares comes true, and his legions of major and minor deities follow him faithfully. If we don't find the king in three days we're in for a battle like this world has never seen."

"Legions? Matt once told me that there were only thirty-three deities," Crystal said, confused.

"Major deities, yes. But there's all sorts of spirits and sprites and imps and other magical creatures around, and the Eastern gods love to raise the monkeys and other critters to the level of minor deity," Stacy said. "Hi, Thor, by the way. I thank you, also. No hugs, though. That fur is itchy."

"Well, we're all in this together, itchy or no, right?" Thor asked.

"Indeed," Crystal said. "Where's Matt?" she asked without thinking, immediately regretting it when both other deities turned disdainful expressions her direction. Stacy's was well-practiced and dripped equal measures of disappointment and contempt along with a pinch of sarcastic humor, but Thor's expression of disdain seemed entirely unnatural for the barbarian god's face to form around.

"Your husband is at your estate, lass, though I'm a bit surprised you felt the need to ask. He didn't feel comfortable entering here with the Jade Emperor around. Said it felt too much like a trap of some sort, and I agree. He told me his girls were in trouble and asked me to come and represent the western deities in his stead."

"His girls?" both Crystal and Stacy said at the same time, and then each glared at the other.

"Oh, get over yourselves, ladies," Thor said. "That wasn't exactly what he said, and you know it. But I dare say you two are the only women he's cared for deeply in his long, long life, and so it felt appropriate enough for me to say."

"So," Crystal asked, letting it go, "I'm confused. The Jade Emperor is at the top, right? And from what I recall of the eastern philosophy, they're very much into both rank and appearances, right? So why wouldn't the Jade Emperor send a subordinate with his warning?"

Thor shrugged, his massive shoulders causing dozens of pounds of fur to shift. "That's exactly why Matthew was concerned about a trap, lass. It's also sort of sideways proof that the Jade Emperor doesn't know what's going on either. If the Emperor really suspected Matthew of treachery, which really could only be caused by partial insanity, he'd think twice about threatening the wife of the god of war without a show of force behind him, no matter how powerful he is personally. But the kings of the five elements didn't show, so we kind of think that Jadey doesn't hold as much belief in Matthew's guilt as he's saying he does."

"Unless it really was a trap," Crystal said.

"But it wasn't," Thor said. "When I teleported in I scanned for a trap, and found nothing."

"Couldn't the Jade Emperor have his—what, generals?—waiting to teleport?" Crystal asked.

"Sure. But so could Matthew. No matter how much dissention you see on Olympus, all eleven of the prime Olympians, plus me, will come to Matthew's defense anytime and anywhere. Trust me, the Jade Emperor wouldn't set a trap he wasn't certain would spring to his benefit."

"Eleven? I thought there were twelve Olympians."

"Eleven deities present and available for action, dear. Subtract Odin. Zeus. Yahweh. The Creator. Whatever you call him, he hasn't been around in a while. Then again, he's as much the east's creator as he is ours, so I doubt he'd take sides. If we were lucky, he'd smack us all on the butt and tell us to sit down, shut up, and quit fighting."

"Okay, so worst case, I hear we have eleven western gods versus six eastern gods," Crystal said. "Is that right?"

"Not even close," Stacy said. "You and quite a few other newer, minor deities will fall into the ranks on Matt's side. That, plus we can probably count on all the sprites, fairies, and other minor beings—several tens of thousands in all. On the eastern side, you have several other deities besides the Jade Emperor and the rulers of the five elements, and those are just the primes. Don't forget the Nine Bright Shiners, the Generals of the Five Regions, the Twenty-Eight Constellations, the Four Great Heavenly Kings, the Gods of the Twelve Branches, the Five Ancients of the Five Regions, the star ministers of the whole sky, and the countless gods of the Milky Way."

Crystal hoped Stacy was being sarcastic, but decided not to ask.

"Indeed, lass," Thor said. "And don't forget that Gaia will do her best to stand in the middle of all this mess and stop it, her being the one to feel the pains of war and all."

"So it sounds like final destruction of the planet that we're talking about," Crystal said.

"If Mother permits it, or is forced aside," Thor said, nodding, "the latter being entirely possible given some of the potential scenarios. But the ultimate answer is yes, lass, if this war happens, we're probably going to see the end of the planet."

"So what do we do next?" Crystal asked.

"I'd suggest you bring in the big guns," Thor answered. "Obviously Matthew isn't likely to be welcome here, but since you're evaluating magical residue, have you considered bringing Michael in?"

Crystal snorted. Matt and Michael were like brothers mostly in their shared mutual antagonism. She could recall as a kid reading that in Greek mythology how Ares, the identity Matt had used, and Apollo, the identity Michael had used, hadn't gotten along. The truth, though, was far more acerbic. Matthew and Michael had apparently hated each other for hundreds of millions of years, their enmity originating back when Stacy had left Matt for Michael's arms, according to the story Sorscha had once related to Crystal. She'd seen some proof of that, as her first test on the path to becoming a goddess had involved learning magic from Michael. The interchange between Matt and Michael had been frosty, to use the nicest term Crystal could think of.

"No, Thor has a point," Stacy said, misinterpreting Crystal's snort. "Nobody knows magic and its uses and traces as well as Apollo. He's a good choice. I'll call him."

"But if he teleports in we'll blow our...." Crystal said, faltering as she realized the folly in what she was about to say.

"The Jade Emperor's visit was pretty clear evidence that your cover is already blown, lass," Thor said gravely.

Stacy snorted, a noise that Crystal found spookily similar to her own snort, and then went silent as she stared off into space for a moment.

"He's coming to help us," she said, and a moment later Crystal heard a familiar popping sound.

"Well, well. How many newbies does it take to read elemental residue?" the newcomer said, his dry tone piercing the room. Apollo peered over his hawk-nose, his glare traveling from Stacy to Crystal to Thor, haughtiness splayed across his face.

"I was wondering when I'd see my favorite asshole again," Thor growled. "Don't you have any colors other than black in your wardrobe?"

"I have mastered all of the elemental hues and thus wear the color that represents the combination of all. Perhaps if you'd come visit for a while I could teach you how to not have to rely on your barbarian-sized muscles quite as much," Apollo sneered in reply.

Crystal suppressed a shudder; she remembered her own visit all too well. Apollo's initiates wore robes the color of the magical streams they were practicing: red robes for fire, green for emotions, purple for healing, and so on. Crystal had spent weeks changing from color to color as she learned to wield the flows under Apollo's tutelage. He'd been tough to get along with, yet he had proven his expertise in the subject of magical flows many times over, and likewise with his ability to impart that expertise to his pupils. As prickly as he was, Crystal nevertheless gave him credit as the greatest magic user on the planet, as well as the greatest teacher of the art, evidenced by how much and how well he'd taught her. She could never, ever share those thoughts with Matt, though.

"Now," Apollo said, "Tell me what we know so far."

"The king is missing," Stacy said drily, drawing out the last word to make her point.

"Oh. So tell me what we know so far that is useful," Apollo retorted, drawing out his own last word in response. After several moments of silence, he snorted and went over to the wall.

"Powerful blast, and luckily so since it's now several days old," he said, attention focused on the remnants of the wall. "I see why people think Matt did it—it has his forcefulness and love of pow-pow fire magic written all over it."

"Do you think he did it, though?" Crystal asked.

"Of course not. First, what would he possibly have to gain by abducting the king? Second, even the war god has enough brains—though only barely, I think—to not leave his own imprint on this. Third, there's just no way Matt would do such a thing."

"So where does that leave us?" Thor asked.

"Well, I understand why none of you picked up on the trail; you're all new gods." When Stacy opened her mouth to object, Apollo waved her off and continued, "Not new as in this cycle or the last, except for Crystal there of course, but none of you were around when the elementals were imprisoned. None of you fought against the sheer power that they represented."

"The titans?" Thor asked, his voice incredulous. "But they're imprisoned, like you said."

"Oh, they get out occasionally," Apollo said with a shrug.

"But Matt said that no one ever got out of the Underworld," Crystal objected.

"And so Matt is wrong. Quick! Tell all the other deities, because that's a phrase they'll have never heard before. Oh, wait—no. No, it's not. Matthew being wrong is like Thor being large."

"Huh," Crystal snorted in return. "So, Prometheus?" she asked, recalling her earlier conversation with Matt and the girls. She hadn't really thought it anything but idle chatter at the time, but now it was coming from the grand master of the arcane.

"Sure. Possibly. He hasn't gotten out before because he's the most closely bound, but the destruction of the wall actually does feel most like his work. It's pure, unbridled, forceful fire energy. Your husband, dear, is known for being—unsubtle—in his manipulations of elemental force, but this is pure unadulterated, unmanipulated power. It is thus my expert opinion that only a titan could have done this."

"Oh. Well, let's go find him, then," Crystal said.

"Just—go find him. Just like that, then?" Apollo asked.

Stacy snorted again.

"But Ap—Michael, that is, you can track him, right? Or at least find out where he is now?"

"No, I cannot. And no, I cannot. If I could just find out where he is now, I'd have done the same for the king, right?"

"Besides," Thor said, "we still don't know what Prometheus, if it was him, hoped to accomplish."

"That, my large furry friend, is actually the correct truth," Apollo said. "And you are quite furry. What breed of yak did you get the winter coat from to dress yourself? I've never seen one that large."

Thor cracked his knuckles and glared in reply.

"Well, I have a project I must return to," Apollo said. "Next time don't hesitate so long to call in the expert, yes? Ta-ta!"

With a pop the god of magic vanished, leaving Thor, Crystal, and Stacy looking from one to the other.

Enlisting the Help of Gaia

"Now what?" Crystal asked.

"Now you find Prometheus," Stacy said.

"Me?"

"Me?" Stacy said, mimicking Crystal. "Yes, you. Who else, sweetcheeks?"

"I was feeling such a fellowship...."

"A fellowship? I don't think so. You're not a hobbit. I'm no elf. And Big'n'Hairy over there's no dwarf," Stacy said.

"Be that as it may, lass," Thor said, "one does not simply walk into the Underworld."

"I'm aware of that, Thor," Stacy said. "But I'm sure that whatever challenges are there, this young goddess can face them all. And besides, it's her ring to bear."

"What do I look like, the goddess of private eyes?" Crystal asked, trying to return a quip with a quip.

"Well—come to think of it, what are you the goddess of?" Stacy asked, hands on hips.

"I haven't thought of anything yet."

"Well, there you go: the goddess of unthinking. Or, better yet, the goddess of investigations. Your symbol can be the magnifying glass. Not that primitives in any cycle will know what it is, but eventually they'll catch on and say, 'hey, that's cool.' They'll call you The Seeker, or better yet, the Seekress," Stacy said, enunciating her last word incorrectly.

"Sea cress, huh?" Crystal said, a scowl on her face.

"Sure! Your symbol can be the owl. A green owl."

"Uh huh. If I recall correctly, the owl is already taken by Athena."

"Oh, right," Stacy said, effecting an obviously fake expression of innocence. "My bad. But I bet Athena will be nice and allow you to adopt the owl as your own."

"You ever met Athena?" Crystal asked, already knowing the answer. "I have. No way she'd agree to that."

"Well, you can still be the goddess of investigation. Do it for a few cycles and you'll get good at it."

"I don't have a few cycles, though. The world has a few days. I need to be good at it now, and you two are my only hope for getting past my own shortcomings."

"Well, fine. So we're your only hope, eh, princess? So what do you want us to do about it?" Stacy asked.

"I'm not entirely certain, but I would suggest that asking the newest goddess in the universe to track down an ancient titan by herself isn't the best choice," Crystal said.

"Is that your way of asking for help and companionship? My, how eloquent."

"If you ladies don't mind," Thor interrupted, Mjolnir cracking the floor as the giant god used it for the clang, "the clock is ticking. I think we all feel pretty strongly for Matt, else we wouldn't be here. More importantly, we all feel strongly against a heavenly war, which is what we're going to have in less than three days if we don't figure this out. Crystal, first thing you need to do is go to Gaia's glade to ask if the titans are still bound, and if not, which one is missing."

"Okay, but why do I have to go to her glade to ask her that? Can't I just telepath the question?" Crystal asked.

"Do ye really not know? Did Apollo not teach you that telepathy between dimensions is forbidden?"

"Well, no," Crystal said, feeling defensive with both of them pressing her. "He didn't. So, why would she be able to tell if the titans are still bound, from one dimension to another?"

"Because she's the earth mother," Stacy explained slowly, enunciating her words as if to a child. "The earthly dimensions, including the Underworld, are actually a part of her. She would know if any of her children, especially the great big thunderous elemental children, are elsewhere."

"Okay, okay. I'm new, not stupid," Crystal said, irritated by Stacy's tone.

"Yeah," Stacy said.

"Uh, huh," Thor said.

"C'mon, guys, neither of you really believes I'm stupid, do you?"

"Crystal, you still don't get being a goddess, do you?" Stacy asked.

"The part about being the ultimate say in the universe? No, I'm not sure she does," Thor said.

"Thor, that hurt."

"So?"

"Well, it's just that I thought you, of all the gods, were my friend," Crystal said.

"Crystal, I'm no one's friend. Well, Matt's, maybe—no, not even Matt's. Oh, I like you plenty, but I'm a god. You know, one of the immortals whose reason for existence is to guide the populations of the planet. Just. Like. You. That's what we're trying to tell you. Why is that so hard for you to understand?"

"I—I suppose I do. Will probably take time to really sink in, but—oh, fine. I'll just go talk to Gaia."

"I thought you would," both Stacy and Thor said.

Crystal managed her first teleportation to Gaia's glade with minimal queasiness. She'd practiced inter-dimensional teleportations in plenty of trips to the bar at Olympus, after all, while showing off her new powers to her husband. Besides, Gaia's glade was somehow easier to locate and teleport to than the bar.

"Welcome to my glade, Crystal, but you really should knock," Gaia said as she stepped out from behind a tree.

Crystal's breath caught as she saw the mother goddess. It always did; Gaia radiated beauty as no other being could. She was petite for a goddess, her trim figure reaching to just over five feet tall. She wore a green dress tied around the waist with a simple silver cord that glistened as though it were made of precious metal, and her dark hair was woven through with flowers of all varieties, colors, and sizes. There was nothing particularly special about the outfit, or the hair, or anything else in Gaia's bearing; the goddess was simply beautiful beyond anything she'd ever seen before. Stacy was beautiful, too, in an alluring sort of way, and Crystal fancied herself to be quite pretty. Neither, though, possessed the same glowing inner or outer radiance as the mother goddess.

Gaia was the mother goddess, after all.

The Mother's calm manner was often combined a wicked sense of humor and a precise expertise at dressing down anyone whose behavior vexed her. Crystal had seen glimpses of that expertise while seeking Gaia's help in becoming a goddess, and she'd occasionally seen both humor and dressings down in later conversations over tea and cookies, a pastime that Gaia seemed to cherish.

Now, Crystal wanted to melt under Gaia's stern gaze.

"I apologize, Mother," Crystal said. "It slipped my mind to request your permission to enter because I came on a matter of urgency."

"Are you out of tea and cookies?" Gaia's arched eyebrow told Crystal she hadn't made any points.

"No, not at all. This is a matter of war among the gods, Mother."

"Ah, yes. The case of the missing Atlantean king that has everyone so riled up."

"Exactly. Mother...."

"Well, I don't know where he is, either."

"I didn't believe that you would, but...."

"So why did you intrude here to ask, child?"

"Well, Thor and...." Crystal stopped herself when she noticed Gaia's eyebrows raising. It was the ultimate tell of the Mother's distaste. Authority, she reminded herself—Crystal needed to speak with authority.

"What I'm trying to get at, Mother, is that Apollo's investigation suggested that it was a titan who blew the walls off of the palace. You have the power above all of us to tell if one of the titans has escaped his imprisonment. I rushed here to seek your counsel, then, and to ask if you could tell me whether any of them have escaped."

"I could," Gaia said simply, eyebrows still raised. Crystal realized she still wasn't being authoritative enough.

"Have any of the titans escaped?" Crystal asked, carefully managing the inflection of each syllable to avoid coming across as either impatient or submissive.

Crystal was rewarded by a blank stare from the Mother as Gaia peered through the dimensions into the Underworld. "I sense all of the titans safely and soundly lodged in the Underworld, dear. I'm sorry to destroy your theory. And really, truly, I do desire to see this war of the gods not come to pass. I know that the Jade Emperor paid you a visit, and that couldn't have been pleasant." Her expression softened as she continued, "I care for all my children. You know that, yes? I cannot take sides, but I can help as requested in order to stave off the coming battle. Surely you are aware how disastrous a conflict on the scale we're talking about would be to the entirety of the world."

"I am, Mother," Crystal said. On impulse, she strode forward, bowed, and kissed Gaia's hand.

"Thank you, daughter. The Eastern gods have fought many conflicts over the millennia, but most have been waged in the heavens rather than on the planet's surface where Matthew and his brethren will make their stand. The Monkey King, in fact, once took on the Jade Emperor himself in a tremendous battle, but much of it was up in the sky. Many of my children were taken prisoner, but none of the living were truly harmed. I fear that won't be the case now; I dread the devastation we will see if battle is joined. It would make the cataclysm you recently survived seem mild—insignificant, even, by comparison."

"I'll do my best to find where the king of Atlantis has been taken."

"I'm sure you will."

"It's just that...."

"You should return to your estate, daughter. Once this crisis is over, I want you to return to this glade, after seeking permission to enter, of course, for some discussions on what constitutes appropriate behavior for a goddess."

Chastised thoroughly, Crystal nodded once and reflexively teleported back to the first place on the estate she thought of, landing in Matt's throne room.

Visit From the Monkey King

"Hi, hon," Matt said cheerfully as he popped into the room in front of Crystal. Klaxons ceased as abruptly as they had probably begun when she teleported into the estate without warning. Matt waved off the thrakkoni who had also appeared in the room as he said, "you know, you should…."

"Signal that I'm coming. I know, Matt, I know. I just felt so stupid after Gaia's comments that I spaced out. I'm sorry."

"Aww. Time with the mother can be intimidating, but why stupid, my love?"

"She said I need to come back after the crisis to learn more about being a goddess."

"Well, you do," Matt said with a chuckle.

"Thanks," Crystal retorted.

"No, really. There's an awful lot to know about being a supreme power, and that knowledge no one is born with. It's no insult."

"Why'd it feel like one, then?"

"I wasn't there, so I don't really know. But she's a stickler for protocol, for one thing, and she also buys into the idea that it's best to say the least when advising."

"Well, she did that. She had nothing for me."

"I have a hard time believing that," Matt said. "Let's go down to breakfast and talk it through."

"Breakfast? I was gone all night?"

"Yup."

"Oh, right—inter-dimensional time differences."

"See? You're starting to get the goddess thing down," Matt said as he led her down the spiral stairs into and through the bedroom to meet the girls in the antechamber.

Breakfast turned in to a huge event as people arrived to hear Crystal's update. They shoved tables together in the center of the room to accommodate all of the magi, even the newest ones.

As Breenda placed a plate in front of her, Crystal looked around. Matt had been busy, she could tell. Every so often her husband rode out from the estate leading a flock—a gaggle?—what do you call a group of dragons? she wondered to herself—out to rescue more packs of humans who'd survived the cataclysm. In the first trip he'd brought close to eight hundred of the college's students and employees with him, plus a small core of people whom he'd somehow sensed would be able to do magic. Birch and Phoenix, the two most powerful, had come in that group, as had RJ and his wife Krista, and they had become Matt's very first battle magi. The god had gone out again and picked up Natalia and her twin sons, who were currently at the table carefully dividing their attentions between Crystal and her daughters. The next trip, shortly after returning from the library where Natalia had worked, had been to rescue her husband Ben, a physicist who it turned out had a bit of skill with spells also. Several other trips had produced more magic-wielders, and then more, to the point where now there were nearly a hundred competent magi seated around the gathered tables. The kitchen helpers served the mages and all ate breakfast quietly as Crystal began her tale.

"Fried okra for breakfast?" Phoenix asked Matt as Sorscha brought his plate.

"Sure. Why not? It's technically a vegetable, after all," Matt said, popping one into his mouth. Crystal knew that the golden-fried nuggets were her husband's favorite food. It was a preference she'd found odd when they lived in central California, but recently he'd explained that it was a delight he'd learned to love eons ago, literally, while traveling through the various equatorial cultures. As gods, neither he nor Crystal needed to eat; they could replenish their bodies through magical means. Still, he often ate for pleasure, and Crystal found herself falling into the same pattern. Not with okra, though. Crystal's version of okra was actually chocolate.

"It's a little strange, that's all," Phoenix replied.

"Eating something I like to eat isn't strange, dear. Eating that gelatinous insult to the world of food that Birch is having is strange."

"What? It's oatmeal," Birch defended his choice. "Back when I suffered from diabetes I was never able to enjoy it mixed as thoroughly with sugar as this is."

Crystal grinned; when they'd arrived she was celiac, Birch and several others diabetic, and quite a few other people had various other medical problems. The lack of pharmaceutical service in the brave new world they entered was, in fact, many peoples' most vocalized fear. Matt's constantly-maintained shell of healing over his estate had seemed nothing short of miraculous at the time, though now that Crystal was confident that she could weave the same energies on the same scale, she saw it as less than a true miracle.

"So, what news, Crystal?" Ben asked, his dark eyes lit up with energy and his deep voice cutting through the clatter. Silence descended; even those in the middle of a bite stopped to pay close attention.

"Well, it's been a reunion of the gods in Atlantis, and quite the party too," Crystal began with a smirk. "At first I spent a day and some hours with Melissa, a cute young lady whom I thought was one of Apollo's trained mages. Then, after I learned that my research partner was actually Stacy in disguise...."

"Wait—what?" Natalia said. "You mean Stacy, as in Matt's ex-wife? The Stacy who tried to kill you?"

"Yes, that Stacy. Sorry, I'd've thought you would have all heard. To be fair, she's the same Stacy that I later tried—and almost succeeded—to kill."

"As well as the same Stacy who did kill me," Phoenix said with a grimace.

"What?" Natalia asked, casting a startled glance Phoenix's direction.

"I got better," Phoenix said, shrugging her shoulders and then wiggling her eyebrows up and down.

"Because I brought you back to us," Crystal shrugged.

"…so that your husband could kill me."

"What?" Natalia asked again, glaring at Matt.

"Oh, quit pouting. I brought you back then, too," Crystal said.

"Pouting?" Phoenix's glare caused murmurs around the table.

"I've never seen anyone who can glare daggers as effectively as you," Crystal said, prompting a couple of chortles. "Perhaps that's why you're such a tempting target for deities who aren't pleased to be glared at by humans."

Phoenix continued to glare impressively. Her nearly six feet in height coupled with a dancer's muscular build made her presence intimidating enough, but when combined with her long black tresses streaked in a single wide stripe of silver, she looked every bit of the powerful sorceress she actually was. Matter of fact, she had looked that way even before the cataclysm, back when her only magic involved leading circles of would-be witches in calling out to powers that never quite seemed to respond. Now that she had direct access to elemental flows, she was both amazingly powerful and supremely dangerous, and she very much enjoyed letting everyone know it.

Matt, though, wasn't impressed. He lazily reached out and encircled Phoenix in a sphere of white ka energy, a trick that effectively cut anyone inside the sphere who wasn't a deity off from the flows. Phoenix's expression didn't change, but the rest of the table, nearly all of whom could sense and mold elemental powers themselves, seemed to shrink back away from the coming storm.

"You were saying, my little battle mage?" Matt asked without looking at her, his voice booming through the hall.

"I was merely saying that I wasn't pouting," Phoenix said. Her voice made it clear that she wasn't interested in backing down. "I haven't pouted for as long as I can remember, but being killed happens to have an impact upon one's psyche. It definitely made me feel a little bit under-appreciated."

"Well, okay, pouting was intended as a joke and was clearly a bad choice of words," Crystal said, hoping to placate her friend and end the tension. "Now, can I continue with the story?"

Phoenix nodded and dropped her glare. Matt, in turn, dropped the shield he held around her. Everyone else sat back in their chairs and took in the breath that most had been holding onto.

"So, where was I? Oh, right—once we figured out that it was Stacy who was helping me look for the king, it felt strange for a minute or two but I really didn't have much time to worry about it, because then the Jade Emperor showed...."

"Actually, first we went to visit Benny, don't forget," Matt said.

"I was trying to forget that vile visitation, but clearly my wonderful, beloved husband doesn't wish for me to. Now, my cherished, would you like to tell the story, or shall I?" Crystal asked, an overly-sweet smile on her face.

"Nah, you're doin' fine," Matt said, popping a nugget of fried okra into his mouth and winking.

"Who's Benny?" one of the mages asked.

"Ben'thra is another of the original gods. The Norse knew him as Loki the trickster, and the Greeks knew him as Hermes, also the trickster," Crystal explained.

"So you're saying he's a trickster," Birch interjected, smirking.

"Indeed. And he and my husband have apparently never gotten along. Remember the story Matt told us—right after we came—about how he and another god split the earth into continents and killed off the dinosaurs in their battle? Benny was the other god."

"Actually, we used to get along, before that. I think," Matt said.

"Before the unicontinent was broken apart and the dinosaurs killed? I'll believe you if you say so, but let's stick to modern history, okay, love?" Crystal said. "So short version of the story—we teleport in, he's in his throne room naked except for his golden winged sandals and his staff...."

"Was his staff—big?" Phoenix asked, smirking also.

"Would you mind letting me tell the story? What is wrong with you people? Are you all in cahoots to keep me interrupted?"

Matt chortled. "Nope, sorry, love. I think everybody here is just really happy to finally be together as a congress of the most powerful mages of the estate—heck, of the world—and thus you're suffering the result of that jocularity. It is kind of historic, don't you think?"

"I'd find it more historic if there weren't a ticking time clock working against us."

"Oh, right. Proceed, then, my love, and the retribution of the god of war will be upon any who interrupt henceforth."

"Hmm," Crystal growled, not satisfied. Continuing anyway, she said, "So anyway, no, his staff wasn't all that big. But once he and Matt reached an impasse in insulting one another we teleported back here for a rest, and then I went back to Atlantis.

What is it now?" Crystal interrupted herself, glaring at Birch, who had once again been smirking.

"Nothing. I just got a visual when you said you came back for a rest, is all. Sorry."

"Gah, fine. Class, does anybody else have any other sexual references or innuendos to get out of your system before I move on?"

Silence fell loudly across the tables.

"Good," Crystal said. "So the Jade Emperor, who is at the top of the eastern pantheon, popped in and told Stacy and I—oh, and Thor, who popped in to support us—that he believed Matt had taken the king and that we had three days to bring him back, or else."

"Or else what?" Natalia asked.

"War. Of the gods, apparently. Boom. Big ba-da-boom and all that. Gaia said that war between and among gods is fairly commonplace with the eastern pantheon, but those battles have always been up in the heavens. Matt, she pointed out, likes to keep his battles closer to the earth—for strategic reasons, right?" Matt nodded, and she continued, "So Gaia is worried that this battle could actually destroy the planet."

"So did you ever figure out whose energy pattern was most likely to have blasted the walls apart?" Ben asked, leaning forward.

"Sort of, yes," Crystal said. "Apollo did, anyway. We initially thought it to be Matt's signature, since the walls were actually melted down rather than blasted, and he's known for being a relatively unsubtle sort of power like that." Matt chortled, a sound Crystal ignored. "Apparently since neither Stacy nor I were gods in the beginning, we missed the years of battle between elementals and gods...."

"Man, were those awesome...." Matt interrupted, and then stuffed another fried okra into his mouth.

Not even bothering to glare, Crystal cocked an eyebrow and continued, "So Apollo recognized the pure energy signal as an elemental's power."

"I've never heard of these elementals," Birch said.

"Sure, you have. The legends and myths call them titans, if you're Greek."

"And giants to the Norse?" Birch asked.

"No," Crystal said, and she explained about the frost giants being made up. Birch looked disappointed.

"So was this a particular titan?" Birch asked.

"The one we knew as Prometheus, probably."

"Ah, yes," Birch said, nodding.

"Don't 'ah, yes' like you knew that was coming," Phoenix scolded.

"But it makes sense. He was the one who got in trouble for giving fire to humans. So all we have to do is track him down and ask where the king is."

"We?" Matt asked Birch. "Powerful as you have become, my little gnome, I'm not sure you'll get anywhere with a titan."

"Birch is not a gnome," Phoenix objected.

"He's your mythology expert, remember?" Crystal said.

"So, back on topic, how does one track down an elemental being?" Ben asked.

"If you're in good with the earth mother, it's easy," Crystal said quickly, hoping to reclaim the conversation. "Once long ago they were all imprisoned in the Underworld, which is part of Gaia just like the planet we know is. Since it's part of her, she can sense whether or not they're still there."

"And they're not, of course," Ben said.

"No, they are."

"Still—imprisoned?"

"That's what she said," Crystal explained.

"Well, that puts a troublesome thorn in the investigation's foot, doesn't it?" Ben said.

"I'd say…." Crystal began and was interrupted again, this time by the jangle of alarm klaxons and a loud roar from outside. "What now?" she growled as everyone at the table jumped.

"I'd say we have a visitor, love," Matt said calmly as he silenced the alarms with a wave of his hands, rose, and swaggered out to the front door. The battle magi followed, breakfast plates forgotten. On his way, Matt thrust open the doors to the mansion with gusts of air and walked out onto the steps, a lightly-glowing red staff appearing in his hands. Crystal recognized the "ready" pose that Thor had taught her.

"I see somebody let the monkey out of his cage," Matt called out as he stood halfway down the steps. Sure enough, across the field in front of the mansion stood what looked like a monkey in black close-fitting clothes.

"Ooh ooh ah ah," the monkey said, scratching himself on his chest and underarms before straightening again to a more human posture. "Atlantis has gone too long without its king," the monkey continued in perfectly-spoken English. "It is time for you to put away the ruse and return the ruler of Atlantis to his people, war god."

"I would if I could, monkey, but I had nothing to do with his disappearance," Matt retorted. Crystal could see and hear that he was ready for a fight; his tone was flat and unemotional, while his lips were turned up at the corner in what she had only recently come to know as battle lust. Looking sideways at him, she could almost see a glow coming from his eyes. "You know that, yourself, don't you, monkey?" Matt continued. "You're not interested in the king of Atlantis, though, are you? You're just here for a fight."

The monkey laughed and pulled something out of its—his?— ear. He shook the hand that had reached up to the ear and a short staff appeared, one that looked to be dark stone lined in gold. It was nearly five inches thick, yet the monkey seemed to have no trouble holding it.

Suddenly Matt let loose a war cry and dashed, faster than Crystal would have thought possible, across the field. The red streak he made ended where Monkey stood, and a loud crash sounded as crimson staff met black cudgel. The ferocity of the charge startled Monkey, and he lost several feet of ground to his opponent.

Monkey answered, whipping through a series of whirls and feints of his own. Though it was shorter than Matt's, Monkey was clearly an expert with his cudgel. The two staves cracked through the air as their wielders danced an intricate duel, both moving fast enough at times that Crystal could see neither the weapons nor the fighters. She could hear the retorts as they met, though, and there were plenty of those.

Crystal could also make out the soft pops behind her as the other deities teleported in. She was comforted by Thor's low growl, but Stacy's appearance beside her set Crystal on edge as she remembered the battle not long ago on the grounds nearby when Stacy had taken advantage of Crystal's ignorance of magic to try to kill her. That time it had been Matt flying in to the rescue, leaping off of Sorscha's back to fight Stacy with magic and sword as the other gods and goddesses teleported in to watch. It made Crystal wish she were capable of doing the same, but just a few moments of watching the opening battle flurries convinced her she was no match for either of the warriors on the lawn.

"Why doesn't Matt use magic?" Crystal wondered out loud.

"The Monkey King is too fast," Stacy answered. "Pulling in flows and weaving them would just distract Matt from the intricacies of staff work."

"But you and he...." Crystal started to object.

"…weren't trying to kill each other," Stacy finished, never taking her eyes off the battle. "Oh, I was trying to kill you—no offense, dear—and he was trying to protect you. This, though, is a serious battle, mano-a-mano."

"And ours wasn't?"

"Again, we weren't trying to kill each other," Stacy said, and then turned her head to look at Crystal. "At least, I wasn't. You didn't know any better."

"Thanks," Crystal said drily.

"You're welcome," Stacy said, missing the sarcasm Crystal had intended as she turned her attention back to the battle in front of them. "Besides, we were all using our preferred weapons, while Matt is using a conjured staff for some reason. Granted, he's okay with a staff, in the same way that Apollo is okay with fire magic, but it's just not his favorite weapon. I think he picked it to answer Monkey's little cudgel trick. Sometimes, after all, size does matter."

RJ's head snapped around to peer at Stacy with narrowed eyes. "You're Venus, aren't you?"

"Guilty," Stacy said. "And who are you, besides tall, dark, and buff?"

"I'm the guy who had to clean up the mess you made when you tried to kill my friend."

Stacy grinned. Instantly her clothing shimmered, changing from the pants and tunic she'd worn when she appeared into a curve-hugging gown that, instead of fabric, seemed to be made of nearly-transparent clouds. Lewdly, she sidled over to RJ and said, "Well, thank you, big boy. I always make such a mess when I'm in a mood, if you know what I mean."

Crystal could see what Stacy was doing as the goddess of love wrapped green energy, the magic of primal emotion, around RJ. Both the former college president and his wife stared at the goddess with enraptured expressions, unable to break the spell.

Crystal thought to step in, but she was too engrossed in watching her husband battle the monkey god to weave any major flows of her own.

"Children. Let. It. Go. Lest you forget, there's a battle raging that needs our attention," Gaia upbraided the group of them.

Venus switched back to her normal clothes and released her hold on green magic, stepping back over to stand beside Crystal with a lewd grin on her face. Both RJ and Krista gasped, and then husband and wife assumed relieved expressions. They reminded Crystal of how a mouse might look if it survived a near miss with a cobra.

Krista leaned in and whispered in RJ's ear. Crystal, rapt as she was at the combat roaring before them, was still curious enough to manage the light flow of air required to pluck the words into her own senses.

"It's okay. Hell, I wanted her, myself, and you of all people know I don't bowl in that lane," Krista whispered softly.

Stacy snickered evilly, earning another glare from Gaia. The glare was shared with Crystal, though, as she hadn't been able to hold back her own snort.

"You'd think..." Crystal started then was cut off by the loud ringing of a rapid-fire attack Matt delivered to Monkey, both ends of the crystal staff whipping around one direction and then another. Monkey fell back a few feet but deflected perfectly and soon regained the offensive. "You'd think that the Jade Emperor would be here to watch, too," she got out.

"He is, daughter," Gaia's voice behind her caused Crystal to jump, startled, and turn. Gaia's eyes darted heavenward, and Crystal followed the mother's gaze to see a collection of deities, the Jade Emperor among them, watching from above while perched peacefully on a white puffy cloud.

"Wow, this is kind of like the Superbowl," Crystal said drily.

"The super what?" Gaia asked absently, focused on the battle.

"Bowl, mother. It was a big sporting event—oh, never mind. Should I be worried for Matt?"

"No, lass," Thor said. "The Monkey God is really, really good, and I'm not sure Matt could ever beat him with a staff, but at the same I'm positive that the Monkey God could never beat Matt. Your husband earned every ounce of that arrogance he carries around on his shoulders like a set of crystalline spaulders, dear. It's not just that he's the strongest of us all; he's also studied combat and warfare for hundreds of millions of years. No, this battle is most likely to come down to a stalemate."

"In what, a million years or so? What about the three day deadline?"

"That's a good—ow—point," Thor said, grimacing as Monkey beat several vicious blows that were barely blocked on Matt's staff. "Come on, Matt!" the giant god yelled, clenching and pumping his fists and then looking embarrassed for doing so. Still, Matt had earned the cheers, coming back from the blows to rain a series of smart raps from his staff on the monkey's cudgel.

No one was winning, of that Crystal was certain. This battle seemed more evenly-matched than any she'd seen before. For every vicious series of blows Matt would swing, the Monkey King answered with deft and apparently effortless parries. The same could be said for the Monkey King's blows, though; Matt was also quite clearly a grand master with the staff. Every swing the Monkey King attempted was either skillfully dodged or forcefully blocked. Both deities, meanwhile, were blessed with super-human strength and speed, which sent the battle spiraling into epic intensity as the combatants traded blows faster at times than the eye could follow.

"Can't one of us step in and help him?" Crystal asked.

"We could," Thor said. "But Matt would be furious. It's his battle to fight, and he's doing quite well. Plus, one of us stepping in to help would bring dishonor to him in the other side's eyes. Besides, all you and the love goddess over there could do is get in his way. Monkey is very, very good, too."

"I see that—ouch!" Crystal said, reacting to a powerful blow Matt had parried while standing nearly sideways. Monkey had inverted his own body, standing on one hand as he twirled the cudgel at ankle-height. To counter, Matt had executed a series of side flips using his left hand while still keeping the staff twirling with his right. He came up behind the Monkey God and launched a blistering combination, but his opponent merely twisted around and countered perfectly.

"On top of that," Thor said, "look around the field, lass."

Crystal did, and saw that the entire battlefield was ringed by Matt's thrakkoni, some of whom had taken on their dragon form already.

Thor followed her eyes and nodded. "Several hundred dragons stand ready to jump to Matt's defense, if he so much as whispers the need. That, plus there's an entire phalanx of battle mages whom Matt has personally trained standing behind you. Granted, one wonders how much good all of them would do against the Monkey King, but in conjunction with the staff of the god of war? None but the foolest of fools would attack the grand master of war on his own turf."

"Yes, but—they're figuring out what it will take to beat him, aren't they?" Crystal asked into the air around her.

"Well, they're more likely trying to figure out whether he's beatable at all," Stacy said. "It's said that Monkey fought off all the hosts of heaven once, but your husband is legendary, dear. I'm sure one of the things they're trying to accomplish is a measure of Matt's skill against one such as Monkey."

The battle raged back and forth as the sun climbed up and over its zenith in the sky. Crystal was worried; the battle, while clearly entertaining for everyone in attendance—including, judging from his whoops and the glow of his eyes, her husband—was costing precious hours from her quest to find the king. She watched Matt perform incredible battle moves and combinations, over and over, and her training with Thor, rudimentary as it was now appearing, had taught her enough that she could easily have been enthralled by Matt's mastery of weapon and form. Enthralled by the mastery of both combatants, actually; Monkey's form was different from Matt's, but it was no less beautiful to watch.

But enthralled, she wasn't. Instead, she was scared, and she grew more so as the hours of combat went on.

"Mother, can't we do something about this? Matt and I need to get back to finding the king, and this battle is keeping us from doing that," Crystal finally said out loud.

"You're right, daughter," Gaia said and swiveled her gaze upward toward the cloud that still floated above with the eastern deities riding atop it.

Suddenly the Monkey King rebounded from one of Matt's attacks not by parrying and striking, but rather by rolling quickly away from Matt. As he came up, he blew a kiss toward Matt and vanished.

Matt stood steady, awaiting a treacherous attack from elsewhere.

"Son, get over here," Gaia said in a motherly tone. Matt obeyed, rising from his ready stance to turn and walk back to his home. As he swaggered across the field of strife, Crystal glanced up to see the Eastern deities gone.

"Of course, you know that they were just testing your abilities, my son," Gaia said.

Matt nodded, the lust of battle still shining in his eyes. He flicked a bead of sweat from his brow, flexing his arm in a masculine move that Crystal found incredibly attractive. "Of course," he said, flexing both arms and then raising the staff above his head, arms held wide, allowing joints all over his upper body to crack and pop in a manly way. "I'm sure they found my abilities quite remarkable," he growled.

"I'm sure," Gaia agreed drily. "But how does that get us any closer to finding the king?"

"It didn't. But it was fun."

"I'm sure," Gaia agreed again.

"So, if I may be so bold as to interrupt," Phoenix interrupted, stepping over to Gaia and bowing deeply, kissing each of the Mother's shoes before rising and continuing. "Yes, we all know you have muscles, Matthew-Ares-God-of-War. But I'm curious about something else. Just before we were called out here, oh wise Earth Mother, Crystal was saying that you could sense the location of the titans, and that they were all still in the right place. I mean no disrespect, but if you can sense their location, can't you also use your tremendous power and wisdom to sense the location of the king of Atlantis?"

"Suck up," Matt said.

"What? The Earth Mother has always been one of my favorite deities. The god of war, not so much. Not," she added quickly and held her arms up in front of her in a peaceful stance, "that I mind the room and board and training you've given me, Matt. You're wonderful in that way. But this—she—is Gaia. I mean, Gaia. The Earth Mother. I was too wrapped up in what was happening when we teleported here the first day to really express my regards to her, but I can't help it now."

Gaia snorted and said, "Are you quite done sucking up to me, child?"

Phoenix nodded mutely.

"Have you ever felt a flea crawling on you?" Gaia asked.

Phoenix recoiled. "Eww. A flea? Of course not. That's—that's disgusting. I hate bugs."

As Gaia's eyes widened, Matt snarled and asked, "Mother, may I do the honor of killing her for you?"

"What?" Crystal asked, unsure she'd heard him right and hoping that he was playing a strange joke. "You do know I'll just bring her back, right?"

"Not from this death," Matt said, his voice full of steel.

"Matthew, Crystal, no," Gaia said, turning to the bewildered Phoenix. "I'll not ask you to destroy one of your most competent mages, especially when she doesn't know what she did wrong. This one has power, indeed. Some day she will be a sorceress to be reckoned with, and a beautiful and competent one, at that."

"Thank you, I..." Phoenix started again in her mildly sarcastic tone but abruptly stopped, glancing over at Stacy and nodding. She dropped to her knees and asked in an entirely different tone, "Please, Earth Mother, will you please forgive me?"

Coaching her a bit, are you? Crystal shot the question to Stacy telepathically.

I shouldn't need to, the reply came. This is Matthew's lesson to teach his followers. That he's taught them so much about magic and so little about their true place in the world is disgraceful. He's always been this sloppy, though, so you might wish to step in and train those you want to see live through future encounters like this.

"Of course, child," Gaia said, smiling at Phoenix, Crystal, and Stacy all at the same time as though she had somehow heard the telepathic messages that had been passed around. "Now please get up. After all, they're going to need you alive and in one piece on the trip into the Underworld. In any event, the question I posed was imprecise. The scale isn't correct. Better would be: can you feel a molecule of air that you brush against?"

"Of course not, Earth Mother."

"But you can feel it when you walk into a wind?" Gaia asked.

"Sure, Mother. I think I see what you're going after," Phoenix said.

"Just to be certain, I'll finish, child. The titans are to humans and naga as a hurricane is to an air molecule. They're even more powerful, in their own way, than the beings you call deities. I recall, in fact, that the god of war whose hospitality you are now complimenting had to be peeled off of a surface or two, himself, during Ragnarok."

Birch, who had been hovering close by, asked, "But Earth Mother, I thought—I understood—that Ragnarok would be the final battle, held at the end of time."

Gaia shrugged. "End, beginning, they're pretty much the same. Now, it is time for me to return to my glade. Good luck, children."

Crystal saw Birch and Phoenix look at Matt, confused expressions on their faces. Matt saw it too and shrugged. "What?" he asked.

Phoenix answered. "Well, since you're our—um, I'm not sure what to call you—patron? Host? Father? Whatever, you're the god we entrust with our training. We were hoping, anyway, that you could explain the beginning-ending thing the Earth Mother was alluding to."

Matt crossed his arms and answered with a smirk, "Well, the wheel weaves as the wheel will."

"What? Now I'm really confused," Krista said.

With Phoenix incoherently sputtering and Birch standing mutely with eyebrows raised, Natalia stepped in. "Shall we adjourn to the library?" she asked, looking significantly toward the holes left by the departing gods and goddesses as they teleported away from Matt's estate.

"Oh, hell. Sure, let's just go to the library, so we can get more non-answers to our questions," Phoenix said. With a flourish of her mage cape, she spun around and floated back inside.

The Library

"Hold," Matt said quietly, stopping Crystal from moving by putting a hand on her arm. She pointed a querying look his direction, and in return he smiled and teleported the pair of them up to the cupola on top of the building. Crystal found herself holding her breath, looking around once again at the lush valley surrounded by the forests butting up against the mountains that surrounded the estate.

It was beautiful.

She'd forgotten about this spot since the night that Matt had teleported with her to Olympus for the first time, but now that she remembered it, she'd have to come up more often.

"I—owe you an apology," Matt said from behind her.

"For what?" she asked. She was pretty certain she knew, but she wanted to make sure.

"For putting you in the situation where you felt the need to defend Phoenix."

"I'm not sure that apology isn't owed more to Phoenix."

"No," Matt said, his voice hard again. "Gods do not apologize to humans."

"Even if we're wrong?"

"Even when we're wrong, we're never wrong to humans," Matt said. "Look, I've set an informal tone with the humans here on this estate, in part because you used to be one of them, and also because many of them used to be my friends and colleagues, but mostly because that's just who I am. I like to laugh and joke, and if the humans run around bowing and scraping all the time then all I'd normally have left to enjoy conversing with is Sorscha."

"She's not exactly Miss Congeniality, I guess, is she?"

"Oh, she's funny enough once you get to know her. A couple thousand more years and you two should be just like this," Matt said, holding his hand up with two fingers crossed.

"I bet," Crystal said, a grin creeping onto her face. "So do I need to be stricter with the humans, myself? Stop hanging out with my former friends?"

"Nah, not at all. Here, it's no big deal. And I usually do train them, but I wait till they're ready to go out into the world. I don't personally care for etiquette one way or another, but other deities are very picky about how humans speak to them. And the Mother—geez, I can't believe how Phoenix addressed her. She's—well, she's the Mother. The Mother, as Phoenix herself pointed out. I had to stand up to that."

"I know."

"I figured you would. Besides, if we don't find the king of Atlantis soon, these will all be your subjects."

"They can't really…."

"Of course they can," Matt said. "And they've wanted to for a long, long time. I can handle the Monkey King by himself, and probably two or three dozen of his compatriots, but if they bring to bear that whole heavenly horde they have—well, I don't think I could withstand that."

"Surely you know that I and the rest of the western gods will stand by you."

"You cannot. To do so would trigger a battle that would rip the universe apart."

"So you expect me to stand by and watch you get killed?"

"No. I expect you to find the king of Atlantis," Matt said.

"Of course. So do I. So, to the library, then." This time Crystal took the lead, teleporting the two of them into the library, targeting a spot about twelve feet off the floor to make sure they didn't pop in on top of any of the dozens of people already there. She caught herself and her husband gently on a column of air and lowered them both to the ground in regal fashion.

"Greetings, oh beautiful and radiant ones," Birch said, bowing as the pair's feet touched down. "We mere humans are ecstatic to behold...."

"Oh, stuff it, Birch," Matt said, walking up to a table. "Get up, please. Look, everybody. I like you all; if I didn't, you wouldn't be here. I like being informal with you. It's how I prefer to be. You've seen me be an asshole, and that's also who I am, but I always try to temper that with a playful side. That said, outside of these walls I'm the god of war, the highest-ranking western deity in this dimension. Never, ever, say or do anything that even looks like it might have been meant disrespectfully, not in the slightest way. Not to me, and certainly not to the Mother. Do you understand?"

"I do, but if you're the highest ranking, what is Gaia?" Natalia asked.

"Gaia isn't in this dimension. She is this dimension. It's tough to conceptualize, I know, but just go with it. I can visit her, and she can in turn visit us, but the person we see is just a representation of her being on the physical plane."

"That's—that's pretty cool," Birch said, grinning.

"Yeah, it is," Matt said. "And by the way, she's also not typically considered either a western goddess or an eastern goddess, but rather one of the three primaries. Be that as it may, though, we need to find the king of Atlantis."

"Is he in the Underworld?" Krista asked. "That's where Gaia told us to go."

"Not us," Matt corrected. "You can't go."

"Why not?"

"Well, there's an agreement that we gods won't enter the realm of Hades unless we're transporting a human soul, so the deities who go will need one of you. But Mother already picked Phoenix, and there's no point taking more than one."

"Why not?"

"You're sounding like a broken record, Krista."

"And I'm going to continue sounding that way till you explain what we're up against, Mister Wheel-weaves-as-it-will."

"Yeah, does that mean there's a Ragnarok every two thousand years?" Birch asked.

"No, it doesn't, Birch. There's a Ragnarok at the beginning of time, and I hear there'll be one at the end of time, and I'm—well, I'm not sure, myself, what what she said really means," Matt said. "And Krista, you're sounding more like Phoenix every day."

"And the problem with that is what?" Krista said, joined almost perfectly in sync by Phoenix and Crystal, both.

Matt held up his hands. "Geez, I can't win."

"So, the Underworld?" Natalia prompted.

"Right," Matt said. "So, the Underworld is a separate dimension and the sole domain of Hades. We don't go there except to deliver him more toys, and he doesn't come here, except to—well, honestly, he doesn't come here ever."

"Why do the gods deliver Hades more, um, toys?" Krista asked.

"To punish them."

"It's bad in the Underworld, then?"

"Well, yeah. If you're expecting roses and harps, you shouldn't go there," Matt said.

"So what should we be expecting there?" Krista pushed the matter.

"Oh, a bunch of demons. Lots of the red devils, breathing fire and carrying pitchforks. They stabbity-stab stab all of the souls all the time, and then there's all that eternal wailing, Demons, stabbing, demons, wailing, stabbing, demons, and wailing, all the time." Matt said, demonstrating the stabbity-stab with his fingers.

"Really?"

"No," Matt said.

"This is no time to be funny," Natalia said. "Can we please be serious about the investigation? The world is literally hanging on our efforts."

Matt said, "Oh, fine. People have all these silly misconceptions about what the denizens of the Underworld must look like, but the reality is nothing like that. Fact is, it's far, far worse. Hades likes monsters of every shape and size around him. Imagine how my place would be if all the thrakkoni hated humans and were made by an insane version of Picasso."

"But isn't there a pleasant spot in the Underworld?" Birch asked. "Elysium, or something like that?"

"Yeah, I think so," Matt said.

"You—you think so?" Phoenix asked, her face incredulous.

"I've never actually been there," Matt said. "Why would I venture into Hades's realm if I don't have to?"

"So all this is conjecture?" Phoenix asked.

Matt shrugged and said, "So, you have a more knowledgeable expert hanging around?"

"No, but..." Phoenix sputtered, then composed herself. "So what's the point of going into the Underworld, exactly?"

"Well," Crystal interjected, "Apollo said that the energies used to blast the castle bedroom apart were wielded by a titan, and Gaia said we'd find that titan in the Underworld. It seems obvious that we need to go talk to Prometheus."

"And he's going to tell you the truth why, exactly?" Phoenix asked.

"I'm not sure," Crystal said. "Matt?"

"Don't look at me. He won't even speak to me," Matt said. "I was one of the ones who imprisoned him."

"I thought that was Zeus, Apollo, Athena, Hades, and Artemis," Birch said.

"Remember what I've said before about the accuracy of those mythological stories? There have been several versions of the tale told over the different cycles. This past cycle there were a few versions circulating, but the only one that survived to modern times was the one Apollo suggested to Hesiod. Of course it included him and his sister and his confidant. The real Titanomachy, though, included all of us original gods. Back then, Apollo and I fought side by side as brothers, if you can believe it."

"You and the twit, brothers? I can't believe it," Crystal said with a smirk.

"But why?" Natalia asked Matt.

"Well, because we cared for each...."

"No, that wasn't what I was asking. Why were you fighting against the titans at all?"

"Well, because," Matt said defensively.

"Because—what?" Natalia seemed to be growing impatient.

"Just—because. They wanted control over the universe, and we did too. We won, and so we got it. Then we banished them to the Underworld. Why is it an issue?"

"It's an issue because we're looking for a king who was apparently kidnapped by a titan, who apparently went to the effort to implicate you in it. I think we need to understand more about the motives at work here," Natalia said.

Matt crossed his arms, clearly frustrated. "Look, motives are all well and good on those TV shows where they take weeks of effort and compress it into an hour of theatrics. We don't have that luxury. Besides, I have no idea how, after all these millennia, a titan could get out of the Underworld without the complicit help of Hades in the first place, much less then snag the king of Atlantis and take him back to the Underworld with him. No idea how, and even less of an idea why. It's boggling my mind, and since I've been around for several hundred million years longer than any of you, I'm not sure you should be wasting your time worrying about that either."

"I guess," Birch said, "that the part of the story about Zeus freeing all the titans except for Atlas is fiction also."

"Sort of. He asked Hades to free them from their bonds. He didn't release them from the Underworld."

"Wait, though—are the titans intelligent beings?" Natalia asked.

"Of course they're intelligent beings. They're extremely, uncannily intelligent, in fact. Why?"

"You've called them elementals, is why I asked. I figured a being made out of elements wouldn't have a separate intellect. What's the difference, then, between an elemental and a god?"

"An elemental is primarily made of energy. That's what makes them so damn powerful. Gods are powerful too, but we're made primarily of flesh and blood. We use magic. They are magic. Both have intellects," Matt said.

"So what keeps an elemental from just oozing out of the Underworld at will?" Natalia continued her line of questioning.

"The mechanics of the place. It's another dimension."

"But don't you teleport between dimensions?" Natalia asked.

"Sure, but that's different," Matt said. "I follow the rules."

"I'm not sure I understand. From what I've observed and read, you follow customs, but there don't seem to be a lot of firm rules."

"But I'm a god. A god, as in flesh and blood. Thus, I'm bound by the rules of flesh and blood. The titans are elementals. Magic, in other words, not flesh and blood. They're bound by the rules of magic."

"Fascinating," Natalia said.

"Yeah, I guess."

"But I still don't get why an elemental wouldn't be able to just slip out of the Underworld," Natalia said.

"The shortest and easiest answer is that they just can't. Hades sees to it, because he personally controls everything on that dimension. So Crystal, Stacy, Phoenix, and Breenda need to get ready to go to the Underworld. I'll ask Thor to go with you," Matt said.

Crystal, who had been silently watching the back and forth, jerked her head toward the back of the library at the list of names. Sure enough, Stacy was sitting there. Matt's ex-wife waved the fingers of one hand.

"Why—" Crystal started to ask a question and then held it back. She recalled the lecture Matt had given her on the relationship between god and human too closely to let herself call his decision into question in front of others. Out of the corner of her eye she saw Stacy smirk and nod. Matt's ex-wife rose and started to walk over toward the table where Crystal sat.

"Dear husband, I'm not sure everyone understands the rationale for the team you've suggested. Would you mind explaining?" Crystal asked, hoping she'd struck the right balance between questioning and authoritative.

Matt's half-grin said she'd come close. He said, "Yeah, sure. I can't go for two reasons, the first being that since I'm one of the gods that imprisoned them, none of the titans will be willing to speak to me. To the contrary, they're quite likely to want to sling me against the wall. The second reason is that there's a chance, slight though it may be, that the party who goes will get stuck there for longer than a day and a half. If I'm going to be attacked by the entire eastern pantheon, I'd much rather it be on my own turf rather than in Hell. Crystal, you've led much of the investigation so far and that needs to continue, but love, you're too new to your powers to go up against titans by yourself. You can't be accompanied by any of the original gods for the same reason I can't be the one to go, but neither Stacy nor Thor fought in the Titanomachy. That said, both have been around long enough to stand by you confidently on this trip. Oh, and Thor has fought elementals before, too."

"So why add a thrakkon on the team?" Crystal asked.

"Thrakkoni are special, remember? We gods can't use telepathy to communicate between dimensions because of the blocks set up between them against elemental flows. Kinda silly blocks, really, but the rules are the rules, and they were set up to protect us from each other. But at the same time we built the thrakkoni to use a process other than elemental flows to communicate, since they can neither touch the elemental flows nor be touched by them. Thus, a thrakkon—Breenda, specifically—represents a telecommunication conduit between your party and me out here. Also, it bears mentioning that she's also another type of asset specifically in the Underworld, since nearly everything there is of an elemental nature. She can't be harmed by much of anything there."

"She also can't harm much of anything there," Phoenix objected.

"That's not entirely true. She can easily transform into a dragon, and as such her breath weapon will be effective against anyone or anything there. Even were your statement completely correct, though, we're not making an offensive strike. If we were, the best practice would be to send in weapons, but if instead we send in agents who cannot be harmed, we confuse those who would strike against us," Matt said.

"Spoken like the true god of war," Phoenix said.

"Thank you," Matt replied, his tone biting. "I guess. Now, are there any other questions before we move out?"

"I suppose I should feel perfectly safe since I'm going to the Underworld with three deities?" Phoenix asked.

"Well, yeah, of course. Only one of those deities has killed you in the past, after all," Matt said.

"And another one brought me back," Phoenix said.

"So what are you worried about, then?" Matt asked.

"Well, there's this small matter of being given away to Hades as one of his toys."

"Toys?" Matt said, a curious expression on his face.

"Right. Toys. You said it, oh wise old man that you are. Toys for him to torture, as I recall your story went. For all eternity, yes? Though, I don't know why I'd be worried about that, honestly. Silly me, worry, worry, worry, fret, fret, fret. You know us high priestesses, we stress out over absolutely nothing."

"I'm sorry, I couldn't hear you very well over all the ambient whining," Matt said. "But if I were to tell you that Hades probably won't want you for a toy, would that make you feel better?"

"Well, of course—wait. Why wouldn't Hades want me for a toy?"

Matt snorted. "Because you haven't lived a long, full, evil life, dear. As wickedness goes you're actually quite deficient. Besides, you're entering his realm on a mission from me, the god of war."

"Oh."

"So, what are you still worried about, then?"

"Nothing. Let's go, my dear friends and honored deity companions," Phoenix said, her voice laced with sarcasm.

"Uh huh. We'll meet in the throne room, then," Matt said.

Minutes later the companions were looking at the gold teleport target circle on the throne room floor with varying degrees of unease. Crystal and Stacy had decided to don normal traveling robes, Crystal's Hephaestus-made war hammer swinging loosely at her side, while Thor insisted on hefting Mjolnir at the ready in full combat armor. Phoenix and Breenda were also there; Breenda wore a simple travel shirt and pants while Phoenix wore her favorite—and most ostentatious—high priestess cloak.

"Quite the expeditionary party," Matt said, grinning. "You do know, Phoenix, that at some point you're going to have to play dead, right?"

"That shouldn't be much of a problem. She can just lay down, hold her breath, and pretend that she's making love to you, old man," Stacy said, drawing a snort from Phoenix. Crystal hid her smile. It was funny.

"Yes, well," Matt said, his grin disappearing to be replaced by a dangerous glare at Stacy. "All that funniness aside, there's only one spot to teleport in to or out from the Underworld. From there, you walk to the castle of Hades and ask to speak to Prometheus."

"That's it? Just walk up and ask? What if Hades says no?" Crystal asked.

"I don't see why he would, but if he does—well, work it out with him."

"How do we know how to get from where we teleport into, to the castle of Hades?"

"Follow the paths. They'll lead you there, from everything I've understood," Matt said.

"So, I've never actually gotten to say 'have fun storming the castle' in real life, or to have it said to me," Phoenix said, prompting a snort from Matt.

"Well, we weren't exactly speaking of storming the castle. Hades is an ancient and powerful god, and he's the absolute ruler of his realm. Storming the castle might take a few more gods and goddesses than you're taking. I wouldn't go in there waving that thing around, Thor," Matt said.

Thor shrugged and hitched the celebrated war hammer to his belt. "Okay, fine. Teleport when ready, lad."

Matt produced an ancient-looking silver coin from his pocket and held it out to Phoenix. "You're the bait, dear, so you have to carry this."

"Payment for passage on the River Styx, I take it?" Pheonix said.

"Hmm," Matt said. "You need to carry it close to your heart." Phoenix placed it atop her left breast, and Matt shook his head. "Closer." She slid it down between her breasts, and Matt nodded. "There."

Thor snorted.

"What is this?" Phoenix asked, holding the coin up to the light.

"It's an old coin," Matt said. "I wanted to see if I could get you to put it in your cleavage."

"For the oldest guy here, you sure do act like a seventh grader sometimes," Phoenix said, flipping the coin back toward Matt.

Still chuckling, Matt hugged and kissed Crystal, prompting a lewd gesture from Stacy. He took a step backward away from the party and nodded, firing up the teleportation spell.

"Have fun storming the castle," he called out as they disappeared.

Into The Underworld

Immediately following the lurching pop of teleportation, Crystal became aware of Phoenix's discomfort. It was hard not to, with her friend sinking to her knees, holding her stomach, and repeating "Je-sus, Jesus Jesus Jesus Jesus, Je-sus" loudly and repetitively. Crystal bent down to help her friend up defensively; it hadn't been that long since her own first inter-dimension teleportation experience, and so she knew first-hand how Phoenix's guts felt like they'd been wrenched into a knot. To make it worse, both of the other gods were laughing at them.

"What?" Phoenix said angrily as she let Crystal help her up. "You've never felt like your stomach was worming its way out through your belly button before?"

"No, no, I can't say that I have," Stacy said, an innocent smile on her face.

"Yes, she has," Thor said. "We all do. It's tough, but you get used to it. I suppose we could've warned you, but that wouldn't have made it suck less for you. And your choice of epithet was entertaining, to say the least."

"What? I—oh. Yeah." Phoenix said. "I don't...."

"Yeah. Time to head out. The castle is over that way, but I think we have to go through that gate first," Thor said, pointing in two different directions.

Crystal peered into the distance. Through the deep gloom she could see, over a towering wall, a black fortress rising from rocks that were somehow even blacker. She could just make out squat towers on each corner of the castle building, mostly by following differences in motion as the air around the castle seemed to be swarming with—something. Something just beyond her ability to see it. No, many somethings, she decided. Surrounding the castle were hundreds or thousands of shadows of creatures of a nature which Crystal shrank away from considering. As she watched, a shadow passed in front of one of the few lit windows, a movement Crystal could only discern because the light from the opening seemed to fade and then return.

To the left of that but much closer was an obsidian gate in a wall that seemed to stretch forever in either direction. Both wall and gate were too tall to climb, though why a spirit couldn't just float over either one seemed odd to Crystal. She couldn't see any joints in the wall; it looked to have been fashioned from one long piece of smooth black stone.

A huge, indistinct black mass lay in front of the gate.

Matthew relays that we should speak out and ask Hades to turn off the sound track, Breenda said through her telepathic link.

Sound track? Oh, right, Crystal replied. She'd been too busy getting her bearings to notice the constant noise of wails, moans, and screams, punctuated occasionally by demonic-sounding cries.

"All right, Hades, we get it. Please lay off the mood music," Stacy called out. It became abruptly silent save the burbling of the black stream Crystal could now hear behind where they stood. Apparently Breenda had broadcast rather than pinpoint her mental transmission.

"Well, that was easy," Phoenix mused.

"Yup. It only gets harder from here. And on that cheery note, I think it's time for us to be off," Thor said as he started walking into the gloom.

Crystal swung her legs rapidly to stay close to Thor, but as she walked she felt the darkness of the realm of Hades wrapping thickly around her. On impulse, she attempted to fire up a light globe above her hand—one of the first tricks Matt had taught her. It fizzled.

"Yeah, that—don't do that, okay?" Stacy said as she strode beside. "This is the domain of Hades, remember? Everything here is elemental. He knew the moment we popped in, and he knows when you try and cast a happy night light into his deep, dark, and mean place. Let's not go out of our way to piss him off early, okay?"

Crystal nodded and settled into a rapid pace through the gloom. She tried working magically within what she knew of how her own eyes worked to enhance the light before it hit the receptors, but she finally gave up when she realized the efforts weren't having much effect. At last she relaxed to let her eyes adjust naturally. She wasn't sure she really wanted to see their surroundings all that well, anyway. Flickers of motion caught her attention to each side, but when she turned her head to look directly at them there was nothing to see. She stopped trying to focus on the shapes, but that made it even worse as her mind began giving her images of leathery wings and shiny red eyes. Crystal could tell she wasn't the only one seeing the shades, though; several times Thor's hand jerked toward Mjolnir, only to relax away when the perceived attack didn't come.

They walked along a flat featureless strip of land that lay between what could only be the fabled River Styx and the wall surrounding the true Underworld. For all its fame, the river gave very little indication of being anything other than a regular undulating stream with a proper amount of gentle splashes of waves upon the bank. The thought of a regular stream back home brought to mind the sound of a fish jumping. Crystal chortled quietly, wondering to herself what kind of fish, if any, might live in the River Styx.

"Have either of you ever met Hades?" Crystal asked.

"Sure," Stacy said. "He comes to all the important meetings at Olympus."

"What's he like, then?"

"He's—like Hades, I guess. Quiet."

"So should I do anything special to prepare myself to meet the Father of Evil?"

"Father of what? Hades isn't evil," Thor said. "He's Lord of the Underworld, but that doesn't make him evil."

"But I've always heard…."

"You've heard wrong, sweetcheeks," Stacy said drily. "What is evil, anyway?"

"Well, it's—it's the opposite of good," Crystal said.

"Okay, fine. So what is good?" Stacy pressed the issue.

"Good is—well, good. Now's not the time for a philosophy discussion."

"You brought it up," Stacy said, shrugging and returning to her quick-paced walk.

"Grunnskólar," Thor said.

"What?" Crystal asked, not understanding the word that Thor said with a heavy accent.

"Grunnskólar. English speakers called it primary school, I think. 'Oh, that's good.' 'Oh, that's evil.' Childish, lass. To an adult, there's no such thing as truly good or truly evil."

"Sure there is," Crystal argued. "I remember taking a philosophy course in college where we learned that relativism doesn't work. There has to be an absolute good, and an absolute evil."

"Why?"

"Well, I don't remember right now," Crystal said, sensing that the debate was soon to be well and truly lost.

"Must've been a terribly strong argument to have made such a long-lasting impact on you, sweetcheeks," Stacy said.

"Would you please quit calling me that?"

"Sure, sourpuss," Stacy said, grinning. "Better?"

Crystal ignored the jab. "That was way back in college. Nobody remembers that stuff. Besides, just because I don't remember the rationale behind something doesn't make it false."

"Correct," Stacy said. "But how many of those philosophy professors were three hundred seventy-five point two million years old?"

"Point two, eh?" Thor said mockingly.

"Look, my hairy barbarian companion, I ruled continents hundreds of times before your sperm won its race."

"Thus making you an old lady," Thor countered. "Big deal. Look, Crystal, let's think about it this way. Is it good, or evil, to be just and equitable in everything you do?"

"It's good, of course," she answered.

"Is it good, or evil, to be cruel in your punishment?"

"Well that's evil," Crystal said, feeling a trap coming on.

"Right. So you just called Hades both good and evil. He's the overlord of the afterlife, such as it is. He punishes those who deserve it, and often quite cruelly. But what would be equitable about letting those who deserve their reward receive it while at the same time letting those who do not deserve it also receive it?"

"Well—nothing, I guess. Okay, you've made your point. I get it," Crystal said.

"So," Phoenix interjected, "Grand discussions of the nature of good and evil aside, it appears that we're coming up on the gate. Do I, as the token human here, need to start playing dead yet?"

"Who said anything about playing?" Stacy asked, a wicked gleam in her eyes. When she received the glare she was hoping for from Phoenix, she continued, "No, you don't have to be dead yet. We'll address the keeper. We've three deities, so we should be able to just walk through. If we have to, though, I can just kill you and he'll let us through immediately."

"Oh, great. Thanks for the comforting wisdom, oh mighty and terrifying goddess," Phoenix said.

"And beautiful. You forgot beautiful. Sexy, too. Exquisitely, radiantly pulchritudinous, if you really want to make an effect with your words. Oh, and don't worry. I'm sure Crystal will bring you back on the other side"

"Not likely. Crystal couldn't even light a globe back there," Crystal reminded the group.

"Oh, right. I forgot about the anti-magic thing going on. I may not be able to kill her either, then, though Hades would probably get a kick out of watching me try. There's probably no need to worry, though. I bet we'll talk our way through easily enough," Stacy said.

"The keeper sure doesn't look like a three-headed dog," Crystal observed as they came close enough to begin seeing details. The huge mound actually looked more like a hill of obsidian than anything else; the only thing that gave it away as a living being was the steady rise and fall of the top of the mound and slight undulating movement behind it that looked like a tail.

"Why would the Underworld be guarded by a dog?" Stacy asked.

"That's what the stories said," Thor replied.

"Some of them said that. Some others, though...." Stacy's voice trailed off as a huge eye opened on the side of the mound of obsidian. A growl sounded, and the hill shook as the creature rose to its feet, two heads turning four eyes to glare menacingly at the group.

"Well, I'll be darned. It is a dog," Stacy said.

"A great big two-headed dog with black dragon-like scales," Thor added, pulling his hammer off of his belt. "And a third head somewhere, if the stories I've heard are true."

"I don't see a third head—oh, wait, there it is," Phoenix said as a third head snaked around from behind the creature to turn the dog's fifth and the sixth eyes toward the group. "I guess it really can look every direction at once, huh?"

Standing nearly twenty feet tall at its shoulders, the massive mastiff growled at the party once again and began sniffing the air.

"Mm, meeeeeeeeaaaaaaat," the creature said, its voice deep and resonant.

"A great big talking three-headed dog with black dragon-like scales," Thor said, bouncing Mjolnir against his left hand. "Isn't that just wonderful. You ladies probably ought to get behind me now." The barbarian god took up a defensive stance.

Breenda stepped out of her clothes and transformed into her dragon form. The process still took Crystal's breath away as she watched the lithe blue-haired woman become a blue-scaled dragon. With wingspan stretching over thirty feet, Breenda wasn't nearly as big as Sorscha, Matt's dedicated thrakkoni servant, but that was because thrakkoni kept growing for as long as they lived, and Sorscha was one of the oldest dragons in existence. Breenda was fairly young, though, which made her a perfect match for the young goddess. Besides, Breenda was a beautiful shade of Crystal's favorite color. With every movement of the dragon, Breenda's scales splayed an azure radiance out into the deep darkness that was the gloom of the Underworld.

"Drrrraaaaaagoooooonnnnn," the creature said. It turned its eyes toward Thor, who was in a battle stance, hammer at the ready. "Goooooooooood?"

"Yes," Crystal said. "We good. We are gods who have come to speak with your master, Hades."

Cerberus, if that was who the creature was, stood silent for several seconds, apparently considering Crystal's words. Finally it said, "Yoooouuuu maaaayyyy paaaassss," and sank to its belly on the soil once again. Crystal watched as its heads twined around the body, folding into crevasses left between leg joints and body cavities. Once the triple-headed guardian closed its eyes, all she could see was a slowly-breathing obsidian hill.

"We good?" Thor asked Crystal, giving her a sideways glare as they walked past the gate.

"What? I didn't figure the dog was much of a grammarian. And hey, lookit, I was right."

"Yes, you were, lass," Thor said, nodding as he put his hammer back into its loop on his belt.

"Well, that was easy," Phoenix mused.

"You keep saying that word," Crystal said. "I do not think it means what you think it means."

"No, I'm pretty sure I know what 'easy' means," Phoenix said, waggling her eyebrows.

"I'll bet you do," Stacy said drily, earning a glare from the human priestess. "Now can we pay attention to the next bit? We have a fair distance to go to the castle still, and now we're inside the realm of Hades, proper."

The path from the gate led straight to a simple square block building that looked like an old country courthouse. Its front doors stood open, and the tall slit windows emitted an eerie red light. Paths led from behind it into the murky darkness to the left and to the right.

"I assume that's where judgment is held, right?" Crystal asked. Stacy nodded mutely, so Crystal continued, "So where is everybody?"

"Everybody who?" Thor asked.

"Everybody waiting to be judged. Everybody being taken off to eternal damnation or eternal salvation. I don't see a single soul, literally."

"They're here. Can't you sense them?" Stacy asked, her own voice serious for once.

"Well, yeah, in a general hair-on-the-back-of-the-neck way. But nothing else."

"We'll have to ask Matt next time we see him. None of us have ever been here, lass," Thor said. "We need to keep moving."

"Matthew says we can't see the souls because Hades doesn't want us to see them," Breenda chimed in.

"Oh, right. I forgot we had a traveling walkie-talkie there," Stacy said.

"Thank you, Breenda," Crystal said, feeling defensive toward her thrakkon. "Could you ask Matthew why Hades doesn't want that?"

Breenda stared off into the distance for a moment, then said, "Matthew says you'll have to ask Hades yourself."

"Of course he does," Stacy said.

After a short discussion, the party decided that since none of them were in need of judgment they should take the direct route, veering off the trail to the right and walking straight toward the castle. Thor was the first to step off of the trail, and an imp the size of a household cat but winged and fanged, promptly leapt onto his shoulders and attempted to turn the giant back onto the path.

A bash from Mjolnir quickly sent the imp flying. Instead of impacting the wall of the courthouse, though, the imp passed right through, gibbering and screeching as it flew entirely without using its wings.

More gibbering sounded to the right as a small army of demons appeared a few feet off the path, their stances making it clear that the party was in for a greater fight if they ventured farther afield. It looked like Hades had taken all of Crystal's nightmares and molded them into one gaggle of evil, since no two of the demons were exactly alike. In the front rank were all sorts of creatures, from one that appeared to be an old hag, warts and rotten teeth and all, leaning on her gnarled staff, to another that looked like a creature from one of the science fiction horror movies Crystal had always avoided watching. Atop its strange body, which featured a humanoid skeleton on the outside of the skin, rested an elongated snout-face that dripped long strands of drool from its long fangs. A loud snap sounded from the back, which must have been eight or nine rows behind, as a large pair of leathery bat-shaped wings unfurled rapidly. Some of the creatures hopped on four legs, and some on two or three; others had three or four arms. The only similarity Crystal could see was that all their eyes set off a malevolent red glare directed at the party.

The gibbering grew louder as the ranks of demons grew longer and deeper. Crystal wondered absently how many demons Hades had at his disposal, but just as quickly she realized she didn't want to know the answer to that question.

"Well, I'd say that's a pretty clear signal from the master of the domain," Stacy said, her flippant attitude returning.

"Ya think?" Crystal said.

"Tell ya what I think. I think it's clear that we're intended to go through the hall of judgment whether we want to or not," Thor said, pulling his foot back onto the trail and shrugging. "I also think that's a pretty good idea, considering the alternative." He continued the march down the path, the rest of the party taking up an easy, regular stride behind him. The gibbering sound continued to their right, but everyone in the party kept their head tightly fixed forward. Even when the imp that Thor had knocked flying into the hall of judgment returned, its little bat-like body bobbing up and down just off the path to the right while it screeched its disapproval at the barbarian, the group diligently ignored its antics.

The party entered the hall safely a few minutes later. Inside it consisted of only one room, in the center of which stood a dais on which an empty wooden throne rested. Three exits led from the building, one on each side and one on the rear wall.

"Kind of anti-climactic," Phoenix said.

"Which part?" Crystal asked.

"The throne. One would expect something either far more dire or far more heavenly, but it's just a fancy chair."

"And nothing on the walls," Crystal said.

"Probably just a blank palette like up in Olympus. Whatever the person being judged expects to see, he'll see it," Thor observed.

"So, like, I'm just curious, but you guys are gods. Why don't the gods know these things?" Phoenix asked.

Stacy answered absently as she walked around the throne, taking it in from all sides. "Well, being immortal, we don't face judgment, and if one of our followers were to ask us we could always just have them see for themselves, and fairly quickly too. But nobody ever asks the gods that question. Instead, they always ask for rain or for wealth or for better sex or, sometimes, for childbirth, and they leave the question of the afterlife to be answered by the weirdos who wander off into the woods, do drugs, and call themselves prophets because they see strange stuff."

"So, like, I'm just curious, too, but will I be as cynical toward humanity after a few cycles as you two are?" Crystal wondered aloud.

"Uh huh," Thor said.

"Yep," Stacy said.

"Well. Such an awesome thing I have to look forward to, I guess. Anyway, let's leave if we can. We still have some walking ahead of us to get to the castle, and we still have time ticking against us if we're going to meet the Jade Emperor's deadline," Crystal said.

"If we can?" Thor asked, and stepped out the right side of the building onto the path that led to the castle. The party followed and then stood looking at Crystal once they were outside.

"Hey, I was expecting a trap of some sort, is all," Crystal said defensively. "I wonder why Hades made us go through here if all we saw was an empty room with an empty palette. It was begging for some sort of grand surprise. A loop, perhaps, back out to face Cerberos again."

"No, Hades's demons are probably just trained not to let anyone or anything off of the path. No point looking for a grand conspiracy when a little consistency will do," Thor said. "And don't risk giving him any of those sorts of ideas if he hasn't already thought of them, okay?"

"Speaking of demons, I kinda expected his demons to actually be thrakkoni," Phoenix said as they started off, drawing a glare from Breenda.

"No, the realm of Hades is entirely constructed with elemental energies," Stacy lectured as she walked. "A thrakkon would be out of place and completely useless to him here. Besides, I don't think that any of the three elder gods uses thrakkoni as servants."

"Matt does," Crystal said.

"Matt's not an elder god," Stacy said, looking at Thor and shaking her head.

"I thought Matt was an elder god," Crystal said.

"Matt is older, certainly, but he's not an Elder," Stacy said. "We're going to have to teach you everything important, aren't we? Matthew and the rest of the original Olympians were created when the universe was, but they didn't do the creating."

"So how was it created?" Phoenix asked. "Was the seven days and seven nights thing true, or was there a big bang?"

"The Creator created a giant turtle who pooped the universe out one day," Stacy said, a wry expression on her face.

"So, I asked a stupid question, I take it?" Phoenix asked.

"No, you just asked another question I don't know the answer to. Ask the Creator yourself if you ever run into him. And, I should add, if you can think of stupid questions like that when you're in his presence," Stacy said, prompting a snort from Thor.

A mile of walking later, they took the left side of a fork in the path. To the right was even darker somehow, but Crystal could just make out what appeared to be dragons that loomed several times larger than Sorscha and had many heads wandering around a large, open pit.

"The Pit of Doom?" Crystal asked.

"Only a fantasy author would call it that," Stacy said.

"So what should I call it?"

"Tartarus was the going term to the Romans and Greeks, and even in some of the other religions' writings. You can call it Hell if you want. But it's down at the very bottom of that pit where the titans stay as guests of Hades. That's where we're most likely going after we get Hades to agree to us questioning Prometheus."

"Long way down?" Phoenix asked, gazing into the distance.

"According to myth, an anvil would fall nine days from this level before it reached the bottom," Stacy said.

"That's a long way," Phoenix said. "Crystal, do you know how far that is?"

"No. Matt would. He's the physicist in the family."

Stacy snorted and said, "No, Matt wouldn't. The distance calculation depends upon the local gravitational constant, which may or may not be the same as the nine point eight oh six six five value that it is in proximity to the earth's surface at sea level, in addition to the more complex consideration of air resistance, which will determine the anvil's terminal velocity and thus set the constant velocity at which it would most likely fall for most of the nine days. We know none of that here in this dimension, nor do we have the time to determine it empirically. Sweetcheeks," she added as an afterthought.

"Yeah, what she said. Now, can we get back to stormin' the castle?" Thor huffed, motioning the party ahead on its walk.

"You've studied physics too, I take it?" Crystal asked as they regained pace.

"Nuclear engineering, sweetcheeks. I was the best on the planet when I was a human. It's.... Well, it's how Matt and I met."

"He was a nuclear engineer too?"

"No, he was a manager. He governed the continent my station was on. Back then the gods were the rulers even in the technological phases. I'll tell you the story sometime if you really want the sordid details, but right now we need to talk to Hades."

"So ya slept with yer boss, eh?" Thor said as they finally strode up to the great black double doors that gave entry into the castle of Hades.

"Stuff it, you," Stacy said and gave the door knocker a few loud raps.

Hades

The doors opened slowly, both of them swinging at the same pace seemingly under their own motivation. Inside was a gloomily-lit entry hall lined with dark grey and black statues, each somehow more morbid than the previous. As Crystal's eyes swept the line of stone figures she saw representations of people going through numerous types of torture, from birds eating their entrails to racks and cages.

In the middle of the grand entry stood Hades.

There was no mistaking the elder god, who leaned on a simple staff made of deep-black wood. His plain black toga was tossed on haphazardly, and his black sandals also were simply-constructed and unadorned. Long shiny black hair curtained his face, with an even longer black beard covering his chest. As his elongated, thin face drew Crystal's eyes and held them, she felt a crushing weight of judgment descend upon her. The light glinted off of obsidian eyes as they latched onto each member of the party and held them while he weighed their souls, immortal or no. Once the trip was over Crystal knew she would have to talk to Stacy about her statement that immortals don't face judgment. Clearly, each had been judged, with the result well-hidden behind the stern countenance of Hades.

Finally Hades flicked his eyes toward Breenda. "An interesting loophole you represent, daughter of stone," he said. "I shall have to consider later whether to close it. For now, though, you have all traveled far, and seemingly with some urgency, so I will ask simply what is it that you are after, wife of Nergal?"

Silence surrounded the party for several long moments. Suddenly a hand—Stacy's, based on where it had shot out from—

shoved Crystal out into the area in front of the party. "Nergal is one of Matthew's old names," Stacy said under her breath.

"Oh," Crystal said quietly, regaining her balance quickly.

"Besides, you're the only one here who could be identified as a wife of anybody," Thor said aloud, seemingly immune to the intimidation that the elder god's presence had cast over the party.

Since the shove and subsequent stumble had released her eyes from the terrible glare, Crystal understood why a canary might stand still in the gaze of a serpent. Clearing her throat, she mustered her courage and began, "Mighty Hades, we enter your realm to investigate a crime that happened on our realm above." Above? Was that right? Too late now, though. She wished they'd worked out how to approach the Lord of the Underworld before arriving. "To do so, we need to interview the titan known as Prometheus."

"No," Hades said.

"No?" Crystal repeated, confusion in her voice.

"No," Hades repeated.

"No, as in we cannot interview Prometheus?"

"That is what I said, daughter."

"But—but why not?"

"Prometheus has been interviewed too often. I will not have the titans continually bothered."

"But our questions are important. My husband is in danger."

"That is not my concern."

"The whole world is in danger if the gods should join battle."

"That is also not my concern."

"Wait," Stacy said. "Who else has interviewed Prometheus?"

"The Monkey King, or so he is called in your realm. He found a way to sneak in and visit with the titan against my wishes. Twice, in fact."

The gods stood silent for a few moments, looking at each other and digesting this new information.

"Look, Hades," Thor said, "we're pretty sure that Prometheus was the one who kidnapped the king of Atlantis. That's why we need to talk to him."

"Impossible."

"Impossible for us to talk to him?"

"Impossible that he kidnapped the king of Atlantis."

"Why?"

"Prometheus has not left the Underworld, that is why. How could he kidnap anyone while he is safely accommodated down in Tartarus?" Hades asked.

The party mulled that over for several moments, and then Crystal said, "Well, that's a very good question, Lord Hades. Now, if we could just..."

"No."

"But..." Crystal persisted.

"No."

"You're making it..."

"No, child. But I will be happy to teleport you from here back to your husband's estate. How is that for a friendly bargain?"

"That would be..."

Pop.

Thor, Stacy, Crystal, and Phoenix found themselves staring at each other in Matt's throne room. A second later Breenda appeared, saying apologetically, "he told me he had sent you all here and that I should follow. At least he was polite about it."

"Well, how was Hades?" Matt asked cheerfully from the door.

"Not very helpful," Crystal said.

"Yeah, that's like saying that you're not very male, dear. Look up 'not very helpful' in any encyclopedia of the gods and I guarantee that you'll see a picture of Hades. So what happened?"

Crystal related the story of their trip, starting over a couple of times as they were joined by Ben and Natalia, RJ and Krista, Birch, and a few other mages as time went on. Matt chuckled at the story of their encounter at the gate and said, "Ah, yes, Cerberus. Good doggie."

"So how did Hercules beat him?"

"Who said Hercules beat him?" Matt replied.

"Well, Greek legend does."

"Oh, of course. The Greeks really liked their heroes to be heroic, didn't they?"

"And their fiction to be fictional, too, I take it?" Crystal asked.

"Mm hmm."

She continued. He nodded when she mentioned the name Nergal. "Ah, yes, that was actually my—well, the closest thing I have to a birth name. It was also my name with the Sumerians. And others in different cycles, of course. But the Sumerians were a lot of fun. I had them convinced I was the god of war and the Underworld."

"Didn't Hades mind?" Crystal asked.

"Nah. What's he care, so long as he keeps his real turf? But they also developed a standard of counting everything by sixties. That was new, and kinda strange, but it worked. For them, at least, since their most advanced physics concept was that things fall downward. They'd've had a bear of a time carrying that numbering system into Hilbert space. Right, Ben?"

Ben chortled and nodded.

"What's Hilbert space, Matt?" Crystal asked.

"It's a mathematical construct, dear, that allows for the translation of frames of reference for general relativity calculations through simple multidimensional matrix algebra."

"I'm—kind of sorry I asked."

"Figured you might be."

"So, were you involved with the Sumerians, Thor?" Natalia asked.

"Yeah, of course. They were a good tough group, and they made some really good beer. Besides, Matt and I have been together with pretty much every culture other than the Greeks and the Romans. Those were both pussies, so I mostly stayed at Valhalla except for when I led a few of the northern tribes against the Romans."

"Oh."

"Speaking of, I think we should probably get back to finding the king of Atlantis," Crystal said.

Matt snorted and said, "Nice segue, dear. So what happened next?"

Crystal related the rest of the conversation with Hades as Matt listened. When she finished, he said, "Wow. Monkey? Why would the Monkey King involve himself in this?"

"It sure seemed like the two of you had a good, solid grudge going," Thor said.

"The little bastard challenged me on my own lawn," Matt said. "Before that, not so much of a grudge match. After, absolutely, yes it was."

"So you didn't sense any animosity before the fight today?"

"Yesterday. And no."

"Yesterday?" Crystal asked, dread gripping her heart.

"Right. You've been gone for nearly twenty-four hours now. Time feels different in different realms, remember?"

"Which leaves..." Crystal said.

"Nearly a day. Plenty of time," Matt said, smiling.

"So, on that note," Thor interrupted, "Why would Monkey speak to Prometheus around the same time as the King disappeared by the hand of Prometheus?"

"Well, didn't you say Hades told you that Prometheus hadn't left?" Matt asked.

"Yes, but…" Crystal said.

"And didn't you say that Gaia sensed that Prometheus was still there?"

"Yes, but…"

"So why are we still even talking about the whereabouts of Prometheus?" Matt asked.

"Well, Apollo said…."

"I know what Apollo said, but why are we doubting the word of Hades and Gaia, two of the three elders, because of what Apollo said?"

"Dad, the one you need to question is Monkey," Heidi interrupted from the doorway.

"Well, hello Heidi! You and your sister surprised me, sneaking up like that," Matt said. "But tell me why you think I need to question Monkey."

"Since the battle yesterday we've been searching the library. Monkey is the trickster of the eastern pantheon, Dad. There are plenty of stories about him fooling around and taking advantage of twisted words or logic."

"Well, okay," Matt said. "So did any of these stories tell how to get Monkey to talk? Or even where to find him?"

"No," Heidi said.

"She has a point, though, Matt," Thor said. "If we're not to be questioning Gaia's or Hades's statements, then we have to assume Prometheus has been locked away. But we don't have to assume anything regarding Monkey."

"Do you really think Monkey could manage to conjure a pure-fire magic signature like Prometheus's when he melts a wall down?" Stacy asked Matt.

"No, I don't. But it's something to check into. I wasn't saying you were wrong in wanting to talk to Monkey, Heidi. I was just pointing out the difficulties."

"Difficulties, but not impossibilities. We need to know more, Dad," Heidi said.

"Indeed we do," Matt said, grinning. "Now that's my daughter. Heidi and Linda, back up to the library. Natalia, Ben, and Birch, head there as well, with Sorscha. We'll all dig into the resources to see what we can find up there. Stacy and Thor, you two mind hitting up Apollo's library for references to Monkey?"

"With pleasure, loverboy," Stacy said. "His, after all, is much, much bigger than...." Stacy stopped when Matt leveled the glare she was hoping for, and then she snickered and teleported away.

"Must she always be like that?" Crystal asked.

Matt chortled and said, "Yeah, she must." He let out a long sigh and then turned and led the family to the library.

Seeking Answers At Olympus

The forces seeking knowledge rallied in Matt's library. Heidi and Linda teamed up reading at one table, Natalia and Ben at another, while Birch and his wife worked at a third. Matt, Crystal, and Phoenix watched from the door.

"Phoenix," Matt said, without looking at her, "must you fidget like that?"

"I'm just not so good in libraries," Phoenix said. "I love to read, of course, but that's books that I select, sit down, and read from one end to the other. This research thing is something I've always avoided. Besides, I'm having a hard time coming up with something to check into that everybody else isn't already reading."

"So go prepare your magic. There is a battle in the future."

"Really?"

"Of course. We have plenty of readers here," Matt said.

Phoenix nearly knocked Crystal over in her haste to get out of the library. Crystal chuckled; her friend had never been very much into serious research in large doses. As intelligent as she was, a few college courses had been all she could stand.

"Dad?" Heidi said, bringing over an old book, Linda following closely. "Looks like we found it. It says here that Monkey is from the Mountain of Flowers and Fruit."

"Oh, awesome," Matt said. "All we have to do now is look for a mountain with both flowers and fruit."

"Are you being sarcastic?" Linda asked.

"Who, me?" Matt said. "Naw. I'm sure there's only one or two mountains in the Orient with both flowers and fruit."

"Matthew Vincent," Crystal said, enunciating her husband's last name more staccato than usual.

"Okay, I was being a little bit sarcastic. The Mountain of Flowers and Fruit is a fictional location, girls. That book you're reading is fiction. Good fiction, but still fiction."

"So were you, Dad, until you weren't," Linda said.

"Touché," Matt conceded. "But I still have no idea where a Mountain of Flowers and Fruit might be."

"That's why we're in here researching, Dad," Heidi said, shaking her head and leading her sister back to their table where Matt's ancient thrakkoni librarian had already deposited more books.

"I thought your library was intended to be a repository of knowledge through the cycles," Crystal said as the pair watched their daughters settling in to reading.

"It is."

"So why would you keep fiction here?"

"Well, Linda pretty well nailed it in her comeback. One man's fiction is another man's mythology is yet another man's religion. Remember how you felt on your first night here, sleeping with a fictional husband?"

"Don't remind me, please." Crystal did remember the alienation, the hurt, the uncertainty of not knowing how much of her life had been or would be truth or fiction.

"So," Crystal continued, "let me guess—that work of fiction the girls found, having true gods in it, was prompted by a god, just like you talked to Snorri and prompted the works of the Norse?"

"Probably. And I didn't prompt all the works of the Norse."

"So, then, how are we—they—supposed to know what and which to believe when you—we—keep nudging the primary works toward one exaggeration or another?"

"They are supposed to figure it out, love. Remember that whole free will thing?"

"Yes, but...."

"But nothing. I've watched through thousands of cycles, and it always plays out roughly the same. These folks will live here in happiness and safety up until they start getting bored with it, and then they'll leave of their own volition or mine and set up the next great civilizations. They'll know the truth—well, some of it, anyway—because they've lived with a true god, but by the time that truth is passed down to their children and their children's children and their great great great great grandchildren's grandchildren it will be all jumbled up into the myths of this cycle that we're in now. You'll be amazed what they come up with. Did you know the Greeks were convinced that Stacy cheated on her husband Hephaestus with me? Who knows, maybe someday you'll hear the tale told of how Crystal the goddess of the tongue came crashing in on the happy home of Stacy and Matthew, drove away the goddess of love, and victoriously claimed the god of war as her husband."

"I'll have to correct them, then."

"They won't believe you," Matt said, his expression making it clear that, for once, he wasn't joking.

"But that's silly."

"Yup. Silly, and incredibly, awfully, and irresistibly humorous when you think about it."

Matt and Crystal watched the research team for several more long minutes. Matt fielded a few questions, but for most of the time, the group was entirely engaged in quiet reading.

Bored, Crystal asked, "So do you know where to find the Jade Emperor?"

"I do," Matt said.

"Why don't we just ask him?"

"You've seen how the western gods are toward a threat to one of our own. The eastern gods are just as cohesive. Besides, the Jade Emperor doesn't particularly want me to win."

"But he wants the king back, right?" Crystal asked.

Matt thought for a moment and then said, "No, I kind of doubt it. If my memory is correct, he's threatened to kill the king himself more than a few times. He'd have been far less offended, I suspect, had the evidence pointed to Monkey instead of me."

"Monkey knew that, didn't he?"

"Yep," Matt said.

"Bastard."

"Actually, the prevailing story is that Monkey was hatched from a stone that became an egg, or something pretty much like that. No parents at all. Now that I think about it, I guess you're right, then. You can also be a bastard if you have no parents; technically it's just the lack of a father that qualifies you for the title."

"Is the stone-to-egg story from your fiction over there as well?" Crystal asked.

"Yep. Same novel Heidi brought over, actually. It's hundreds of years old, which as novels go is amazingly long-lived."

"So you've read it."

"I've read most of it. I skipped the boring parts."

"Correct me if I'm wrong, but haven't you read all but the boring parts of pretty much every book in here?"

"Once or twice, sure. Except for the newer ones."

"Well why are they taking time to look, then?"

"Oh, I might have missed something."

"Like hell," Crystal said derisively.

"No, that place is too big to miss. You've been there, now, remember?" Matt jerked his head toward the door as he finished the quip and then turned and walked toward it. Crystal, catching the cue, followed.

"Where are we going?" Crystal asked, suspicion blooming, as Matt's path lead upward toward the cupola that sat atop the main estate building.

"I'm thirsty," Matt said. "All that hard research makes a guy parched, you know?"

"Possibly the biggest battle the universe has ever seen is coming up, and you're stopping to get a drink?"

"Hey, it worked for the Scots," Matt said.

"So did eating pig organs minced up with vegetables then boiled in pig intestines, and then wearing skirts into battle," Crystal said. "And actually it didn't work for them; they still ended up losing to the English."

"Kilts, love," Matt corrected. "And it's sheep organs that haggis is made from, and sheep stomach it's boiled in. For that matter, haggis is actually quite good, especially on the morn of a glorious battle, though I still prefer my fried okra." As they stepped out into the bright daylight in the glassed-in area atop the mansion, Matt grabbed Crystal's hand. "So, ready?" he asked and then teleported them without waiting for an answer. Crystal let down her guard and allowed herself to be led into the quiet bar, suspecting as she did that Matt was after something other than a drink.

"Would you be willing to wear a kilt for me?" she asked.

In reply, Matt grinned and glanced down. She followed his eyes to see a green and blue checkered kilt around his waist, high socks in matching pattern covering his calves. Shiny black shoes and a shiny black leather strap holding up a furred sparran completed the ensemble.

Crystal smiled and pulled Matt's hand to her mouth for a kiss as they found a table.

Olympus was unusually empty and quiet. The dive bar of the gods was usually filled with bored major and minor deities socializing, its copious artwork along the walls morphing from one image to another to suit the nearest occupants' moods.

Those same walls were now covered in sable canvas.

"You're the last one I'd've expected to see here, Matt," the bartender said.

"Hey, if the final battle is about to go down, might as well face it after a good drink, right? And you do mix 'em good, my friend." Mike, the bartender, grimaced; there was nothing mixed about nectar.

"Nice skirt," Mike said.

"It's a kilt," Matt replied.

"I thought you were Irish," Crystal accused.

"Lass, I've been around since the universe began, back when there were no Irish. I'm only Irish because it amuses you, and that, in turn, amuses me. Regardless, that tartan isn't Irish."

When Crystal looked questioningly at Matt, he shrugged and replied, "It's Black Watch. Scottish, technically, and a military organization rather than a clan. You didn't say which kilt you wanted me to wear, and this is more appropriate for who I am, I think." He sipped twice, slowly, at his nectar and then continued with what Crystal could tell was forced indifference, "So, you haven't seen the Jade Sternyface or Monkey hereabouts lately, have you, Mike?"

Mike grimaced again; Crystal hid her own expression behind a sip of nectar. Her husband was many things: mighty warrior, powerful mage, awful actor. Still, she couldn't believe she hadn't thought of this herself. If anyone would have a clue to Monkey's whereabouts, it would be the tender of the bar at, literally, the center of the universe.

Mike shook his head slowly. "Can't help you, Matt. They haven't been around for a few days."

"Any idea...."

"Nope, no idea where they can be found," Mike said. "Well, Jade is probably in his Imperial Palace, but I don't know where Monkey is, and he's the one you're really looking for, isn't he? From what I'm hearing, neither one is really going to welcome a visit from you right now."

"I couldn't really care less what they welcome," Matt growled. "I have a battle to stave off."

"Yes, you do, Matthew. You certainly do," Mike said pointedly and then walked to the other end of the bar to wipe its spotless surface down.

"Well, I'll be. Matthew, what a surprise," a voice from behind said. Crystal recognized the voice, spun around, and dashed over to hug the grizzled smith god. Part of her quest to become a goddess had involved mastery of the test of Hephaestus, and she had spent several weeks at his manor, deep within the bowels of the largest active volcano in the world, learning the basics of his trade. In doing so, she'd developed a strong back, strong arms, and an even stronger bond not only with the god but also with his chief journeyman Angus and the journeyman's family as well.

"Aye, lass, it's good to see you too," Hephaestus said, wobbling slightly.

"Had a bit of a nip?" Matt asked, a grin on his face.

"Not had. Hav-ving. More like it. Mike, how about another?" Hephaestus roared.

Properly served, they all went back over to the table where Hephaestus had been sitting alone. Crystal noticed on the way that the mood-indicating artwork above the smith's table was still black.

"So how's it going?" she asked the smith tentatively.

"Ah, fine, fine," he said. "Gettin' finer every sip. Matthew, how's preparations for the big battle comin' along?"

The smith to the gods had no Scottish blood in him at all as far as Crystal knew, but he'd chosen the population of his grove from there this cycle due to their intense work ethic. It was hard not to adopt a little of the charming brogue while you were surrounded by it, of course, but Crystal hadn't ever heard him slip in and out of the brogue randomly; she took it as a sign of the number of nips he'd already had.

"There won't be a battle," Matt said quietly, steel in his voice.

"Oh? You find the king?"

"No," Matt said. "Not yet. But we are getting closer."

"Closer won't hold off the hordes."

"Yeah, true enough," Matt said. "Still, we'll make it. Always have. Speaking of the hordes, by the way, you wouldn't know where Monkey can be found, would you?"

"Me? No. I stay deep down in my hole, beatin' on iron all day. I don't get involved in these things, lad, and I sure don't know where anybody can be found these days," Hephaestus said. His expression turned even darker.

"How's Angus and Donna?" Crystal asked, hoping to switch topics and lighten the conversation.

It worked. Hephaestus smiled as he said, "Oh, they're doin' great, lass. Donna is expectin' and everybody's real excited about it."

"Even little Robert?" Crystal asked. Robert was the precocious son—an only child up to now—of the journeyman smith and his wife. Crystal wondered what his reaction would be.

"Aye, he's the most excited of all. He keeps runnin' around camp braggin' about how he's 'gonna have a baby brudder.'"

"So it's a boy?"

"Too soon to say, and besides, I dinna believe in usin' magic to check those things an' neither do they. Robert is either goin'ta get his wish of a baby brudder, or he's goin'ta get a beautiful surprise of a darlin' little baby sister. Either way, he wins, aye?"

"Aye," Crystal agreed. "I need to come by sometime to say hi and remember how it is to swing a splitting maul." Truth be told, once she'd gotten over the muscle aches she had come to enjoy the soothing repetitiveness of the chore of splitting cord after cord of wood that the forge needed to be turned into charcoal to continue its operation.

"Aye, that ye do," the smith agreed, his face darkening again. "Only, ye'll have to wait. We haven't fired the forge in a week."

"Oh, that's too bad," Crystal said. "Why not? Surely you haven't run out of projects?"

"Heck no, lass, we've got enough projects on the log to keep us goin' for eons. But we can't work, because the volcano's been eruptin' for a week solid. Thrakkoni can't fly up it to get ore or wood, and it's too much to teleport enough ore in."

"A week?" Matt interjected. "That volcano's never actively erupted for that long before. I don't think any of them have, for that matter."

"She's never had a damned titan playin' around in her belly before, neither. I've been thinkin' about askin' him nicely to quit, but you know how they are. He's just as likely ta smash right through my wards and flood my chambers with lava as anythin'."

Matt and Crystal's eyes met, four eyebrows raising.

"A titan?" Matt asked. "How do you know?"

"How could I not? I wanna see you put somethin' that powerful 'neath your home and see if ye dinna know it."

"Which one?" Crystal asked.

"Which what?"

"Which titan?"

"Which titan? Why, the big one, of course," Hephaestus said. "Hell, I dinna know their names, lass. I think I'll call him Steve."

"Better to call him Prometheus," Matt said drily.

"That's Prometheus?" Hephaestus said, a thoughtful look crossing his face in spite of the drink. "He's a big one, Matthew."

"Yes, he is," Matt said, the expression on his face vacant as his mind raced ahead. "He's the biggest, in fact. Say, do you mind if Crystal and I visit your place to chat with him?"

"So long as you can get him to quit floodin' my volcano with lava, I don't care if you tap dance in my dinin' hall wearin' damn magical slippers an' tassels."

The Search Heats Up

"What's wrong with tap dancing in the dining hall?" Crystal asked once they were back at the estate. After the revelation of Prometheus's location, the pair had said quick farewells to the smith god and vanished nearly immediately, neither able to contain his or her excitement very well.

"I have no idea. Hephaestus has his own expressions," Matt said.

The pair teleported to the forge inside the volcano.

"Wow, it's hot," Crystal said.

"Uh, yeah. We're inside of an erupting volcano. Of course it's hot. Hephaestus's wards can only handle so much," Matt said, leaning down to touch the earth. His hand passed right through the illusory grass and settled on the rock floor of the cave in which Hephaestus had constructed his forge. His face went blank for a moment as he projected energy through the granite below.

"Sense anything?"

"I do. He's here, alright," Matt said, a worried look on his face.

"So Hades was lying."

"No."

Crystal waited several moments, hoping Matt would explain. Finally she challenged him. "Why no? He said Prometheus was still in his place. Prometheus wasn't. That's a lie, right?"

"Hades doesn't lie."

"But he did."

"No. Listen to me. Hades does not lie. Hades cannot lie."

"He said something that was a lie, then. What's the difference?"

"No. He didn't. He couldn't. Clearly, he told you something that was not correct. So did Mother, if I remember what you said. Both of them have been known to speak in riddles before, and both have given their listener one idea when a more careful listener would adopt a different one. But neither has ever, to my knowledge, uttered an untruth with intent to mislead. To do so would be foreign to their natures as elder deities."

"Well, one way or another, we were misled."

"Yes, that statement is correct, and to be honest, it kind of worries me. I think that you need to be extremely cautious when you go down there to talk to Prometheus," Matt said.

"Me?" Crystal squeaked.

"Yes, you. Why do you ask?"

"Oh, um, well," Crystal's tongue fought briefly against her reeling brain, "to be honest, it never occurred to me that I might need to dip into lava to accomplish this. Isn't there any other way?"

"No, love. As much as I'd rather it be me going into the lava, it has to be you. Remember that Prometheus despises me for putting him in prison in the first place. I can pretty well guarantee that a conversation between him and me would be extremely short and, in addition, would add nothing beneficial to our situation."

"But he's in a big pool of lava," Crystal said. "Couldn't I get him to come up to the surface?"

"Highly unlikely. And that would be a bad idea, anyway."

"Why? And—why is he down there playing in the lava in the first place?"

"He's an elemental, dear. All the titans are. Water titans play in water. Fire titans play in fire. It's where they're most comfortable. And there's very few fires available that are as hot as molten lava at a volcano's core. Besides, the last time Prometheus was loose on the surface was when the Father decided that we needed to capture him and all his brethren in the first place."

"I thought it was because he brought fire to the mortals. That's what the stories say," Crystal said.

"Well, that's kinda, sorta true. He did bring fire to the mortals," Matt said, nodding. "In fact, he brought a lot of fire, in a very large way. If we hadn't intervened he would've set the entire surface of the planet ablaze. Granted, it also had the effect that was central to that story, because some of the mortals took one look at the fire and said 'hey, we can use that' and then they went off to invent hot dogs and marshmallows and those fancy roasting forks. But I could've shown them how to light a bonfire; that wasn't a big deal. Extermination of all organic life on the surface of the planet—that was a big deal. The big deal, in fact."

"Oh. I see. And you want me to talk to that creature, the one that nearly extinguished all organic life on the surface of the planet in his gleeful playing." Crystal said.

"Yep," Matt said, nodding. "More accurately, I need you to talk to that creature. If it helps, think of it this way: the future of the entire universe is hanging on whether or not you manage to talk to that creature. And, if it matters, creature is a bit far off from the truth; he really is quite intelligent. It's a little different kind of intelligence from that displayed by you and I, but he's an old, old titan. Don't approach him as a creature, but rather as an ancient god. An ancient god who's a little slow of speech, but—well, you'll get it when you chat with him."

"Okay, ancient, intelligent, slow of speech, I get it. That's all fine, but we still haven't addressed how I'm supposed to get close to an ancient god who's swimming around in a massive underground pool of fricking lava."

"Dear, you're not really going to make me remind you once again that you are, in fact, a goddess, are you?"

"No, Matthew" Crystal spat. She had actually been about to do that very thing, but she wasn't going to admit it now. "No, I'm quite aware that I'm a fricking goddess. I'm perfectly cognizant of my amazingly fricking awesome powers of pow-pow. After all of the hell I've gotten, I'd never, ever ask you to remind me of my supreme fricking goddessness, never, ever again. No, Matt. What I'm really going to do is ask you what spell you recommend that I use to protect my goddess-pure complexion from sixteen-fricking-hundred-fricking-degree fricking lava."

"Actually, dear, the lava in the middle where Prometheus is swimming around is closer to two thousand fricking degrees. Fahrenheit, of course," Matt said drily.

Crystal's irritation with her husband grew to where she could only growl at him. As she stood in the middle of Hephaestus's glade, a growl gurgling through her teeth, Matt defensively raised his hands in peace. "Okay, okay," he said, actually looking cowed for the first time that she could recall. "Just, um, kidding? Seriously, love of my life, partner in my eternity, mother of my children, here's what you need to do," and he showed her how to combine flows of water and earth with a little bit of air, weaving them just so to form a shield bubble around her. When she was done attempting it for herself, he stepped back and walked around, examining the protective sphere on all sides. At first, he shook his head and showed her how to weave a little more water into the flows to protect from the intense heat. She made the changes, and after a few iterations he finally nodded.

"Nice work, as usual," he said. "Keep it a little bit fluid, though. If Prometheus decides to play with you and push some heat your way, you need to be able to shift the cooling quickly to meet it. Don't expect any push to come from the front, by the way. He's been messing with gods for millennia, even just counting the time before his imprisonment."

"So what should I ask him?"

"Oh, I don't know," Matt said. "Maybe you could just say, "Hey, I heard you were in Atlantis. Did you happen to see, or maybe take, the king while you were there?"

Crystal glared at Matt, and he shrugged. "What?" he asked defensively. "You've lost all your sense of humor in your fear of the lava, dear. So seriously now, there's really no point in dissembling with a titan. He's as ancient as I am, and he's been imprisoned long enough that he's probably not nearly as patient as me. Just say what you want to say. He can't really hurt you, can he?"

"He can't hurt me, I think, but can't the lava?"

"Well, um, that part hasn't actually been tried."

"Oh, great. And he's not nearly as patient as you?" Crystal asked, her voice sardonic. "Oh—well, hell. Well, here goes. Wish me luck, oh patient one." She walked around Matt, a smug expression on her face, and stepped confidently through Hephaestus's wards and into the stream of molten lava.

Crystal felt the resistance of the lava flow as she stepped into it, a turgid flow of liquid stone not wanting to allow the entry of her sphere of protection. She also felt the heat intensely, despite the protective bubble. As she took breath into her lungs the heated air singed the hair in her nose and seemed to set her sinuses afire. It felt like she'd walked in to an oven on Thanksgiving morning, and she was the turkey.

The heat wasn't a big deal, she reminded herself. She'd conquered it with her protective spells. It was uncomfortable, of course, but no matter how hot it became the temperature couldn't become too high for a goddess. She certainly wouldn't melt, and she'd never stoop to complaining. Not in front of or anywhere close to Matt, anyway.

Her focus on the heat was broken when her protective bubble bounced against a small rock outcropping on the side of the chute. It jarred Crystal, bumping her off balance momentarily, and she caught herself and turned to watch as the offending granite hump moved down and then away from her.

Wait—the rock moved down, she thought. Either the mountain was falling downward, an unlikely proposition at best, or her bubble was being swept by the current rapidly upward toward the sky and away from Prometheus. It made sense; she'd watched footage of volcanic eruptions showing tons of lava, rock, and ash catapulted miles into the sky and never really thought about how fast the material had to be moving upward in the volcano's throat to accomplish that.

She'd also never thought about how to swim against a dense current that was as forceful, viscous, and rapid as this one was. She'd never had need to.

But she had need to now. If not, soon enough she and her protective bubble would be cast up and out of the volcano in the opposite direction from where she needed to go. She was certain she could survive the trip, but she and Matt—and the rest of the world—didn't have time for her to figure it all out while flying through the air.

Setting her mind to the task, Crystal found it simpler than she'd feared it would be. She reformed her bubble on the fly into the shape of an angelfish with longer and more flexible side fins. By causing the tale to wiggle and the fins to move like oars, she was able to move through the current. What she didn't know was whether she was moving downward faster than the current was moving upward. Was she getting closer to Prometheus or farther away?

Suddenly she realized that her brain was urgently signaling that she'd run out of oxygen in the bubble. The exertion of getting the fins to flap had caused her to breathe deeply, and she hadn't made any contingencies for how to get more oxygen into the bubble once she was inside of the lava flow. Crystal tried slowing her breathing back down, but there was now nothing useful for her to take into her lungs. The massive muscles around her lungs spasmed, and she saw spots before her eyes.

Unable to catch a breath, Crystal did the only thing she could think of—she panicked.

Matt, help! She called out to her husband, inserting as much panic into the telepathic thread as she could manage. With a soft pop he teleported in beside her, and then with another pop he teleported both of them back to where she'd stood recently just beside the forge of Hephaestus.

"There, there, love," Matt consoled Crystal softly and rubbed her back as she sank to hands and knees and gulped at the air that now was so freely available around them.

Finally she found herself able to stand up. The spots were gone from her vision, and though she felt a little weak still, she also felt her magic healing spell taking over.

"Wow," Crystal said. "Thank you, love, for saving my life."

"Wow is right," Matt said. "And you're certainly welcome. I'll do that anytime. So what happened?"

"I ran out of air is what happened," Crystal said. "There's got to be a way to rejuvenate the oxygen inside the bubble."

"You—ran out of—air?" Matt asked, his voice tinged with something Crystal couldn't quite identify. Was it surprise?

"Well, yes, Matt," she said. "Or technically for the physics majors, I guess, I ran out of oxygen. My bubble only had a certain amount of oxygen in it, and once that was used up there was nothing but carbon dioxide for me to breathe. It's actually a problem with that biology that you said you always found so boring."

"Oh, right, I forgot all about that," Matt said, his expression clear that he hadn't really forgotten anything. "So, you're suggesting that a goddess can live through tremendous trauma and go without food interminably, but...."

"Oh, shut up, you," Crystal said, crossing her arms in frustration. She'd realized where he was going with the statement before he'd even really started making it, and she was disgusted with herself for not thinking of it on her own. Reaching inward, she plucked the purple healing energy oscillation a little differently, causing a new vibration that would allow her brain to continue functioning entirely without oxygen.

Matt watched closely. "That's right," he said. "Sorry, I thought you would have already figured that out. But you probably ought to turn off the brain's automatic breathing signal too. And turn it back on later, of course. If your lungs continue to pump air you'll use up the oxygen in the bubble anyway, which will still cause your body to pretend like it needs oxygen and go into shock. The involuntary reflexes are pretty powerful. Later, if you don't turn it back on, you just won't feel right. Nor will you look quite right to anybody. Have you ever noticed that in every movie adaptation showing a god, the god still breathes? That's not just because there's a human playing the part. It's because somebody who isn't breathing looks weird to humans. And, frankly, it looks weird to us too."

Crystal nodded and did what Matt suggested.

"Dear," Crystal asked, "where do you learn these things? Is there a goddess finishing academy I've somehow missed attending?"

Matt chuckled and said, "That's why you've been called to Gaia once this is all done, dear. But no, most of us learned these things over time. Time, as in hundreds or thousands of years. Honestly, you're still a baby as goddesses go. In a thousand years or so you'll be an expert. I know the peerage is tough on you now, because that's what is expected, but you shouldn't be too hard on yourself till then."

"Gotcha," Crystal said sardonically. "So I need to mark my calendar to check my expertise a thousand years from now."

"Mm hmm. Maybe a thousand and one or a thousand and two, just to be safe."

"Because a goddess should always be safe, right?" Crystal asked, a sarcastic twist to her voice.

"Now you're getting it, love," Matt said, a bright smile on his face.

"Heh," Crystal said, looking back toward the lava flow. "Well, I suppose there's no time like the present to go once more unto the breach."

"Boy, if Prometheus were allergic to clichés, you'd slay him dead," Matt said.

"He's not?" Crystal asked, feigning ignorance.

"Not unless he's gained some weird allergies since his imprisonment. But maybe the demons read Shakespeare plays to him every day for the past few hundred million years? That would build up quite the allergy, I'd bet."

"Shakespeare hadn't started to write back then."

"Well, there's that problem," Matt said. "But even a hundred years of Shakespeare would be too long."

"Hey, I love Shakespeare's writings," Crystal objected.

"Not for a hundred uninterrupted years, you won't."

Yielding Matt the point, Crystal walked slowly back toward the lava flow, going over the problems she'd experienced during the first attempt in her mind. Inability to breathe was taken care of; oddly, it felt really strange for her body to not be breathing. She knew it shouldn't really feel any different, of course, but she'd been either taking a breath in or pushing one out nearly every moment of her life, waking or otherwise. The lack of activity in her chest was just—strange.

The challenge of swimming against the current she'd pretty well conquered the last time. This time, instead of shaping the bubble like an angelfish, she broadened the rear fin to provide greater propulsion.

Location, though, was an interesting question. How would she know whether she was making headway against the current or being slowly swept along in spite of her efforts with the swimming bubble? How would she know which direction to go to get to Prometheus?

"Matt?" Crystal said.

"Yes?" Matt's voice came from behind.

"Never mind," Crystal said. Instantly she decided that she was going to figure this one out on her own. She knew Prometheus was a fire-based elemental, so she reached tentatively downward with the same mix of air, emotional energy, and healing energy that she'd seen Matt use, pressing it through the rock gently.

Suddenly she felt a presence, one that clearly felt her. She gasped and jumped back to avoid the magical backlash she felt coming.

The quiet chortling sound behind her irritated her to no end, causing her to spin around, glaring. Matt held up his hands and said, "No, no. That was a good effort, actually, my love. A very good effort. It's just that sometimes it really is okay to ask questions first. I wish I knew when to tell you that was, but I don't. You remember your time in the classroom, not knowing for certain what your students didn't know?"

"My students were third-graders, Matt. Unlike your college kids, they had no problem asking questions."

"Oh. Right. Anyway, in this case the purple energy in the probe that you saw me press downward was actually a part of my own harmonic oscillation, the addition of which allowed me to sort of perch my own awareness at the far tip of the probe. That let me sense where Prometheus was before I actually came into contact with him. The not coming into contact is important, since he's an awfully powerful and magically-sensitive titan, as I'm sure you realized."

"Oh," Crystal said, seeing her error. "I did realize that, as a matter of fact. Okay, so let me try again. When I bumped into him, he felt like he was turning his powers about to send something back at me."

"Huh," Matt said, a worried look finding its way onto his face. "Well, that's bad. It means he's likely in a combative mood. The only thing he could send back at you is fire energy, but his resources are so immense in that one primal that he would likely crush and destroy Hephaestus's little retreat here."

Crystal thought of Angus and the rest of the smiths and their families in the clearing. All of those—her friends—would perish if what Matt described happened. "That would be horrible, Matt. To be safe, should we evacuate all the people back there?"

"No time, love."

"They're just humans, anyway, right?" Crystal started feeling defensive for her friends' sake.

"Well, yes, but that's not why I say no to evacuation. They're my friend Hephaestus's humans, for one thing, and many of them are highly trained—irreplaceably so—craftsmen. They're also friends of yours. But it would take hours to convince them to leave and get everything they wanted to take up to the surface. Despite my bluster back at the bar, we really are running up very close on the time limit. We don't have time to be as careful as we should, so you'll just need to proceed with extreme caution on your end."

"Okay. So don't piss him off? That's your suggestion?" Crystal asked.

"Nah, not really. You can't help it. He's been imprisoned for hundreds of millions of years, love," Matt said. "I doubt there's anything you could do to piss him off any further."

"So why am I even bothering?"

"Because we need to find out where the king is. Prometheus may not know the king's final location, but he was the guy who took him away. We know that much, at least. If you can somehow talk him into telling you who he turned the king over to, we're a major step ahead."

"So I don't need to talk him into going back to Hell?" Crystal asked.

"Tartarus, technically, and absolutely not. That issue is for Hades to deal with once he realizes that one of his wards is out without his permission. And Hades, more so than any other deity in the universe, has the resources to deal with it. Assuming, of course, that Prometheus doesn't have Hades's permission. I really hope, anyway, that Hades didn't grant Prometheus exit; that potentiality just opens up wayyyy too many issues for me to deal with right now."

"Why?"

Matt sighed and said, "Because Hades is a member of the triumvirate that I and all my brethren look up to. Mother is one, Hades is the second, and the Creator is the third. More significantly Hades's disposition has always been one of absolute fairness, his role of ultimate judge based on his reputation of perfect justice and complete honesty. Hades just doesn't play favorites. Nor would he just let a titan—or anyone else, for that matter—out of Tartarus without something of equal weight going in to balance. And he certainly wouldn't lie about it. It just wouldn't—couldn't—happen. It's unimaginable. The capriciousness required to let Prometheus out of Tartarus would, in most of our eyes, drop Hades down to the level of me and my peers, out of the elder triad."

"You keep referring to Hades in absolutes, Matt. Gaia isn't an absolute. Why should Hades be, if they're peers?"

"You can't compare Gaia and Hades, love. I mean, they're two—three, including Zeus—very different entities, with three very different purposes of existence. Zeus is the creative force, and as such will always behave as the creative energy, flitting from one creation to another and leaving the maintenance of those creations to his lesser gods. Gaia is the earth mother, and will in turn always behave as a mother in all things. She can't flit anywhere else, because she is this place. Meanwhile, Hades is the judge, for this realm and for untold others, and to perform that role he must be fair in all his decisions. He would never, ever, just let someone out of Tartarus. He's let someone out before as part of a trade, but only because it was an equal trade. Well, that, and he's let someone out of his domain for periods of time because of the trickery of other deities, but only because he'd given his word and then only with others having high prices to pay later."

"Like Persephone?" Crystal asked.

"No, that was a myth," Matt said.

"Oh," Crystal said, a little disappointed.

"Hey, it sounded good. Cool love story, right?"

"Yeah, but after having a mythological god turn out to be both real and married to me, it's kind of disappointing to find out that a beautiful love story was just a myth."

"Yeah, well, love stories are Stacy's business. You should take your complaint to her," Matt said.

"Not likely. Hey, wasn't—isn't—Apollo the god of literature? He'd represent the better choice of complaint department for love stories."

"Hermes, actually, but only high literature. Love stories have never been high literature, dear, and there didn't exist any romance novels back then."

"Love stories have never been high literature," Crystal said in a mocking tone. "Spoken like the god of war."

"Heh. True. By the way, the volcano isn't getting any cooler."

"I know. Now I'm just wasting time because I'm nervous," Crystal admitted to her husband.

"I know. And what a nervous wuss you are, too. I mean, all you have to do is step into the two thousand degree molten lava flow, navigate yourself to an extremely powerful and ancient elemental being, and talk him into revealing his secrets without angering him enough to blast all your friends out of existence. What could you possibly be worried about?"

"Matt, if something does happen down there to my shield, would…."

"The lava eat you?" Matt finished her question. "I don't know. It's never been tried. Your healing spells are strong enough to handle nearly any trauma, but a dip in lava is something else entirely. You'll want to keep a teleportation spell at the tip of your tongue. And while you're doing that—just don't let anything happen, okay?"

"I'll try not to," Crystal said drily and turned back toward the flow. To keep from giving any more ground to her fears, Crystal wrapped herself quickly in her bubble and stepped into the flow.

It was as much of a shock as it had been the previous attempt, but Crystal knew what to expect this time. She shaped her shield as she'd planned and reached downward with her energies, carefully scrying for Prometheus's location. As soon as she sensed him, she pressed the energy flows in the fins into a rhythmic undulation that propelled her surprisingly rapidly through the molten rock. As she went, she pushed her senses out to the sides also, finding to her delighted relief that she could actually get an idea of the shape and features of the channel in which she swam. It wasn't quite the same as seeing, but it was close.

The volcano's throat widened abruptly as she came to a vast chamber. Idly Crystal wondered if scientists pre-cataclysm had ever discovered the forces that powered a volcano. The pressure and heat in the lava-filled chasm were immense. It was no wonder; tremendous forces must be needed to push molten rock all the way to the surface. Still, Crystal reveled for a moment in the pleasure of knowing that she was very likely the first person to ever experience the heart of a volcano. Goddess, she corrected herself with a smile. Then again, from what Matt had said, it was likely she was the first goddess to experience the heart of a volcano, too.

A very large presence swam beside her, the disturbances in the viscous lava jostling her shield and knocking her slightly off-balance, reminding her forcefully of the mission.

Prometheus? She sent her mental voice out tentatively, trying to sound a little bit submissive. She realized, belatedly, that she hadn't asked Matt which attitude might work best, and a split second later it occurred to her that he probably wouldn't have known what would work any better than she.

LITTLE ONE, Prometheus's voice rang in her head. Okay, he hadn't smashed her immediately; that was a good thing. In fact, he sounded kind of playful, and sort of curious as well. The tone continued as the massive mental presence of the titan said, *YOU SHOULD NOT BE HERE. YOUR MAGICAL SHIELD IS INSUFFICIENT TO HOLD BACK THE ELEMENTAL FORCES FOR LONG, AND YOUR FLESH WILL MELT IN THIS FIRE NO MATTER HOW MUCH HEALING YOU ATTEMPT.*

I will not bother you for long, mighty Prometheus, she answered. If the titan could smash her like a bug, and most likely knew it, then it couldn't hurt to suck up a little, and besides, he'd started the conversation being nice. Pulling from Matt's vast repertoire of analogies, she might as well—what was that phrase, swing for the end zone? Whatever that meant.

Mighty Prometheus, I come begging your help in averting a battle that may destroy the planet. You are the only one with the answer I seek. Will you grant me your....

FOR ONE IN A PRECARIOUS LITTLE BUBBLE, ONE WHO PROMISES NOT TO BOTHER MIGHTY PROMETHEUS FOR LONG, WHY DO YOU MAKE SUCH EFFORT TO AVOID COMING TO THE POINT, LITTLE ONE?

I need to know where the king of Atlantis is being kept, oh mighty titan.

NO.

But....

NO. I WILL NOT RETURN TO THAT PRISON.

No one is asking you to return to the prison, Prometheus. It's....

HADES WILL REQUIRE IT.

But I won't tell him where you are. You have my word.

YOU FOUND ME. HE WILL FIND ME EASILY, LITTLE ONE.

But the gods will fight. Millions will die. The world....

THE WORLD WILL CONTINUE, LITTLE ONE. THE MOTHER WILL MAKE IT SO. THE PUNY ONES YOU CALL GODS, ONCE THEY'RE DONE WITH THEIR PETTY SQUAB-BLES, WILL CREATE MORE MILLIONS TO LIVE ON THE WORLD. BUT YOU HAVE SPENT TOO LONG DOWN HERE ALREADY. YOUR LITTLE BUBBLE IS BREAKING UP.

Crystal felt a push, just a slight nudge, from the titan's di-rection, and his prediction came true. With an audible pop the powerful energies she'd held wrapped tightly around her gave way to the immense pressure. Molten rock rushed toward Crys-tal's skin.

Luckily Crystal had caught the warning in Prometheus's comment. Seizing hold of enough ka for the fastest teleport spell she'd ever cast, she flung herself back into the forge. Collapsing onto her hands and knees from the effort, she felt Matt at her side immediately, his powers wrapping flows of air, water, and healing energies around her to cool the skin she was slowly coming to realize was on fire. She gulped in a huge breath of cool air to replace the searing hot gases that had gathered in her lungs despite her lack of breathing. Finally the burning sensations covering all of her body subsided and she stood up, shaking the bright spots of flame from her vision and turning to Matt. The pair wrapped each other inside tight embraces for several long minutes.

"You did good, love," Matt whispered into Crystal's ear.

"Don't sound so surprised," Crystal said, teasing. She wasn't sure whether she wanted to dance in the joy of surviving the experience or just stand still inside the safety of her husband's embrace.

"Do I?" Matt responded seriously. "I'd have never let you go down there if I weren't certain of your ability to get out. You know that, don't you?"

"Oh, of course I know that, Matt. I was teasing you. Sometimes I'm just not sure of my own abilities."

"Love, you're the smartest woman I know, save one named Gaia, of course."

"What's a gal gotta do to not be compared with a guy's momma?" Crystal joked.

"Marry a guy whose momma isn't the earth goddess?"

"Yeah, but I'm stuck with you," she teased.

"Mm hmm. For all eternity, right?"

"Yes, indeed. Literally, even," Crystal said, nodding. Years before she and Matt had used the phrase "for all eternity" to signal the strength of their love to each other. She had never, in her wildest dreams, meant it entirely literally, yet she was overjoyed to do so now.

"Love, I don't mind your nakedness at all, but the smiths have come and gone a couple of times since we've been standing here. Would you mind conjuring up something to shield your rapturous beauty from those who don't deserve it?"

Crystal looked down, confused. She'd had clothes on. Looking back up into Matt's eyes, she followed his gaze to the lava. Oh, right....

"The lava was pretty hot, I guess," she admitted as she conjured a white Greek-style toga for herself.

"Pretty hot?"

Crystal shrugged and danced away across the field, singing "Doesn't matter. I survived it, and now I know where the king is, I know where the king is."

"Oh? Do tell, love," Matt said. His arms were crossed and his voice stern, but on his visage Crystal saw the radiant smile that hadn't visited her husband's face for several days.

Time Runs Out

The sun set peacefully to end the third full day after the Jade Emperor's pronouncement. The halls of Matt's estate were filled with tension as battle mages prepared for the inevitable fight, but Matt made rounds to urge them to get a good night's sleep. "Only the darkest of the eastern gods," he assured the most nervous, "do battle at night. This attack will be led by the Jade Emperor himself, so it will definitely occur during the light of day."

"Tomorrow, sunrise, that's when to look to the east for the onslaught," Matt said several times, a twinkle in his eye and battle lust spread across his face. "They won't attack by surprise. We'll meet them out front. Get a good night's sleep, folks."

"But Matt," Krista objected to his speech to the head table over dinner, "what can we do to prepare for tomorrow? There's got to be something we can do to shield you, or us, or something. The Jade Emperor said they would kill you."

Matt shrugged and said, "If it comes to that, frankly, there's nothing you all can do to stand up to the power of the Jade Emperor."

"What do you mean if it comes to that? You haven't done anything all evening long but lounge around the estate. How can it come to anything different?"

"I have a plan," he said and returned to popping fried okra nuggets into his mouth.

"But Matt," RJ said, moving in to back up his wife, "we're all really nervous here. The coming battle could devastate us, our way of lives, everything. Yet you're so calm. Your life has been threatened, yet you don't seem to care much. Don't you real-ize...."

"Don't you realize who you're speaking to?" Matt interrupted, his face growing stern. "I was organizing military campaigns long before your great-grandfather's great-grandfather's most distant ancestor in recorded history became an organic combination of a sperm and an egg cell. I said I have a plan."

"Whom, dear," Crystal said.

"Whom what?" Matt said, swiveling his head toward his wife, sternness melting into confusion.

"It's whom you're speaking to, not who. If you're going to snap your best supporters' heads off, you should at least use proper grammar while you do so," Crystal said with a smirk and a wink.

"Hmmph," Matt grunted, and then he rose and stalked out of the dining room.

"A little touchy tonight, isn't he?" Phoenix asked.

"Wouldn't you be?" Crystal said.

"Yeah, I guess I would."

"Crystal, does he really have a plan for tomorrow, or is he just making us all feel better?" Krista asked.

"I think we'll be okay," Crystal said. "RJ, he worked for you for several years. Did you ever hear him say that things would work out when they didn't?"

"No," RJ admitted. "But there's a big difference between an accreditation visit and a universal war of the gods. Armageddon, I think it's going to be called."

"Ragnarok," Birch agreed. "I'm surprised Thor isn't here partying the night-before away with Tyr."

"Thor is indisposed tonight, or he likely would be here," Crystal said. "But I'm sure he'll be here partying the night-after away with all of us. If, that is, we can get him away from his own hall. The Valkyrie are pretty darn good partiers in their own right. Regardless, if Armageddon or Ragnarok, either one, is truly what is coming tomorrow, then Matt is correct that we'll all face it much better if we're well-rested. It's time for this lady to hit the hay, and I'd recommend the same for all of you as well."

"Mom?" Crystal heard as she entered the master suite's antechamber. Heidi and Linda sat on the couch with Steve and Corey. "Is everything going to be all right?" Linda finished her question.

Crystal's mind flashed briefly over her own feelings. Was she confident in the outcome of tomorrow? She was pretty certain. She knew Matt's plan, had even helped him come up with it, and didn't see much that could possibly go wrong, unless, of course, something went wrong. That was the problem with plans, though. Still, she was pretty certain at least that she was confident. If she wasn't, faking it would be obvious to the girls, who would just be more scared as a result. She had to be honest with them, which meant she had to be honest with herself first.

"Yes," Crystal said after she'd taken a moment to think while seating herself in her arm chair. "I think everything is going to be all right. Your father has a plan, and what I know of it is extremely sound."

"What if something goes wrong?"

"Nothing…," Crystal started, and then thought better of not speaking the whole truth to the kids. "Your father and I have been over the plan several times, and we think we have all the major contingencies covered. Trust me, it's a good plan, and everything will work out fine tomorrow as a result."

"Is there going to be a battle?" Steve asked.

"I don't know. Possibly. Knowing your father, he's probably looking forward to at least a skirmish. He is the god of war, after all," Crystal said.

"And gods can't be killed, can they?" Linda asked.

"Not without dipping them into the lava of Mount Doom," Crystal joked. She'd been gone all day, so she hadn't had a chance to tell the girls yet about her meeting with Prometheus and the associated near-death experience in the lava of Mount Etna. Now wasn't the time.

"Would that really work?" Corey asked. Crystal grimaced; she hadn't intended for her quip to raise a question that was both too real and too close to her own comfort level.

"I—we—well, it's never been attempted, Corey. I'm certainly not volunteering for that experiment," Crystal said, laughing it off. The kids joined in with her laughter.

Kids? The boys would have been voting next year if there were still the opportunity, and the girls were already old enough to drive if there had still been functional cars around.

"You four probably ought to stay inside tomorrow morning, though," Crystal said. "No, really. If there is a skirmish, there's no telling what strong magical forces will be tossed around. You remember how to get to the cupola on top of the building, girls? You can watch it from there."

"Yes, mom, we remember," Heidi said and glanced briefly over at Steve, whose blush was unmistakable.

Crystal caught the lapses. Well, well…. "I take it you four have done some exploring around the estate?" Crystal asked, not sure whether she'd rather kill the boys right there on her couches or break out in laughter. She could remember being their age and exploring, and part of her wanted none of that nonsense for her own daughters. Another part, though, was happy they'd found something to enjoy. And it was kind of natural, after all….

When all four tentatively nodded—she wished the boys could have read her mind when she'd envisioned their burned hulks resting on the sofas—she smiled wickedly and said, "Well, then, you won't have any trouble finding the cupola again to watch the battle from. It's heavily warded and will protect you from harm, but you should also be able to see everything that happens. And I'm sure that you won't mind a thrakkon or two watching over your safety, either. Right?" She glowered at them, playing the game that she figured had been forever played between mothers and daughters.

"Right, mom," Linda said timidly.

"And because tomorrow's such a big day, and will probably start very early, it's about time for everybody to be getting to bed. Right?"

"Right, Ms. V.," Steve said as the pair of boys caught the mother's tone correctly and shot up off of the couch.

"Right, mom," Linda said, a little less immediately and with a touch of disappointment in her voice. The girls rose and slowly walked the boys to the door, stepping out into the hall and closing the door behind them. It was—cute, Crystal thought. A very little bit dangerous, true, but cute nonetheless. She'd stolen her fair share of kisses outside of entry doors at that age, and it was rightful that the girls have the same opportunity.

Sighing, Crystal thought about how important it was that Matt's plan worked, not only for their own sakes but for that of the kids she'd just shooed to their beds. Putting her concerns away behind a façade of conviction, she rose and entered her own bedroom where her partner, husband, best friend, and lover awaited.

A Kidnapper Exposed

Dawn broke the next morning with the sun sending its first tentative rays over the roof of the mansion and across the field before it. At the bottom of the steps leading up and into the estate stood a lone figure still shrouded in the night's darkness. Other figures slowly gathered on the steps above, each hidden in the shadows of the looming building.

As the rising light slowly unwrapped the gloom from the lone figure it revealed the armored and armed god of war, a long ebony pike set in one hand and a golden buckler bearing a crimson serpent in the other. Matt's torso, legs, and arms were covered in what appeared to be bright red leather armor, protection both ceremonial and practical that when Crystal had helped him don it that morning had felt different from any leather she'd ever touched—enormously pliable, but stronger. Much, much stronger than leather could be, in fact, a quality that Matt had insisted that she demonstrate using her own war hammer (to quiet her doubts, she was certain). On each shoulder rested what could only be a black dragon's scale bearing the shining golden chevrons of a battle commander. From his left hip hung the broadsword that Crystal had assumed was merely ceremonial on their first trip to Olympus, though now her more-attuned senses could feel the elemental fury that pulsed from its black blade and red gemstones. Having been through the crucible of solo combat against the barbarian god, herself, she was now fairly certain that the powerful weapon at Matt's side would be an even match for Thor's war hammer, Mjolnir.

As the receding gloom slowly resolved the scene in front of the mansion, a *whoof* sound echoed across the clearing. The source of the loud disturbance became clear as Matt's shoulders sprouted huge black feathered wings that unfurled majestically, extended to their greatest length, and flapped loudly twice, and then settled down through the disturbed morning air to the ground beside him. Crystal smiled despite the tension; she could only imagine the intimidation Matt's wings would effect upon the average warrior who might be intent upon charging against the god of war.

The waxing light also revealed two goddesses standing just behind Matt, each of them two steps above and farther from the battle. On his right hand was Crystal, the goddess of lava survival, resplendent in a blue gown with glimmering golden filigree, a Vulcan-crafted war hammer hanging from a cord looped simply around her waist. To his left stood Stacy, the goddess of love, apparently unarmed and wearing a green gown that very closely matched Crystal's in cut and ornamentation. Crystal glanced over at the other goddess, allowing her thoughts to wander briefly on her amazement at how their relationship had come full circle. The other woman had tried to kill her. Several times, in fact. But the trials of the past few days had revealed a side, and a strange bit of logic as well, to Stacy/Venus/Aphrodite that had completely changed the way Crystal felt about her, to the point that Crystal had unconditionally welcomed the other goddess's help in preparing her husband and herself for the coming battle.

Behind the goddesses, stretched all along the massive stone porch, fidgeted Matt's battle mages. Some, including Birch and Phoenix, had mantled themselves in the robes that they associated with the powerful sorcery that all imagined might be called for during the day's events. Phoenix, undoubtedly the most resplendent in her silver-embroidered priestess gown of sable velvet, stood in the center, while others, including some adorned in everyday clothes, were on either side. All stood as though they'd never been to battle before, shifting weight from side to side or quietly clearing their throats.

On the ground to each side of the mansion were most of the thrakkoni who served Matt, standing ready in humanoid form but already disrobed, all but Sorscha clearly ready to shift into dragon form to meet whatever combat came their way.

Quiet pops indicated the arrival of others. Thor, disheveled and aggravated, appeared on the ground to Matt's left. "You owe me one, Tyr," the giant barbarian god grumbled as he glared over his shoulder at Hades, who had also teleported in and now floated a few feet over the front doors right beside Gaia.

Matt chortled silently, reacting to the name he'd used during the Norse days. "Remember the kettle, my friend," he whispered.

"That kettle gig has been repaid many times over, and you know it," Thor growled under his breath.

"Aye, it has. I suppose a mere thank you will have to do. That, and a reminder that while the kettle quest was for your benefit, what you've done this day will benefit the whole world. For this, I thank you, my friend," Matt said, looking across the field to where other figures were appearing.

Thor's grunt was his only reply as the giant barbarian god stood ready for battle beside his old friend, Mjolnir loose from its belt loop and twirling in the god's right hand.

Before long the stage was set and the Jade Emperor, enrobed in a stunning multicolored kimono with bejeweled obi and borne on a small cloud, processed ceremoniously across the field. Surrounding him were nine standard bearers, each hoisting a gold-fringed white banner hung from a long pole. The banner in front Crystal recognized as the traditional yin-yang symbol with white and black sinuous shapes equally dividing the area of a circle. Unlike any symbol she'd ever seen, though, this one undulated independently of the fabric on which it seemed to be painted. The effect was hypnotic, but too far away for Crystal to make out the flows involved in its creation.

The other eight standards bore simple designs, each with three horizontal lines. Each design had the lines broken in half in different combinations; in the first pair, one flag's three lines were all unbroken while in the other flag's design all three were split. In the next pair, the top two lines were whole in one set and broken in the other. The middle line was the broken or unbroken difference in the third pair, while the final pair combined one symbol with the bottom two lines whole with another with the bottom two lines broken. The symbols on the eight banners nagged at Crystal; she'd seen them before but couldn't place the memory. She tucked it away to ask Matt about if—no, when—the day ended with the plan successfully carried out.

To the right of the Jade Emperor hopped the Monkey King, dressed as before in a simple black fighting uniform. Despite the distance, Crystal was certain she could read the glee on Monkey's face. Behind the top leadership stretched the horde Matt had told her would come: thousands of major and minor deities, sprites, and other mythical creatures. There looked to be a small legion of tiny dragons, platoons of several different types of monkeys, and companies consisting of humanoid versions of many different animals. To one side stretched a host of beings that seemed to be nothing but energy-based, small and glimmering against the forest backdrop.

"There's thousands of them," Crystal whispered to Stacy.

"Yes, there are. So?" Stacy shot back.

"We don't have that many," Crystal said.

"Eh," Stacy said dismissively, shrugging her shoulders slightly, "we have a Matt, and we have a Thor. You haven't lived till you've seen them fight side-by-side, sweetcheeks," Stacy said quietly and almost gently.

Matt looked over his shoulder past the unfurled wing to glare the goddesses into silence.

Halfway across the field the procession stopped. Thor growled softly and shifted Mjolnir in his grip; Matt waved his hand slightly, signaling his friend to stand down.

Sorscha picked that moment to emerge from the mansion. She walked silently down the stairs to stand behind her master and the two goddesses. With her right hand she gently led a hooded figure.

The Jade Emperor called from the center of the field, his magically-amplified voice echoing from the mountains behind the mansion, "Matthew, Western God of War, is it you that I see standing before us?"

"It is," Matt said, amplifying his voice rather than putting any apparent effort into raising it.

"Then you stand before us accused of kidnapping and murdering the king of Atlantis. What say you to the accusations?"

"Well, I—wait. Murder? Has someone found His Majesty's body?" Matt replied.

"No, but that is only a matter of time."

"Without a body, though, how can it be a murder?" Matt asked.

"Don't waste our time with semantics, war god. We're aware that one with your powers would have no difficulty disposing of our dear murdered king's body. It is, as I said, a mere matter of time, though, before we learn of its disposition."

"So, let me make sure I understand," Matt said. "Your conjecture is that you haven't found the body because I would have no problem making it disappear, yet you're also saying it's only a matter of time before you find it. Isn't that a bit of a contradiction?"

"It—it is largely irrelevant," the Jade Emperor said, irritation creeping into his voice. "For now, we'll just say kidnapping.

I accuse you, Matthew, of kidnapping the king of Atlantis. What say you?"

"Well, I say that even if you somehow were to prove my guilt, your threatened punishment is unjust. How is a kidnapping punishable by death, as you warned when you threatened my team?" Matt asked. "More specifically, if I am found guilty of the crime of kidnapping, how is it equitable that I be rewarded in turn with death? Is death not a greater crime, especially when pressed upon an immortal god? That sort of sentence is revenge, not justice. Do you not agree?"

"This is his plan? He's going to wrangle his way out of it?" Crystal heard Phoenix whisper to Birch.

The Jade Emperor glared over Matt's head for a moment, annoyed at the interruption, and then continued, saying, "There were others who died, God of War."

Matt shrugged and said, "Servants. Guards. We gods kill servants and guards all the time; are we now to redefine the act in this case singly as murder? More vitally, are you suggesting that it is just to change the nature of the way we view an act, after the act's commission, into a crime, and then punish the act in a manner that it would not have earned had it not been redefined?"

The Jade Emperor shrugged and replied, "It is my opinion that the sentence of death is just."

"Well, it is my opinion that it is not," Matt said. "That puts us at a bit of a disparity of opinion, doesn't it?"

"Well—in that case," the Jade Emperor said, pointing to Hades. "I see that King Yama has illuminated our morning with his honorable and august presence. He is an appropriate entity to render such judgment, would you not agree, God of War?"

King Yama? Crystal asked Stacy telepathically.

King Yama is the judge of the eastern pantheon. Of some eastern pantheons, anyway. He filled a very similar role to them as he did to the Greeks as Hades, if I understand correctly.

"Well, yes! Yes, I do. Why, I find that a splendid idea. Lord Hades, what say you?" Matt gleefully called over his shoulder.

Monkey bounced up to the Jade Emperor and whispered something in his ear. The Jade Emperor brushed him away and motioned for him to resume his place.

"I accept," Hades said gravely, nodding once. Atop his head appeared a simple rounded black cap embroidered in gold with a vertical stripe intersected by three horizontal stripes, the bottom stripe slightly longer. "Now, the charge, as I have heard it spoken, is kidnapping. Matthew, I believe, has the right of it; death of an immortal is a vastly unjust penalty for the kidnapping of a mortal, no matter how high the mortal's rank."

Crystal barely held back a cheer.

Hades continued, "Kidnapping is, at its core, a crime involving the forced removal of freedoms from the kidnapped party. It seems just for the penalty, then, to also involve the forced removal of freedoms from the kidnapper. Thus, I suggest that the penalty for kidnapping a mortal king, in this case, shall be eternal imprisonment in Tartarus where I and my staff can ensure the removal of the appropriate number of freedoms. Keep in mind, however, that this judgment, once enacted, sets forth a precedent in all cases involving the relations of gods and mortal heads of state. Do you still wish to proceed, Jade Emperor?"

With the distance Crystal couldn't be certain, but she thought she saw a flash of panic stretch across the Jade Emperor's visage. He opened his mouth to say something, but a squeal and a few chirps from the Monkey King apparently changed what he was about to exclaim. In a subdued tone he said, "I do."

"Well. That determined, how do you plead? Are you guilty of the crime as charged, Matthew, God of War?"

"No, I am not." Matt said, echoes of his statement ringing from the opposite mountains.

"So what evidence do you bring, Jade Emperor?" Hades asked.

"King Yama, the western god of war has the motive, in that he has long despised the king of Atlantis, a fact evidenced by the frequency with which he's attacked the king's castle. He's also long wished to see the king's brother on the throne. Further, the magic used to blast through the castle's defenses bears his typical magic signature. It must, therefore, have been him."

"Were there any witnesses to the crime?" Hades asked.

"Only the king's guards, who are now in your kingdom abiding by your wise judgment," the Jade Emperor said.

So, Jade Emperor, have you no direct evidence? Do you bring charges to us that are based on motive and magical signature alone?"

"I do, my lord eternal King Yama, and I pray that your wisdom will see through the lies of my opponent."

"Your opponent? Sometime in the future we need to consider how it came to pass that deities became 'opponents.' But be that as it may for now. Matthew, what is your response to this charge?" Hades asked.

"I didn't do it," Matt said.

"Well, yes, I believe that you've already said that. Now tell me why I should believe you."

"I could," Matt said, and then he allowed a pause to spin along after his short statement.

"But?" Hades asked after a short wait, his scowl deepening.

"But it's better to let the king himself tell you," Matt said, and as he spoke, Sorscha pulled the cowl off of the figure beside her. The illusion of a human-sized battle mage melted away with the cowl, leaving the mighty form of the naga king towering behind Matt. Gasps were audible across both sides of the field.

"Well, this does simplify things, indeed," Hades said, a half-smile playing across his face. "Or perhaps it complicates them. King Takshaka, I presume that is you?"

"It is, King Yama," the naga king said.

"Are you well enough to give testimony?"

"I am, King Yama. I have been Matthew's guest overnight, and have been quite pleased with his hospitality and that of his servants."

"So the two of you are now friends?"

"I wouldn't go that far, Your Immortal Highness. The western god of war still has a few attacks upon my home to answer for. For now, though, I am happy and well and looking forward to returning to that home."

"I see," Hades said, a full smile encroaching across his normally-stern visage. "Well, let us bring the matter to a close so that your return may be arranged. Tell us who kidnapped you."

"The titan Prometheus kidnapped me, King Yama."

"But that is impossible," Hades said. "Prometheus is forever chained in Tartarus."

"No, he is not, King Yama. He was released through trickery, and after his magic was used to kidnap me, I was made to stand in his stead, under the clever spell of a master illusionist."

"How do you know of how Prometheus was released from Tartarus?"

"Prometheus told me. He said he had nothing against me, but his own freedom was too dear to turn down an opportunity like the one which he was presented. He seemed to believe that the suffering of a mere naga would be nothing compared to that of a titan. And who knows, he may have been right."

"And so you were released to spend the night here at this estate? Just—released? How is that possible, when I do not allow prisoners free exit?" Hades asked.

"That god took my place for the night," King Takshaka said, pointing to Thor. The onlookers gasped again; Thor shrugged.

"What're friends for, right?" the giant god said.

"But that—that is impossible," the Jade Emperor said. "There is no one who can sneak in and out of your realm at will, King Yama."

"There is one," Hades said. "He does it by dreaming himself in and out. He has done it before, and I suspect that he is the one who has done it again. King Takshaka, I ask you now to identify for us the illusionist who imprisoned you."

"It was Monkey, King Yama."

All eyes turned toward the center of the field, where Monkey was jumping around and entreating the Jade Emperor for something the western pantheon members couldn't hear. With one shake of his head, the Jade Emperor abandoned Monkey, rising on his cloud with his standard-bearers into the sky. The Monkey King was left standing alone.

"Monkey," Hades said, "The testimony I have heard is in accordance with evidence of events from within my own realm that is already known to me. The case against you, then, is quite unassailable. It is clear that you used the titan known as Prometheus as your weapon to kidnap the king, and thus it is my judgment that you bear the weight of punishment for the crime. By the powers granted me, then, through agreement of the deities gathered here today, I hereby…."

"Hades, wait," Matt said.

"Wait? For what?" Hades said, exasperation in his tone.

"For this," Matt said, and he charged at Monkey while spinning his pike over his head. Thor followed his old friend into the fray, screaming a war cry.

To Battle

The rough CLANG echoed off of the surrounding mountainsides as Matt's pike met the short staff that Monkey, as quick as he was, barely had time to shake out of his ear and bring up to a guard stance. The meeting of the two rods presented such force that the Monkey King flew back several dozen feet, landing on his back with a whoomph. He somersaulted backward and flipped back up onto his feet, simultaneously swatting away Thor's thrown Mjolnir with his cudgel.

Monkey wasn't without allies, though. As he took up a position ready for Matt's next attack, six huge animal-like humanoids roared and rushed the pair of western gods.

"The bull, the roc, the macaque, the salamander, the camel, and the lion," Matt said. "Those would be the six Sworn Demon Brothers."

"I got 'em," Thor said. "You get Monkey."

"You by yourself against the six demon kings? Hardly a fair fight," Matt said.

"Oh, I know. But don't worry, I'll go easy on 'em," Thor said. He wound up his hammer, which had reappeared in his hand moments after being deflected by Monkey, and tossed it at the oncoming band. Lion and Macaque leaped out of the way, but the hammer caught Bull in the chest and slammed him backward into Salamander, both into Camel, and the trio into Roc.

"Nice throw," Matt complimented as he dropped the pike and drew his sword. The blade gleamed bright red as Matt spun in a couple of times and then rushed at Monkey, covering the dozen yards Monkey's flight had opened up between them in less than a second. The blade and the cudgel made the nearby mountains echo again with the sound of their impact.

Monkey went into a series of spins with his club, his form looking similar to the previous time Crystal had watched the pair battle, but this time Matt was having none of it. The glowing red sword seemed to be able to move much faster than the conjured staff he'd fought with before, and so it met every blow Monkey attempted with ease. Meanwhile the ancient god of war blasted Monkey in the face with elemental energy every time the creature paused; first an air blast knocked Monkey off his feet, and a few moments later a fireball enveloped the ape.

Thor, for his part, was enjoying his own battle, singing joyfully along to the rhythm of his hammer's strikes against his foes. Each of the six demon animals had a different style and a specific strength, but each also had a distinct weakness, and Thor had already proven to Crystal his mastery in the combat art of pinpointing and exploiting weaknesses. Bull was the first to be embarrassed; his great strength was in the momentum he applied to a strike, yet the same momentum made it difficult to change course of an attack once he'd committed to it. This had Thor literally running circles around Bull as he charged, then stopped, then charged again. With each charge Bull received a thunderous whack on the flank from Mjolnir.

Crystal felt Stacy tense and followed her gaze upward to where an uncountable number of dragonlings had sprung up into the air from the other side and were headed right toward Matt. The sky filled rapidly, though, as the nearly eight hundred thrakkoni who were standing ready for this very moment shifted to dragon form and sprang into the air to meet the demons. Sorscha whooped joyfully, marking the first time Crystal had heard such a grand expression of any emotion from Matt's sidekick, as she tossed her own clothing to the side and kicked off the stairs, transforming as she leapt upward into her massive silver dragon form and joining the fray. Even Breenda touched Crystal's mind with a questioning presence.

Yes, go, Crystal sent, and the blue dragon also whooped and joined in. The dragon flight swooped in as one in a huge semicircle and blistered the thousands of smaller demon-dragons with a withering blast of fire breath. Not waiting for the air to cool, they charged in physically and entered into a grand aerial melee. It was actually a beautiful spectacle to watch. The dragonlings supporting Monkey were all shades of black, red, or white, but Matt's dragons presented a rainbow of different colors, all of which glistened brightly in the morning sun. The combatants roiled together in the sky, a chaotic kaleidoscope of aerial battle.

Monkey blocked another of Matt's blows and spun out and toward his own lines. Clear for a moment, he took up a defensive posture and called loudly, a yell that was answered by a sea of monkeys who charged onto the field.

"Geez, how many fighters did he bring?" Crystal wondered aloud.

"Enough to subdue Matt, or at least I suspect that's what he thought. But we're not exactly playing fair either," Stacy said, looking meaningfully from one side of the field to the other. Crystal followed her gaze to the left and saw, to her amazement, the company of human barbarians she'd trained with at Valhalla surging onto the field, swinging war axes and mighty hammers while singing their praise to Thor and to Tyr. She knew, having faced them herself in the sparring ring, how tough those men were, and their ferocity and devotion to her husband and to their master brought a cheer to her lips. The cheer turned to a gasp as she watched a formation of Valkyrie swoop in above the charging barbarians. Crystal could hear similar gasps from Matt's battle mages behind her in reaction to Valhalla's version of thrakkoni, shaped into their battle maiden form and supremely decked out in their gleaming silver armor, their great white wings propelling them into the fray. Their entry was a spectacular sight, and she saw how the Valkyrie earned their deadly reputation as they joined the battle, using hoof and sword both to cut a wide entrance into the line the monkeys were hastily forming to that flank.

"Once you're done yelling, look over there," Stacy pointed to the right. Crystal did, and was thrilled to see a phalanx of Apollo's red-robed adepts conjuring fireball after fireball as they held a line against the monkeys' opposite flank. Just past them, a silvery streak of arrows caught her eye, and she watched Artemis's hunters lined up firing volley after volley of magic arrows into the host of monkeys.

"Oh, my god," Crystal exclaimed, overtaken with pride as Matt's own battle mages entered the fray, choosing through some unspoken agreement to use sonic balls as their primary weapon and launching them over Crystal's and Stacy's heads. The massed explosions to the front shook the stairs of the mansion.

"Careful with that phrase around here," Stacy said as the pair of goddesses watched the firepower being brought to bear on the host in the clearing to their front. It had, on peaceful days, seemed to stretch forever, with nearly a mile to travel to reach the opposite tree line and nearly nine miles from end to end. Now, though, it was full, and Crystal as she watched could almost see where Matt got his lust for grand, tumultuous combat.

Two distinct but related battles raged in the center. Matt and Monkey fought as expertly as they had two days previous. Neither gave much ground to his opponent as both passed through series after series of attacks that slipped smoothly from offensive into defensive postures. This time was different, though; Matt felt confident enough in his superiority over Monkey, given the weapons being used, to bring magic to the fight as well. The god of war sauntered in with a lazy-looking sideswipe of his sword that was easily blocked by Monkey, but then he rapidly inverted his elbow in a move that would have dislocated a mortal man's shoulder, bringing his broadsword swishing around, over his head, and down. Monkey barely got his staff back to the right to deflect the newly-angled attack, and that was the time Matt chose to throw a fireball to Monkey's left, spin, and bring his sword back up and over in a double-handed blow that rocked Monkey back a step. The red glow from the sword was exciting to watch as it flashed up and over and around, carving out a show that looked more like a lighted children's play sword than the solid hand-and-a-half bastard sword that it was.

Thor, for his part, seemed to be having a much easier time in the other central battle. Four of the animal demon kings had already submitted in defeat, and the barbarian god fought the fifth by itself. Salamander's sinuous style was proving a challenge for a barbarian who preferred straight-on attacks, but Thor had fought too many battles to be put off for long. He changed his own style, holding his hammer out toward Salamander and taunting the beast to come at him. When the demon gave in to Thor's taunts, the giant showed his amazing speed in swinging Mjolnir out and around and back in to bash whatever body part his opponent brought closest. The bashing caused Thor a great deal of joy, an emotion he showed by roaring in laughter again and again.

The onslaught of dragonlings ended abruptly with all of them vanishing at once. What had been a thunderous soup of overhead aerial melee suddenly resolved into individual dragons circling and landing. Several nursed wounds, Crystal could see, but none appeared serious, much less life-threatening. Meanwhile the giant silver winged serpent that was Sorscha continued to circle overhead, bellowing a dragon-song in triumph every time her master landed a blow on the Monkey King.

Breenda landed gracefully nearby and sprinted over to Crystal, picking up her clothes as she ran. "That was so incredible!"

Breenda trilled, her voice modulating the sing-song of thrakkoni amusement.

"Yes, and it's still going," Crystal said, eyes locked on her husband's weapon-based ballet with the Monkey King. Breenda's enthusiasm dimmed as she moved quietly to the side.

The monkey horde wasn't doing very well either. The combined onslaught of barbarians and Valkyrie had ripped its right flank asunder, sending those monkeys scurrying toward the middle. Apollo's adepts' fireballs did the same to the left flank as the monkeys proved to be terrified of the eruptions of flame. This left the compacted center to be a slaying field for the arrows of Artemis's archers and the sonic explosions of Matt's battle mages.

As Crystal watched she recalled Matt's lessons on the difference between fire and air energies in battle; it hadn't made sense to her at the time, nor had it really settled in to any of the other mages in training, but watching it played out suddenly made the strategy clear. Because of the elemental control required, the fireballs had to be started at the caster and trained in to the target, which required some concentration and also allowed the target advance warning of the impending danger. Sonic explosions, though, happened instantaneously wherever the battle mage wanted them to, so long as the spot had air in it. Thus the group of Matt's battle mages directed by Phoenix were able to march a line of explosions back and forth through the ranks of monkeys, leaving entire platoons of the creatures stunned and listless.

The front few ranks of monkeys somehow managed to get through the magical onslaught and charged the party on the stairs leading to the mansion. Crystal realized it was her own time to put her powers as a goddess on display, and she strode forward onto the field and stood her ground before the monkeys. The horde of apes charging at her numbered nearly a hundred and were each sized significantly larger than an average man.

No matter. She gathered magical energies in preparation for their arrival.

Don't use ka, Stacy cautioned. *It is forbidden.*

I know, Crystal replied. The battle between Stacy and Matt so many months ago had featured the use of ka, and that, more so than the battle itself, had been what had caused the entire pantheon of western deities to teleport in and surround them, and it had then forced Gaia to step in and end the fighting.

As the monkeys drew nearer, Crystal pulled together a net of air energies that spanned from ground level up to waist-high. She solidified it with a flick of her mind, making each monkey suddenly look like he was wading up to the shore from the sea.

Crystal lightly tweaked the strands in the middle to make them give less resistance than the ones on the edges. The monkeys continued to struggle against her magic, still gaining ground but slowly, becoming slower with every step. In their effort to continue moving forward they failed to notice that she was drawing them inward, bunching them closer together.

Finally Crystal was satisfied that the monkeys were close enough together to spring the trap. Smiling wickedly, she gathered green emotional energy above the monkeys and laid it like a tablecloth over the entire troop. She watched as terror beset the horde, each monkey's primal fear lit up by Crystal's spell, each panicking and trying to run, and each held firm by the bonds of air around its legs. They screamed seemingly in unison, their eyes wide and their hands, each held menacingly earlier during their charge, now waving in front of their faces to ward off terrors they could feel but not see. In their absolute horror they flailed at each other, each monkey beating its neighbors, pulling hair, gouging skin and ears with their sharp claws, each strike adding to the terror spell's effects.

"Nice," Stacy said softly. Crystal heard Stacy's approving tone and smiled.

The goddess who had yet to finish the phrase 'goddess of blank' walked forward slowly. The apes in the front row noticed her approach, but they were too absorbed in their magically-induced panic to pay attention to what looked like a mere human approaching. Finally Crystal decided she was close enough, and she lit a glow around her, using the elements of fire and air to give her body a blazing corona similar to the glow lights Matt had taught his mages to use but much brighter and grander. At the same time she intensified the green energy weave while ripping away the air energy behind the apes, allowing them to flee.

Raising her arms, she let rip a terrifying scream.

Flee the apes did, dropping to all fours and speeding across the terrain back to the safety of the side they had come from. Some, heedless of where they were going, bowled into the Monkey King as he attempted to bat them aside with a frustrated growl. Others ran right into and through the line of fire of arrows, fire, or sonic explosions, trampling their shocked comrades as they quit the battleground as fast as they could.

Crystal chortled quietly. What had been Monkey's vanguard, his largest and strongest apes, she'd not only neutralized but actually turned into a weapon against him, using them to press his forces back out of the battle.

"Nice job," Stacy repeated, and then added telepathically, *just don't get too cocky, sweetcheeks.*

"Enough," the Monkey King suddenly said as he fell to a knee. "I submit. My host is beaten, and I am bested." The battlefield suddenly became very quiet, Thor having already beaten all six demon kings down to one knee and the hosts of Ares, Apollo, Artemis, and Valhalla instantly ceasing their offensives.

Matt stopped a blow mid-swing, folded quickly into a guard stance, and nodded once, sharply. "Lord Hades," he called over his shoulder, "I yield to your judgment. A freedom for a freedom was the agreement. Yes?"

"Yes, indeed," Hades said from behind Crystal. "Judgment has been rendered and shall now be carried out." Suddenly an enormous creature with more arms and hands than Crystal could count appeared behind Monkey. Each of his limbs was grasped by a separate hand, and the black creature pealed a wicked-sounding laugh. The Monkey King screamed as he and the creature vanished.

The rest of the defeated forces quickly retreated unhindered as Matt sheathed his sword and sauntered back across the field to the estate, Thor plodding just behind. Crystal made ready to run into his arms to celebrate, but something in his expression held her. Her husband's gaze was anchored solemnly to a spot above her head, and as he reached the immediate area at the bottom of the stairs, the Western God of War, Champion of Olympus and top of the pantheon, went down onto one knee.

"Welcome back, Father," Matt said reverently from within the folds of a deep bow.

Cleaning Up

Crystal turned and gasped. Beside the earth mother and the overlord of the Underworld floated a wizened old man. Stacy and Thor also turned and joined Matt in kneeling, the pair followed immediately by Crystal. She glanced around and saw that all across the acres of clearing, everyone—gods, humans, and thrakkoni alike—were bowing in respect to the Creator.

"My newest daughter," a deep rumbling voice said, "So recently ascended to the pantheon, and yet such good work already. To have gained immortality and then risk it so soon by leaping into a lava stream to help prove your husband's innocence and determine the truth about the kidnapping! I am pleased."

"Thank you, Father," Crystal said, not really certain what else to say. She'd never seen Matt bow to anyone before; quite the opposite, actually, as she'd watched him saunter and quip in response to deities across both major pantheons. He even flaunted his powers around Gaia, who obviously had special spot in her heart reserved for him. But the respect that Matt felt and displayed for the Creator went well above and beyond anything he'd shown to anyone else.

"Rise, everyone. Rise, please," the Creator's voice rumbled across the clearing. "My immortal children, I shall see you all in Olympus two earth-days hence, when we shall celebrate this great victory over wickedness. Until then, my sons and daughters, fare thee well."

The Creator vanished.

Crystal said, "I—kind of expected...."

"What, a burning bush?" Stacy asked derisively. "Or a big booming voice with a British accent coming out of a chalice? Or perhaps you expected a bumbling old wizard with a kender sidekick?"

"Well, yes, as a matter of fact I did expect one of those. Look, I know I'm a victim of all of the Hollywood garbage of my time, but it's my fantasy, darn it," Crystal said.

"Indeed, love. But it's not his," Matt said, coming up behind and putting his arm around her. "We should rejoice that the Father is back. For now, though, I'm hungry. Mother, Hades, Apollo, Artemis, Thor, Stacy, and anybody else I don't see, I'd love to have all of you at my table for, um, a late lunch I guess," Matt said, looking overhead at the sun. The golden orb had traveled far across the sky. "A very late lunch."

"Don't mind if I do," Ben'thra said jovially as he popped in beside them. "By the way, Matthew, that was well played. Very well played. You even had me fooled when you submitted to the judgment of Hades."

Matt leveled a quasi-appreciative grunt toward Ben'thra as the parties filed into the dining hall, Matt taking up the rear. Crystal started to follow her husband into the grand hall, but stopped briefly to turn and survey the battlefield. Some of the creatures they'd been battling had been magical in nature, she guessed by the lack of their bodies, but the sight of dozens, or possibly even hundreds, of dead apes brought tears to her eyes in spite of the fact that not that long ago she'd fought a company of them.

"What's wrong, love?" Matt said.

"I was just thinking how sad it is to see all the bodies of the apes who lost their lives in the battle, now scattered about the lawn like that."

"Yeah, battlefields are rarely pleasant places to be after the fact." Matt draped his arm gently across her shoulders.

"I guess you've seen your share of them, haven't you, Mr. God of War?"

"More than, to be honest. But let's go inside and leave the thrakkoni to clean up the lawn."

"Okay," Crystal said, and then the meaning behind Matt's words hit her. "Wait. You mean clean up as in—eww."

"Eww what?"

"You mean that the dragons are going to eat the corpses of great apes, the closest relative to humans in the animal kingdom. Eww that. Those are apes."

Matt shook his head. "Those were apes. Now they're ape-shaped piles of flesh and bones, which just happens to be one of the dragons' favorite food groups."

Crystal turned toward Matt, disgust and shock on her face. "You can be such a monster sometimes, you know," she said.

"I do know. Large with blue fur is what scares the kids most, but I can do plenty of other monsters when I need to. Now come on, let's go eat. People food, of course. If, that is, you're willing to call fried okra people food, and I certainly am."

The human followers of the different gods filled the main hall to bursting, but Crystal felt even happier because of the crowding. It was the first time the cavernous dining room had ever seemed truly occupied to her as they settled down at the main table, Matt's senior battle mages shoved to a second main table due to the presence of so many deities at the regular one.

It was over. Her husband, and the world, were both safe, and she'd had a fair hand in accomplishing it. This was a party, and a high table, at which she'd earned her spot.

Goddess of What?

Clink

Several glasses and one large mug came together in a divine toast over the largest table in Olympus. Somehow, despite the forcefulness of the toast from a couple of the gods involved, not a drop of nectar was spilled. Less surprising was that all the glasses had come together over the middle of the eight foot diameter table, hefted by gods with arms that were only about three feet long—hey, they were gods, after all.

Gathering for a drink (or several, really) had seemed the thing to do after suffering through an interminable meeting featuring accolades for her efforts in saving the uuuuuniveeeeerse (as bellowed by Zeus in rather loud and somewhat obnoxious approbation) followed by a lot of other nonsense that made Matt's administrative audiences in his throne room back at home seem downright thrilling. She'd been surprised, though, at some of the deities who'd decided to join the new heroine goddess and her husband.

"So, Crystal," Thor said after quaffing a deep drag from his mug and slamming the vessel onto the table, "tell us. What's it like to swim deep into the bowels of Mount Etna?"

"Hot. And claustrophobic," Crystal said, downing her own shot of nectar. "I almost panicked at first when I realized I couldn't breathe. Matt showed me how to turn the involuntary respiration off, but that took some getting used to."

"Yeah, but how did you keep from being melted?"

"With a shield, of course. It was pretty easy once...."

"Once she figured out the right combination of flows," Matt interrupted, winking at his wife. "It was so epic that someday we'll have to teach it to the bards. There I was, feeling around under us to see if Prometheus were really there, and I turned around to see her bravely launch herself into the two thousand degree abyss. In-credible! And by the way, hon, you probably ought to turn that breathing thing back on sometime soon. It's been kinda strange over the past few days watching you not breathing."

"Oh—yeah. I got so used to it that I forgot," Crystal said.

"How, dear girl, did you figure out where the king was? I'm led to believe that Prometheus was less than forthcoming," Benny's voice slithered into the conversation. It was his eagerness to join the group that had surprised Crystal the most, considering the enmity between him and, well, pretty much everybody else there.

"It was the only way Monkey's scheme would've worked. I caught the answer when Prometheus refused to tell me where the king was and argued that it was because he didn't want to go back there. It was in the wording the titan used, but it made perfect sense. After all, Prometheus didn't care about us or the king. If the king had been cloistered anywhere else, you have to assume that the titan would've been perfectly fine with telling us where, but since the king was in the one place he didn't want us to go, and the one place he was afraid to return to, he just said no."

"Very nice," Benny purred.

"Don't even think about it," Matt said, glaring at his nemesis.

"Think about what? I was merely complimenting the brilliance of your spouse."

"I know you, Benny. You were thinking of ways to use that brilliance against us all in the future."

"Bah. Here I am, innocently being nice, and you assume I'm not. I suggest that the plotter here is you, not I."

"So how'd ye get 'im ta settle down, lass?" Hephaestus interrupted Matt's attempted retort, the smith god quite drunk again but with an entirely different aura than the previous time they'd run into him. "I dinna' think I'd ever get ta use me forge again."

"I didn't," Crystal said. "That was part of the deal with Hades."

"Hades did that?"

"I believe so. When we went back down to the Underworld to explain what we knew, he didn't believe us at first. Said there was no way Monkey could've fooled him again. You should've seen the anger in his eyes when he came back from inspecting the prisoners in Tartarus. 'Monkey!' he screamed, over and over. The Lord of the Underworld was absolutely furious at having had a prisoner stolen out from under his nose and an innocent slipped into his place. You know, he actually did look like the stereotypical devil several times during his rant—bright red face, steam rising from his black hair, lips curled up like this." Several chuckled as she demonstrated, and then she continued, "He was perfectly happy to agree to take Monkey in exchange for the titan, but we asked him to use his status as Prometheus's former jailer to convince the big guy to go farther underground and quit disturbing everybody within several hundred miles of the mountain."

Apollo asked, "But how did Monkey fool Hades into thinking the king of Atlantis was Prometheus? He fooled Gaia, too, I recall you saying. Those two are widely regarded as entirely unfoolable."

"C'mon," Matt said, "You know Monkey." Apollo shot Matt a withering glare that was merely shrugged off. "Okay, I guess you don't. He's more my grand warrior type than your bookish type, anyway. But he's a master illusionist. That's how he earned his immortality in the first place, learning the thirty-six earthly transformations."

"It's the seventy-two earthly transformations," Apollo corrected.

"Hah! See? You do know what he can do. And in an energy zone like Tartarus he was able to build up enough fire energy around the king to create the illusion of a titan. It wasn't enough to fool somebody who actually looked in the cell, but it fooled the senses. I suppose Hades likely had a nice long talk with his hecatoncheires after he got back."

"His cat whats?" Crystal asked, captivated by the swirling purple vortex in her glass and, having lived the story, only partly paying attention.

"Hecatoncheires. His chief jailers. And tormenters, too, or so I've heard. The guy with the hundred hands who showed up to collect Monkey was one," Matt said.

"Oh. I thought that was a demon," Crystal said, and then glared across the table to where Stacy had just snorted in derision.

"Sweetcheeks," Stacy said, "they're all the same thing: demons, angels, spirits, sprites, li'l wee folk…." Stacy said the last in a poorly-done brogue while leering between a thumb and a forefinger at Hephaestus, who glowered in return. "They're all the same, all gatherings of energy that take on a life of their own."

"Yes, but the hecantoncheires have been around since before the titans," Matt corrected. "One must assume they were created from the primordial stuff in the creative soup that Father cooked. They're actually the same kind of being as the titans, ish, but much, much bigger."

"That makes sense," Crystal said. "And by the way, when, dear Stacy, are you going to stop calling me by that annoying and childish nickname?"

"Oh, probably right about the same time you start acting like a goddess," Stacy retorted.

"So, that thousand years that you and I were talking about," Crystal asked, looking at Matt.

"Not really. Knowing all the spells is a different thing, love," Matt explained gently. "Just because Apollo didn't do his job thoroughly," Matt paused, smirking in response to the huff that Apollo had just let out, "doesn't mean you shouldn't take on the attitude of a goddess, ruler, and guiding power of the universe, as well as peer to those of us seated around this table."

Crystal looked around the group uncomfortably. Thanks to her relationship to Matt, and later to her completion of what she now saw as a fairly mild line of quests, she was seated at a table comprised of the foremost powers in the universe, many of whom had been in existence since the universe itself had begun.

"I'm not even sure I...." Crystal began, about to give voice to her fear that she wasn't even qualified to sit at the table, much less call herself equal. But Matt interrupted her with a grunt and a look.

"Crystal," Apollo said in his dry, lecturing tone, "I'll say this one time, and one time only—you need to banish any human thoughts of inadequacy that may still be swimming around in that head of yours. To continue holding onto such nonsense is to lower us all. We will consider you a peer, if you make us do so. Do not, and we will not. Understand?"

Crystal took a moment for introspection. She had, in fact, walked into the core of a living volcano. She'd earned accolades from both the Mother and the Father. She'd done the work to earn the spot. She'd battled Stacy to a decisive win. And, for the first time, she truly understood what Apollo was getting at.

Looking him directly in the eyes, she said, "I do. Thank you."

Apollo nodded once and went back to disdainfully sipping his nectar.

"So, Crystal, I understand that you've decided what you'll be the goddess of," Matt said. Her husband winked at her over the cup he'd raised to his lips. She'd been asked at the meeting but she hadn't completed making the decision at that time. Now she had, and he was giving her the opening she needed to announce it.

The table became quiet as all the drinkers looked at Crystal, everyone apparently eager to learn the newest goddess's primary interest.

"I have, indeed. It was difficult to narrow the choices down, as there were so many. Goddess of investigations didn't work out because, frankly, I'm not all that interested in private eye work unless I have to be. Goddess of the tongue, meanwhile, didn't suggest the appropriate gravity. So I settled on something that the eastern pantheon actually has two of, yet it doesn't exist in the west: Goddess of Protection."

Everyone at the table nodded appreciatively except for Apollo, whose thin-lipped expression, always dour, turned down even farther. "Goddess of Protection. Hmm. Protection of what, precisely, dear one?" he asked.

"Protection of life in general," she said. "That includes gods and goddesses, of course, but we don't really need protection, as my hubby so ably demonstrated a few days ago. I'm speaking mainly of protection of human life. In the time that I've known you all, you seem to exhibit quite a bipolar relationship with the sanctity of human life. 'Oh, we love humans,' you'll say, but when one steps out of line you're quick to cut them down."

"Hmm," Apollo said, his eyes narrowing. He looked at Matt. "You approve?"

"I do," Matt said, glaring at his ancient counterpart across the table.

"Well, then, all I can say is welcome to the pantheon and we're glad to receive you, Goddess of Protection," Apollo said, his voice bearing neither welcome nor reception.

"Hmmph," Matt said, his grin one of bemusement. "So, Thor, you got to spend a night in Hell," Matt said. "How was that?"

"Glad you asked," Thor said. "Where the titans are kept is pretty much the high rent district. A lovely lass—a demon, of course—comes around every so often and gives out tea or beer for those who want it. They even had this little entertainment box they called a tee vee that showed pictures all night long."

"Mm hmm," Matt said after a few moments of silence. "Did anybody here buy that story?"

"Not at all," Stacy said. "We're too used to your B.S. to not recognize it from a friend of yours."

"My B.S.? Ah! I'm—injured," Matt said, pouting, hand over his heart and face screwed up in pain.

"Ah! Me too," Thor said, attempting to match Matt's expression. On the bearded giant, though, it looked comical. Everyone but Thor laughed, Matt leading the way.

"So, no, really, Thor, what was it like?" Stacy asked, stifling a final chuckle.

"It was like nothing, really. There's not much in the way of torment and wailing in that part of the dungeon, I guess. It was just dark and quiet."

"That's all?" Stacy asked. "Just dark and quiet?"

"No, not that's all. You try staying against your will in a place that's completely dark and obscenely quiet for a while, missy," Thor said. "I was going stir-crazy."

"I can imagine," Apollo said, his normally bored tone sounding animated. "So tell me, why did you have to spend the night in Hell? I mean, I've seen some of the women you've spent the night with, but those aside...."

Thor growled and said, "There's never been a lady's companionship that's ever been a bad thing. Ain't I right, Matt?"

Matt threw up his hands defensively and said, "Hey, I can only recall my current lady's companionship, now, and it's certainly the most incredibly glorious thing in the world. In the earth or heavens, even."

Stacy snorted and said, "So it appears that after millions of years he can be taught. Well played, Crystal."

Crystal nodded and hid her own smirk behind a sip of nectar.

"So, um, yeah. Right," Thor said, trying to regain his dramatic momentum. "So anyway, Hades required me to stay. Well, he required somebody to stay. See, there's this rule about how he can't let someone out without taking someone else in to take their place."

"But the king of Atlantis wasn't there rightfully," Apollo objected.

"Correct, but he was there. He had replaced Prometheus. Granted, that was through trickery and deceit, but he was still there. Hades couldn't just say 'well, my bad' and let the king walk free," Thor said.

"But there was a promise to admit the Monkey King in his stead," Apollo said.

"There was an intent to admit the Monkey King in his stead, but the only way to promise that was to leave someone else to basically serve as a surety bond," Stacy jumped in. "Hades said he'd be at the battle to collect Monkey himself—though granted, he meant himself through his own minions—and that he'd bring Thor. I think Thor was his guarantee against things going south; had Matthew failed to capture Monkey, Thor would've gone back with Hades."

"No, that's," Thor said and stopped when he saw Matt nodding. "Is that right, Matt?"

"Yep," Matt said. "That's Hades to a t. Or it would be, of course, were there a t in Hades. That's why I arranged the battlefield as I did, putting myself out there as such an inviting target for Monkey to come after. I wanted to make sure he was there, and then I wanted to see him left bare of all eastern deity support when his duplicity was revealed so that I—we—could battle him down and let Hades take him."

"For one left bare of all eastern deity support, he sure had a lot of supporters," Crystal said.

"Yeah, in the eastern philosophies there's always been a lot of call for making things into quasi-deities," Matt said. "None of those were real animals, except the ones that were, well, real. And those made it so I don't have to use my herd of cattle to feed the dragons for a while. I do appreciate, in any event, all of you coming to my assistance. That would've been a difficult battle to wage by myself."

"It's what we do, Matthew," Apollo said and held his glass up for another toast.

"Yes, it's what we do," Artemis, Apollo's sister, agreed.

"Indeed, it's what we do," Benny's voice snaked in, earning him a brief glare from Matt.

"Well, let's hear it for the combined might of the gods of Olympus," Thor bellowed, and everyone at the table yelled "Hear, hear!"

Clink!

ABOUT THE AUTHOR

Dean by day and writer by night, Stephen H. King grew up being asked whether he was "that Stephen King." "Not the author," he'd say until his writing addiction took hold and made that into a lie. Now he writes and reads and blogs as The Other Stephen King—you know, the one who writes fantasy and science fiction. When he's not writing, he enjoys thinking about writing while going on hikes or long road trips. When he's not thinking about writing, it's usually because he's fishing.

Find other Stephen H. King works at:

http://TheOtherStephenKing.com

Read his ongoing thoughts about writing, authorpreneurship, and other key parts of life at his blog:

http://TheOtherStephenKingOnWriting.blogspot.com

www.ingramcontent.com/pod-product-compliance
Lightning Source LLC
Chambersburg PA
CBHW070440120726
47910CB00003B/865